IN STONE:
A GROTESQUE
FAERIE TALE

Visit us at www.boldstrokesbooks.com

IN STONE:
A GROTESQUE
FAERIE TALE

by

Jeremy Jordan King

2012

IN STONE: A GROTESQUE FAERIE TALE
© 2012 BY JEREMY JORDAN KING. ALL RIGHTS RESERVED.

ISBN 10: 1-60282-761-3
ISBN 13: 978-1-60282-761-5

THIS TRADE PAPERBACK ORIGINAL IS PUBLISHED BY
BOLD STROKES BOOKS, INC.
P.O. BOX 249
VALLEY FALLS, NY 12185

FIRST EDITION: NOVEMBER 2012

CREDITS
EDITOR: LYNDA SANDOVAL
PRODUCTION DESIGN: SUSAN RAMUNDO
COVER DESIGN BY SHERI (GRAPHICARTIST2020@HOTMAIL.COM)
COVER ARTWORK: JEREMY JORDAN KING

Acknowledgments

This book wouldn't exist without the support of many friends, family, and colleagues. Thank you for enduring endless ramblings about things that don't exist and allowing me to be crazy. More specifically, much gratitude to…

Len Barot and the entire Bold Strokes team for believing in this young author and giving books like *In Stone* a home. My editor, Lynda Sandoval, for making the editing process an absolute joy and helping me find more magical moments than I thought possible. My agent, Monika Verma, for attention, guidance, and enthusiasm for the rest of the Immortals. Mom and Dad for giving me an overactive imagination and being patient while I figured out what to do with it. My sister, Kelley, for being my constant champion. Aaron Glick for reading everything I write (and for managing my life). RJ Jordan for pushing me to find *my* voice in a story about an ancient gargoyle. Gregory Maguire for being my idol and offering kind words exactly when I needed them. Various co-workers at day jobs in events, yoga studios, and theaters for being interested in my work outside the hourly wage. Every teacher I've ever had for making me feel smart enough to write a book.

And finally, to Natural Wonders at the Freehold Raceway Mall for selling me the real-life Garth who keeps me dreaming safely every night.

Dedication

To my mother, lover of beautiful stories.
To my father, teller of fantastical tales.

Prologue

W hat will it feel like to finally die?" he wondered, gripping the hand of his only friend. In some ways, he'd been dead since he'd learned to love. Childhood was difficult. Adulthood would never see fruition. Wayward glances led to ridicule, then torture, and culminating in an irreversible act of violence the likes of which have always been committed but never prevented.

He entered a life of entitlements, fineries, and glory. He would die depleted of those things, left to pass away like a beggar in a storm drain. Would he too be washed out to sea with the other waste?

Broken, bleeding, and beginning to rot, he lay under the most perfect of star fields. Leaving this world while beholding such splendor gave him some peace. "It must be better there," he said to himself. He didn't really know what it was like but one must project the best before the end.

He did not think of things he'd never come to see, for there were too many to even grasp.

Hardly a word was wasted on praying to his father's god. What god would let a boy drown in his own fluids on cold stone with hardly a soul nearby to hear his cries?

Time passed without so much of a whisper of the real sins committed there. "This isn't so bad," he thought. His biology had numbed him through the worst of it but the finale proved too much for nature's graces. The hemorrhages surged, entrails slipped, and hot iron filled his mouth, eyes, and ears.

"What will it feel like to finally die?" It felt like too much to comprehend. Bodies weren't meant to feel so much.

The last thing he heard was laughter: unfriendly and victorious.

That is how I died. I just didn't know it yet.

1. Happy New Year, Faggot.

I was wearing rainbow suspenders, a green pleather cap, and a t-shirt with "FRANK" scrawled across the front. The name referred to the wieners that I was slinging from a rented hot dog cart at the bat mitzvah for Miss Spencer Blatt. The catering company that I worked for was hired to do the food. Our team was part of the tens of thousands of dollars spent on bringing the theme "A Spencer State of Mind" to life. Two busses full of the birthday girl's closest friends and relatives walked into one of NYC's event spaces to find a Disney Channel version of Manhattan, complete with a hot new club (the dance floor), a chic bar (a soda fountain manned by real, live jerks), and Restaurant Row (elaborately constructed buffets). My hot dog cart was, just like real-life, parked at the gate to faux Central Park, which was really just an excuse for Spencer's parents to spend even more money on exquisitely stupid flower arrangements and imported tree branches.

So there I was, a bright, attractive, and talented twenty-two year old gay kid wearing rainbows and hawking sausages. Offensive. The fifty-third time a child wearing nicer shoes than me called me "hot dog man" was the moment I decided that I might hate my life.

I'd graduated in the top ten percent of my college class. Sure, I went to a tiny liberal arts school with a concentration in theatre, but still. I was smart. I even had sixty thousand dollars in debt to prove it! Yes, I took out a bazillion student loans to pay for my education, but so did the rest of the country. At least I learned something and didn't just buy a giant house for my nonexistent family of three. Things in 2008 generally sucked. Everyone was poor and frustrated and ready for the new President to take office and clean things up. That melancholia and hyper-awareness of the social climate made an extravagant party for a child even more insulting. I became enraged in thinking Spencer would probably never have to worry about student loans and credit cards and scraping tooth and nail to make rent for a shitty apartment in Spanish Harlem. And in several years, after her gigantic graduation celebration, she wouldn't have to worry about her major at university because she wouldn't be the person paying for it. If nothing panned out, she could just learn something else or have daddy buy her another degree or an internship or a not-for-profit focused on saving sea turtles or something else rich people think is important. She'd never have to wear a costume at work and then go home smelling like hors d'oeuvres and children. That little bitch would float through life unaware of how ridiculous it was for a thirteen-year-old to receive a city for her birthday when most of us couldn't even afford a cupcake. I hated her.

"Whoa, Jeremy. I haven't seen a death stare like that outside of a scary movie." I snapped out of my secret rant and saw Robbie, one of my co-workers. He was blessed with the more humane position of bussing glasses in a standard uniform. His brown hair and eyes melded into the blackness of his clothes, enhancing his pale winter skin. He looked like a pencil sketch by a fashion illustrator. "You probably shouldn't look at the birthday girl like you're putting a hex on her," he said with a laugh.

"I hate her," I told him.

"Is that anti-Semitic?"

"I don't hate her Jewness. I hate her life."

"Dark much?" he asked, seeming slightly repulsed by my feelings. His outlook was always sunnier than mine.

A mother of one of the kids asked for a hotdog with ketchup. When I handed it to her without any topping, she looked at me like I was defective. I coldly pointed to the self-serve squeeze bottle in front of her tightly pulled face, my eyes letting her know that she was the numbskull. I turned back to him. "Anyway, doesn't all of this make you angry?"

"I try not to think about it. We're young. It's just a job." His tongue poked out of his mouth and his eyes went crossed, clearly trying to convey how utterly goofy our employment was.

He obviously didn't understand what I was getting at. I knew it was just a silly job but it was the principal of...ugh. There was no use explaining myself. I wasn't getting anywhere by focusing on the rotten. I closed my eyes, and with a deep breath, I tried to drag myself out of the gutter. When I opened them, Robbie was smiling. The grin washed away any residual annoyances. "So...going home for Christmas?" I asked him.

The brightness in his eyes diminished and he looked to the ground. "I wish. I'll be here. With Nick. We'll do something fun."

I feigned ignorance. "With who?"

He shot me a look.

I knew perfectly well who Nick was. Nick was the dick he'd been fake-dating for months. They barely liked each other. If the relationship were serious, Robbie wouldn't flirt with me so hard.

He was flirting with me, right? Again I found myself going to that dark place...

His hands were busy holding discarded glasses so he bumped me with his shoulder. "Well, let's get together after the holiday," he said.

Yes. Definitely flirting. I returned the gesture. "Is that code for your desire to be my New Year's Eve kiss?"

Robbie rolled his eyes and went back to work.

I had to stop falling for unattainable men.

I found it hard to look forward to another year. Like everyone else at that bar for New Year's Eve, I could have affixed an artificial grin to my face and vowed that the next three hundred sixty five days would be mine to conquer. But life after college was detrimentally uneven. It was like being thrown from a moving train and left in the desert called Life. Fueled by free drinks from my bartender friend, my inner monologue reeled forward as my body slowed into a sloppy gay mess. Soon I was mumbling something aloud about being an unsuccessful actor or loan payments or chasing boys with boyfriends.

"Stop it. You're being tragic," said my friend, Dan. Because Dan was a bizarre little spitfire himself, when he was able to recognize tragedy in another person, you knew it was bad.

"Sorry. New Year's is a terribly depressing holiday."

He grabbed my shirt collar and walked me to a vacant corner. "Listen, you used to be fun but you've been a downer for months. Snap out of it. Self-deprecation is my thing."

A woman came around with a tray of champagne. The countdown would soon begin. We both grabbed a flute. Dan snatched mine and drank half the glass. "Hey! That's for midnight."

He smacked his lips in distaste for what was definitely cheap sparkling wine. "That's your ration for the rest of the night. You're drunk enough," he said before walking back to our group of friends near the bar.

"Ten! Nine! Eight! Seven!" The crowd slurred numbers together and began to position themselves near the objects of their affections. Even girls and gays without boyfriends wrapped arms around one another. The point of celebrating that midnight was simply about togetherness. Not everyone needed the love of his or her life by his or her side. My friends were great. Really. I just wanted something else. If I couldn't have a good job or a nice apartment or fame or fortune, couldn't I at least have a boyfriend, a companion to draw focus from my more superficial problems? I wanted Robbie there. I wanted to see his goofy smile and shaggy hair and that permanent pimple on his chin.

I imagined him with Nick, a guy I know only through stories. Robbie often complained about him. "Nick's jealous of everyone I talk to," or "Nick's mean to my friends," or "Nick and I don't have much in common," were his typical examinations. When I asked about his reasoning for being in such an unhappy relationship, he'd change the subject. The version of Nick he'd led me to concoct in my head resembled a comic book villain with mean, slanted eyebrows and fiery pupils. In reality he was just a fairly bland, reasonably attractive boy from Pennsylvania. In my mind, I saw them together on a balcony overlooking the city, clanging crystal glasses and kissing under a silver moon.

Then I saw myself alone, staring vacantly into space as everybody around me cheered and blew paper horns. I'd missed the ball drop.

I fled to the restroom and looked at myself in the mirror. There was something different about me. The six months of true adulthood I'd just lived through had been tough. My friends were getting jobs, booking shows, and reveling in grownup things like decorating apartments and dating on a Tuesday because there's no class to go to on Wednesday. I was stagnant. My life was still, caught in the panic-stricken moments after tossing my black square cap in the air. I doubted my abilities, decisions, and path. Even the slight curl to my hair had deflated to a sad clump of mousey tendrils.

"Come on, Jeremy," I said to myself. "Cheer up. It's 2009. New start." I forced a smile onto my face. I'd heard that if you smile for several seconds, you automatically feel better. My cheek muscles scrunched up against my eyes and accidentally activated the waterworks that I'd been holding inside all night. I bawled into the sink and silently thanked everybody for celebrating outside and leaving me to cry in solitude.

My phone let out a little chime. A text message from Robbie let me know that him and Nick were thinking of relocating to another party. He wanted to meet up with us. In a second message he added, "You two can finally meet!"

No. That would NOT happen. I was already feeling shitty. I didn't need to have Robbie, the shiny carrot, dangled in front of my face. I didn't need to make small talk with his boyfriend because his boyfriend was someone who I wished would get vaporized by extraterrestrials. I slammed my phone shut. I wondered where that shot girl was. She could pour tequila down my throat to the point of almost drowning, and then I'd bolt.

By the time I stumbled out of the bar, my complexion was a color somewhere between my gray cowboy boots and my green jacket. I found myself smoking some menthol thing that I'd bummed off a girl with sparkles on her eyes. Despite her clownish appearance, she appeared to be confident in her look. She probably viewed me with equal judgment.

"What if I have to move home to Jersey?" I rambled aloud, my woes partially projected for all of Twenty Sixth Street to hear. "What if I have to be a waiter forever? What if—?" A minty inhalation of that cigarette swallowed the other half of the question.

I realized I was drunkenly weaving across the sidewalk. I tried to confidently strut in a straight line but I ended up stumbling into a brick something.

And then into someone. Two someones.

In the haze set in by alcohol and tobacco, I vaguely remember hearing derogatory, hateful slurs before a fist hit my face.

Sounds of late night traffic and the few lingering celebrations of the night roused me back to consciousness. My eyes tried to peel open but my still tender face forced them closed again. "Give me a sec, will ya?" it seemed to say. Memories began to seep back to me: I saw figures approach me from the darkness of a scaffolding-covered building. They appeared like hyenas, laughing at their victim before going in for the kill. Just before an almost fatal blow, the memory disappeared. That must have been the one that knocked me out.

Mortified. Sick. I'd just been hate-crimed…or attempted hate-crimed. I didn't know the specific definition. Did such a crime have to result in death or did the pain I felt from a beating count? Did I have to report the incident to the police? Would they just look at me as some drunk faggot who daintily stumbled into the wrong place at the wrong time? How was such a simple crime committed in a neighborhood as sophisticated as Chelsea, in a city as progressive as New York? I wasn't on Main Street, U.S.A., where people value bibles more than sanity. I was in the capital of the human universe, where gays are more common than pigeons.

How could such a thing happen in such a place?

And to me?

How embarrassing…

I began to cry. Salty tears sizzled their way down my face, uncovering wounds I didn't even know I had. I cried not only from the shame and the insult and the aches, but from thinking about how depressed I'd been earlier that night. I cried because I'd let myself become drowned in misery, a misery that was escapable. It distracted me and brought me to unsafe places where others could bring me pain. Real pain. I'd made it through twelve years of schooling in the suburbs and never let anyone make me suffer. Emotionally, I shut everyone out. Physically, I was nonconfrontational. But there on Twenty-Sixth Street, I was finally greeted with the hate and the prejudice I'd been so conscious of deflecting. Regret and an open bar had blocked my defenses and all that was left to do was cry.

Someone sweetly hushed me. The soft sound forced me out of my head and into the world. My eyes finally made the effort to open. They were met with darkness. I felt beneath me, expecting to touch the starchy linen of a hospital bed because the *only* place a person should go after a violent attack is to the emergency room. But to my horror, my fingers found smooth cement. The space seemed more like a hospital's parking garage than its urgent care unit. My overactive imagination took over. Could I be the sacrifice for a secret society? Was it gang initiation week? Possibly I was in my attacker's secret lab where he'd saw me into pieces? I would have hyperventilated if my ribcage weren't so tender. Where was I and who was I with?

I heard it again. "Shhh…" It came from a darker shadow than the one I lay in. Astonishingly, the simple sound of air through lips had emotion. It was too warm for a sadist.

Only my rescuer could produce a sound so loving, so full of concern. I felt the obligatory pangs of gratitude but still-unknown injuries kept me from running into the darkness and throwing my arms around him. "Who are you?" I asked though split lips.

"It does not matter," he said. His reply was almost too soft to register.

"It does matter. You saved my life. Who are you?" He was silent. "Who are you?" I grunted. My voice echoed through the room. It was very empty and very large.

"I am a Guardian." His full voice grumbled with the deep resonance of timpani. It reverberated against my bones and made my hair stand on end.

"Come out."

He ignored me. "I am glad you are safe. I will leave you now."

I heard him begin to shuffle away so I mustered some strength and forced a hand into my skinny jeans to retrieve my phone. "Wait!" I yelled as I tried to activate the screen. When its light was about to fill the space, his hand flew by and batted the device across the room. I was left just as blind as before.

"What'd you do that for?" I yelled.

"Guardians are not meant to be seen."

"Huh?"

"Guardians are—"

"I heard you." He had used the title a few moments ago, but I'd failed to recognize it. "What the hell is a Guardian?"

"Of the Immortal race."

Any easiness that I'd felt suddenly diminished. Panic spread. Immortal race? Was I in the presence of a crazy person? He was probably the same homeless man that sits on the subway platform drawing symbols sent to him from another planet. Next he'd get out his Magic Markers and start doodling over my major organs in preparation for a divinely inspired autopsy. I needed to get out of there. "Please! Someone! Help!" I pleaded to the ceiling as if it would scoop me up and take me away.

"I am not going to hurt you," he assured me.

"Sure, sure. You're just going to suck out my life force so you can stay Immortal, isn't that right?"

"I am afraid I do not know what you speak of..."

"I've seen movies!" I screamed. I sounded loonier than him.

He didn't know how to respond. Hell, I wouldn't know how to respond, either. Deep down I felt deserving of some mild overreacting, but I didn't want to alienate him because he had all the answers. I'd spent the last God knows how long passed out and had little to no idea of my condition. My legs could have been replaced with mermaid fins for all I knew. For the first time since I was a child, I felt completely reliant on somebody else.

"Am I going to be okay?" I asked.

"Yes. You are injured but nowhere near death."

I tried to let that sink in. "I'm fine," I kept repeating to myself. "I'm fine." And then I asked, "Did you save me?" That sounded funny coming out. It's a question people rarely have to ask.

"I did."

I pictured him stumbling upon Twenty Sixth Street and seeing my pathetic self being tossed around like a Hacky Sack. What had sprung him into action? What sad whimper had alerted him that I was truly in danger? "Why did you help me?"

I still couldn't see him but I could feel the look on his face communicating the ridiculousness of my question. "They were hurting you," he said. The silent coda to his response would have been, "So of course I helped you, you idiot."

"What were they doing to me when you got there?" I needed to know. I wanted him to recall every second of the attack, to draw all of the pages in the flipbook. Each word and strike were precious treasures I'd dropped, treasures that would help pay my way through the processing of the assault. The details of one's fall are crucial in coming to terms with one's new place on the ground. If I knew exactly what had happened I could replay the events over and over again in my head. I'd search for the moment I'd screwed up, the air between punches in which I could have reacted. If I could understand exactly why and how I ended up in that state, I could move past it. That's what I thought, at least. My eyes fixed to where I imagined his would be.

I never saw them but his voice communicated the desperation I'd probably find in them. It was a different sadness than mine, one that couldn't bear to recount what had been witnessed. "I do not remember," he said with a slight stutter. As much as I needed to know, he needed to forget.

"What were they doing?" I knew he knew.

"That does not matter. All that matters is that you are safe now," he insisted.

I threw my aching body in his direction. "It does matter. What did they do to me, Guardian?"

"Do not move," he said. "You are hurt. I will help." His speech was accented with a myriad of languages that begged me to wonder which one was native. He was careful to stay in the darkest shadows of the room, but in my blurry periphery I saw an orange Home Depot bucket sit down beside me. His hand dipped a torn cloth into it. "You had fallen to the ground. They were kicking you. Two men." His large, heavy fingers dabbed a wound on my face. The touch was too hard but I didn't dare comment on the bruises he was probably inflicting. That was all of the information he could give me. Who'd have thought that the witness could be just as injured as the victim?

I waited for another rush of emotion or jolt of pain to tear me from reality but I just stared up, dumbfounded and numb like an invalid plugged into life support. Even after closing my eyes and summoning myself awake, he was still there. I was still there. I wasn't sleeping. A slight breeze rustled my hair and stirred up dust from the floor, temporarily attracting my thoughts elsewhere.

"But we're inside," I slurred after the dust settled. "Why is it so windy?" Again, my delusions did somersaults. What wacky locale could I be in? Why were the elements free to harass me? As I moved my head, something within me snapped back into place, allowing me to sit up without screaming. He moved backward into another shadow. I ignored his coy game so that I could put an end to my wondering.

Several stumbles later, I found myself in front of the glassless window of a construction site. The wind stole my breath before I could even manage a gasp. How did I get there? I was so small and helpless against the majestic city that sprawled before me.

Who knows what could have happened down there. I'd always looked at that skyline with wonder but for the first time, I feared it. Mean spirited people lurked in those streets and inhabited those buildings. People who didn't even know me felt hate for me. They should have at least let me grant them a reason to throw punches. I could have belittled their education or made fun of their clothes but I hadn't even seen them. They peered at me from shadows with judgment and motives unnatural to man. Humans don't hurt one another without cause. We don't kill each other for fun.

At least, I used to think that.

But there were good people. I was in the presence of one. He'd recognized evil, torn me from it, and had given me shelter in—I glanced around to get my bearings—an incomplete luxury high rise? My evening had become some strange version of the knight in shining armor and castle in the clouds story.

I could feel him lurking behind me. "You should not be alone in this city, especially so late at night," he said.

"What, I should have a Guardian, like you?" I asked in a combination of snark and fear. I turned around and he was gone.

Waking up the next day in my bed was confusing to say the least. Through barely open eyelids I was forced to question what had happened. Admitting the truth would hurt more than any wounds inflicted by homophobes. In order to stay in my place of denial, I had to lie perfectly still under my sheets. I thought if I stayed that way, I'd never feel my bruised ribs and be reminded of the horrors that greeted me on 2009's doorstep. I tried to hold that sleeping position like I'd been cryogenically frozen that way. Soon, playing mannequin became daunting and the morning after pains of nearly every part of my body, every part of my being, forced themselves out of the covers and into real life.

Okay, so I knew I was sore. But a number of things could have caused it. I could have run laps or worked out really hard or climbed a long flight of stairs. Or I could have drunkenly stumbled into something, perhaps a medieval torture device someone had left lying around. Aches and pains did not a hate crime make, right? After several minutes of this mental trickery, I got out of bed and made it to the bathroom.

I kept a low head as I entered, averting my gaze from the mirror that typically greeted me. My reflection was destined to be terrible enough to confirm my deepest fears, so I temporarily became a vampire and avoided the damn thing.

The front door buzzer blared through the apartment and shattered my brain, which felt as if it was suddenly made of glass. Finally, in addition to my battle scars, I was feeling that inevitable hangover. One more thing to add to my list of hurts. "Wait a minute," I yelled as if it were a real person. When I arrived at the intercom, Dan's high-pitched voice greeted me.

"Good morning, sunshine!" he sang. "The Gluttonfest Express is here to pick you up!" Then he hooted an irritating train sound that made me want to reach through the intercom and slap him across the face.

Gluttonfest was our group's official celebration of New Year's Day. We spent all of January 1st lying around, eating junk food, and watching movies. Nothing else. Dan and I had always been the festival's biggest proponents, so he was arriving early to discuss which trashy films we'd bring over to our friend, Asher's, apartment. "Well are you going to let me in?" he added.

"Um...Dan, I'm not feeling well. I think I'm going to skip this year."

Silence from his end.

"Dan?"

"You. Will. Not." He was deadly serious.

"I'm just not in good shape."

"Jeremy, we're all hung over. The entire world is. Get over it and let me in!"

A little coal started to burn within my heart—the beginnings of a panic attack. He couldn't come in and see me like this. Even I couldn't bring myself to evaluate my condition. For a second I contemplated climbing out the window and running down the street, or hiding under my bed until he left, or making vomit sounds into the speaker to convey how much I really couldn't stand to have anyone near me. A loud knock on the front door beside me made me jump, and hurt, and wince.

"Your neighbor let me in. Open the door."

Goddamnit. Why were the inhabitants of the building so trusting? He could have been a rapist. We were in Spanish Harlem, after all! You can't just let anyone into your building in a neighborhood like this. He continued pounding and my anxiety rose to a level that threatened to make me either pass out or have diarrhea all over the living room. "Dan, I'm not kidding. You can't come in!"

"I will march myself down to Asher's place and get your spare key, which I know he has, come back here and drag your gay ass to his couch and force you to watch movie musicals if it's the last thing I do! I will, Jeremy King, I will."

I opened the door.

He screamed at the sight of me.

I screamed at his startling scream.

"What happened to—"

"I fell. After I left the bar, I fell into scaffolding on Twenty Sixth Street. I'm terribly embarrassed." Technically, not a lie. I did end up there.

"Did the scaffolding then proceed to roll you down a mountainside? You're a mess."

"I know. Come in." I stepped away from him and began collecting dirty dishes from the kitchen counter, as if I cared about tidying up. The more I could hide my face, the better. "So what movies do you have in mind?"

"You're really going to graze over what happened to you last night?"

"Yep."

"Okay," he agreed. "I found this little known Sarah Jessica Parker movie about a ghost. That could be fun and weird." I was too preoccupied with old food to notice he'd snuck up behind me to examine yet another bruise on the back of my neck. His hand landed on my shoulder.

That was the first time in my tender state that I'd been touched and it was startling at best. My skin seemed to twist under my shirt and send my body into an intense knee-jerk reaction that led me to whirl around and hit him straight upside the head with sandwich dish. It shattered on his square noggin.

"What the hell?" His hand flew up to touch his temple.

"Ohmygod, I'm sorry…"

"Why did you do that?"

"I don't know."

"You don't know why you broke a dish over my head?" He pulled his fingertips away, checked for blood, and finding none, cupped his palm around his skull.

"You scared me."

"I was trying to comfort you. You're crying into the kitchen sink."

"No, I'm not."

"Yes, you are. Tears are pouring from your eyes, you psycho!"

I touched my face. He was right. I was weepy and didn't even realize. My mental status was obviously more delicate than I imagined. "Dan, I'm so sorry. I don't know what got into me."

He peered at me with caution. "Did you lose brain cells in that fall?"

Aside from the lump on his forehead, he wasn't too badly injured from the flying ceramics. He then mentioned the unwritten rule, that after trying to kill your best friend with dinnerware, one must go along with anything he asks. I had no choice but to accompany him to Gluttonfest. All I had to do was shower and then I'd be ready.

Again, I gingerly entered the bathroom and successfully climbed into the tub without passing the mirror. The water couldn't get warm enough. It was as if all of the blood had been drained from my system and been replaced with cold liquid fear. I shivered under the stream, occasionally jumping out of its range when a drop of water rolled down my body and into a still fresh scrape. Bathing was quickly turning into a jerky modern dance routine. Eventually my skin grew accustomed to wetness and I began to relax. I closed my eyes and pretended the water was a rainstorm. Those had always brought me peace.

The serene world inside my head quickly grew ominous and I sensed a presence in the room. I'd never realized just how scary a shower could be. The curtain wasn't clear, but an opaque white that formed a barrier between the rest of the room and myself. It might as well have been drywall. I was on one side of the divide, in the most vulnerable possible state. On the other was the unknown. Well, not the complete unknown, but it certainly wasn't impossible for somebody to have planted themselves in the room while I was distracted by lathering up my loofah. I wouldn't be able to hear the door open over the whoosh of water. Riffraff could have waltzed in from off the street, slaughtered Dan, and been waiting for me behind the towel rack without me ever realizing. Totally feasible.

And then I looked at the small window next to me. On its ledge we kept our bath supplies. In warmer months we'd crack it open to let the steam escape. I stared at the foggy glass and began to think about how scary it'd be to suddenly see a face peering in at me. I pictured a little demon child pressing its pointy nose and claws against it, breathing hot breath and drawing a "666" with the end of its tongue. What would I do if I saw that? Would I scream? Would I make the sign of the cross and then jump out? No. No, I wouldn't because there could be a murderer or another demon child waiting for me on the bathmat.

Why was I thinking that?

Even more distressing, why was the preposterous idea actually upsetting me?

I looked away from the window and closed my eyes. "Rainstorms, rainstorms," I chanted. "Peaceful jungle rainstorms. Rainstorms on a tin roof. And me, in bed. With Orlando Bloom." But my mind couldn't hold those images. It wanted something more disturbing. My dashing movie star turned into a scary man who punched and kicked and laughed as I bled on the cold, wet ground.

Holy crap.

I had to break out of this steaming den of death. I took my chances with the imaginary crazy person on the other side of the shower curtain and ripped it open. Unfortunately I failed to exercise the same care with which I'd entered the room, and the mirror landed right in my line of vision.

I gasped.

What I saw was more terrifying than anything my mind had recently concocted. My left eye was the color of raw denim, the surrounding skin a pee-stained yellow. The rest of me was the color of my grandfather while in hospice. My lips were swollen and a gash accentuated what seemed suddenly to be very prominent cheekbones. The scariest injury, though, was the handprint of my aggressor stamped across my neck. It waved at me, reminding me of what he'd done. I collapsed to the floor and cried so hard I thought my tears would swallow me up like Alice's had, but I didn't want them to wash me away to another world, I wanted them to drown me and put an end to what was destined to be a life of traumatic visions and memories. When that obviously proved impossible, I pressed my head into the tile floor, trying to concentrate my pain to one place. Maybe if it gathered there it'd pop like a pimple and I'd be relieved.

There against the grout, an unexpected sensation shivered through me. The cool, hard floor reminded me of heavy hands cleaning my wounds. My sobs vibrated in the hollows of my body like someone speaking from within a deep cave. The sound soothed me. For the first time since it'd happened, I recalled that someone had helped me.

I'd been saved.

I stopped crying, pulled myself up on the sink's edge, and looked in the mirror.

Momentarily, I felt safe.

Like the ingénue's lyric in that musical comedy about pen pals-turned-lovers, I didn't know his name or what he looked like, so my imagination would be my guide. It told me exactly what he looked like inside. Basically, I couldn't stop thinking about my rescuer. His appearance, personality, and history changed depending on what I found desirable or intriguing at any given moment. Sometimes he was an off-duty cop, other times a vigilante. My favorite version of him was that of a man scorned, prowling the night for fag bashers to avenge the death of his soul mate. His anger about the crime fueled him to do anything, everything to save the defenseless boys on the streets of New York. His sensitivity made him vulnerable enough to love.

Of course romantic daydreams aren't complete without eye candy. Even more enjoyable than constructing his character was the opportunity to create his form. The bass in his voice led me to believe he was a large man. Maybe even fat. But that wasn't my style so I envisioned him more on the brawny side. Or he could have been really tall and fit, kind of like a pro basketball player. Their hands are also gigantic, which could account for the feeling of bricks being laid on my head when he was cleaning my wounds. Then again, he could have just been clumsy, with motor skills better suited for beating up gangsters than applying butterfly bandages. In my heart of hearts, all of his talk about being a "Guardian" had me hoping that he was a perfect, superheroesque specimen. After all, he did bring me to a safe haven high above the city. Obviously he had to have used a cape to fly there, right?

I gravitated towards the superhero version of him because it made me feel the safest. The first several days of January are supposed to be a fresh start. Optimism should exude from every pore. That year however, my experience was far less peppy. Dark clouds of despair gloomed over me. The thunders of apprehension kept me uneasy. Each "next step" I took seemed destined to be my last. Each corner I rounded was an outpost for criminals. Every eye that looked upon me judged to the core. Imagining a superhuman in my wake was the only thing getting me through the day.

My attack had detonated something fearful in my brain. The part that deals with reason and the way we're meant to perceive the world was damaged. The dial on the evil saturation meter had been turned way up, causing me to see blood reds and putrid greens when most people saw sky blues and sunshine yellows. Screeching bats replaced chirping birds. Flowers became thorns. The descent into insanity was quick and I wasn't far from the bottom. I forecasted I was only a matter of days from a complete mental crack.

My first day back at work was for an event celebrating the twelfth day of Christmas. Unfortunately it was only five days after I'd had my face beaten in and I still hadn't adjusted enough to work the floor.

Unfortunately, I realized this fact in the *middle* of the party.

A small concert of twelve drummers drumming on various trashcans, pots, and trunks was in progress on stage. I was bussing glasses from a nearby bar. As I walked into the kitchen area to dispose of them, the performer's beats became more intense. Choreography ensued, which heightened the violence of their pounding. Two men clashed their hands together to recreate cymbals. Another rolled cans across the stage to make a snare. One guy even threw another into the wall, a unique way to achieve bass.

As I watched them, I went into the kind of flashback mode usually reserved for war veterans. Memories of my assault that I thought I'd lost bubbled to the surface.

The names they'd called me rang in my ears. The unabashed ferocity of their punches nailed me in places that had just begun to heal. Images I didn't understand, like an abundance of blood and broken bones and guts, assailed me.

Without considering the tray full of glasses in my hands, I grabbed my stomach to make sure my insides were still on the inside. A crash as loud as the ones coming from stage tore through the room. Thankfully it didn't interrupt the performance. The audience believed it to be part of the show. However Robbie was standing nearby and saw the whole thing.

He waved at somebody to clean up my mess and pulled me to the side. "What just happened?" he gently asked.

I still wasn't completely aware of myself. I did a cartoon shake of my head to try and put the pieces of my brain back in place.

"It was as if you blacked out...but while standing up," he continued. "I've never seen anything like it."

I wanted to concoct an excuse but I was still too shaken. All I could do was say, "I don't know," in the most desperate tone imaginable. The concern in his eyes made me weak. I thought I was crying but my body couldn't even manage that. All it could do was shudder and fall into his arms.

"Hey, hey," he whispered. "I think you should go home."

Robbie talked to our catering captain and convinced him to cut me. It probably wasn't a hard decision. The thick layer of foundation to hide my bruises was already a scar on the perfect cosmology of the party, so any recommendation that I'd do better at home had my boss leaping for the sign out sheet.

"I'm putting you in a cab," Robbie said. "You have cash?"

"Yeah. Of course." That was a lie. I didn't have funds for a cab all the way to Harlem, but I didn't want him forking over money for me, which I knew he would have. My crush was already witnessing me at one of my lowest points. I couldn't have him emptying his pockets as part of it.

On the street he hailed one and opened the door. "Get some rest, mister. Call me tomorrow to let me know you're well, okay?"

I agreed. He kissed my cheek and helped me inside. The driver asked me where I needed to go.

"Wait one second," I told him. I watched Robbie run out of the cold and back inside the concert hall.

"Hey, man. Where to?"

"Nowhere," I called out, as I slipped from the cab and ran toward the subway.

I entered on Broadway and Eight Street. That particular entrance to the station only has a single turnstile onto to the train platform. During rush hour this set up is the bane of every New Yorker's existence because it forces us to walk single file, like kindergarteners. God forbid a train arrives and the person in front of you has trouble with their Metrocard. I'm surprised commuters haven't torn off one another's heads for that offense. Luckily there wasn't a line behind me because the scanner was having difficulty recognizing my fare. I kept swiping, entering the turnstile, and getting stopped by its irritating beeping. "SWIPE AGAIN" read the display. So I did. "SWIPE AGAIN" it repeated. I noticed a shadow cast over me. A tall, scruffy man in a tan suede coat waited behind me.

"Oh, I'm sorry. Go ahead through," I said as I stepped aside.

"Thanks," he said gruffly. He swiped his card and the turnstile approved. Just as he was about to walk in, he grabbed my arm and swung my body firmly against his. He pushed both of us through.

We popped out the other side, and I didn't know whether to thank him for his strangely forceful assistance or scream. When his rough grip tightened on my arm, I decided the latter would be the most appropriate reaction.

"Hel—!"

"Shut up," he said through gritted teeth. He forcefully walked me to the left, behind a column to mask us from other riders. Before he whipped me around, I looked over my shoulder. We were alone. He was just being careful. "Get down there," he commanded.

"What?"

"On the track. Go or I'll throw you."

Somehow I gathered some bravery and asserted, "Absolutely not."

"Fine," he said, delivering on his promise with a shove.

I fell flat on my ass, in the big gap between rails. The splintering of my tailbone made me lurch. I rolled to my side and faced the infamous third rail. It hissed with one thousand volts of electricity. I swallowed my sick and backed away.

A crash blast from around the corner, as if a taxi had backed into hot dog cart. A millisecond later, the turnstile flew through the air and knocked out the lighting fixture above the platform. The guy in the suede jacket ducked against the wall as it fell nearby. In the darkness I made out a figure coming upon him.

"What th—?"

The figure picked him up and threw him down onto the track with me, except the man who'd thrown him had better aim. He landed him right on target: the third rail.

Heat radiated off his body as the supercharged rail cooked him through. Blood gushed from his eye sockets. I turned away.

"Up here," said the shadowy figure above me.

I knew that voice.

My superhero.

"Hurry!"

I struggled to my feet, clenching my teeth against the shooting pain in my tailbone.

"There's not time!" he insisted.

"Give me your hand." I reached up.

He backed away.

"I need help getting up. Give me your hand!" His reluctance confused me. Was I really supposed to climb up out of that hole myself? I was injured. If he were in such a hurry, a helpful hand certainly would have expedited the process. Once more I yelled, "Give me your hand!"

He reached out to me. Without really looking, I grabbed hold.

You know that feeling when you plop down in a subway seat without really looking, and the shock of finding it's wet? That horrifying moment of realization, then panic, then revulsion, and finally resignation as you take an investigative look as your rear end? That's what happened to me when I took his hand. Our skin touched, but his wasn't soft or even warm.

My heart dropped to my ankles.

It was shaped like a hand, but it definitely wasn't any hand that I was used to. Did he have a prosthetic? Was he using a prop? Eighteen possible explanations shuffled through my mind and I was disturbed by at least ten of them. I worked up the nerve to pull myself closer and get a look at our entwined fingers. Most people would have considered me pale, but my skin was bright pink compared to the pallor of his complexion. His hands were so rough they didn't seem to be made of human skin at all. In fact, they felt exactly like…stone.

I jerked away, scraping myself on his "fingers." It felt like road rash.

A cacophony of footsteps and urgency arose from the other end of the platform. "Is everyone alright down there?"

I glanced over. MTA employees and several delayed riders ran toward us.

"Come," my hero demanded, his deformed hand still extended in my direction.

I looked from him to the approaching crowd, and back. "What are you?"

"It does not matter."

"Yes, it does!"

"Do you want my help or not?"

"But you're a…a—"

"Grotesque," he said with an equal mixture of sadness and anger.

The swinging beam of a flashlight illuminated my face. I could tell its next movement would be toward the object of my attention who felt like…a *monster*.

Part of me wanted to wait for the light to reveal his self-declared grotesque figure, but another part of me knew he'd done everything to conceal his deformities. How ungrateful of me to destroy all his efforts due to my own selfish fear? Thanks to his assistance twice in one week, I was alive. Injured, but strong. Certainly strong enough, brave enough, to take his stony hand.

So I did.

He swung me out of the track and onto his back. In a flash, he dashed down the platform and onto the narrow walkway workmen use to enter the subway tunnels. The little iron staircase at its end is always tempting, but anyone with a brain realizes the world beyond is treacherous. Charged wires. Moving tracks that can sever a human in half. If we were spotted entering that zone, extraordinary trespassing fines awaited us. So needless to say, I screamed the entire way through.

Once we were a decent way into the network of tunnels, he veered onto a detour and clanged up a ladder. I dangled off his neck as he ascended. Miraculously he seemed unaffected by a grip that would have crushed most people's windpipes. "I'm sorry. Am I hurting you?"

"No," he replied without a hint of strain. We reached the top of the ladder and entered what appeared to be a dark passageway under the sidewalk. He put me down. "Surely you can walk this yourself."

The only light came through metal grates overhead, and he avoided the glow. "Thank you," I said, after a moment of stunned muteness.

Without a word, he headed in the other direction.

"Wait! Please don't go. I don't know the way out."

"Just follow this path. The grate at the end can be pushed up. You will be in Washington Square Park."

"Wait! Why is this happening? Twice now." My voice cracked. "Is someone trying to kill me?"

"Bad luck," he grunted and took another step toward the ladder.

"You can't do this," I yelled. "You can't just show up out of nowhere and be all…made of stone and expect me to be fine. This is anything but fine."

He stood quiet for several seconds before adjusting his weight. His feet pounded the floor like dropped cinder blocks, and I flinched.

"Are you—?" I stopped, realizing that there wasn't a complete thought behind my words. The pieces were still too jumbled.

"I told you. I am a Guardian."

"Five minutes ago…you said 'grotesque.' What does that mean?"

"It matters not."

"No, it matters yes." That didn't make any sense but I was flustered. "Come into the light."

"I cannot."

"Come into the light!" My voice hurled its echo down the hall, escaping the tunnel clear enough for the train passengers to hear.

We stood, neither of us moving, until the last of the echo stilled.

Very slowly, he walked forward, stopping just outside my field of vision. Wan light from the street poured through a grate above and speckled the floor with little white squares.

I held my breath.

He stepped onto them…and revealed himself. Through the plaid shadows cast on his body, I just barely made him out. My superhero wasn't a man at all, but some humanoid monster thing, hunched over and ancient.

I muffled a gasp in my hands, then said, "You're a…a gargoyle?"

He sighed. "We are called grotesques. Gargoyles are drain pipes."

I would have laughed had it been the least bit funny. Or sane. This had to be my imagination, a psychedelic chemical reaction to getting bashed. Mind you, it was common for my family to hallucinate in order to get through difficult times. My elderly Nana used to see her dead little brother, Tommy, strolling around the house or sitting beside somebody at the dinner table. Once she swore the little African girl she had donated money to was hiding in the china cabinet. So, in this moment, when my hero stepped into the light, I realized I'd clearly inherited Nana's crazy gene.

I backed away and pressed my palms into my eyes. "This isn't real. You're not real."

"That belief would do you well. For years I have tried to convince myself of the same thing. But here I am. Real." He hobbled backwards and hopped onto the ladder. "Keep telling yourself I am not, though. Hopefully one day you will convince yourself."

"I don't want to convince myself," I yelled after him, panicked that he'd disappear. Panicked that I'd never see him again, grotesque or not.

He paused.

"This…this might sound weird, but knowing that you exist has been the only thing getting me through the day."

His hands gripped the metal rungs. "I doubt that someone like me could be that important to someone like you."

"We don't even know each other. Don't make broad generalizations like that." The remark barreled aggressively out of me, as if my speech had been holding onto my tongue for dear life before entering the room with a monster. When it landed, I turned red.

I looked at him looking at me. Even though his eyes lacked depth, color, and gloss, I could see into them. True kindness shone in those eyes. They searched my face until he seemed to realize he'd been staring. Then his glances bounced from the tunnel below him, to his shoulder, up to the grates, and then back in my direction. His stone body clearly wanted to leave but those eyes forced it to stay. What was behind them? Before I could contemplate them further, the ladder he hung from began to groan. Bolts tore from the wall as the steel buckled under his weight.

Just as he was about to fall out of sight, he hurled himself up and back into the corridor with me. His rusty escape route landed in a twisted pile fifteen feet below.

"Most objects cannot support me," he huffed. "I try not to stay in one place for very long. You distracted me." He looked at me with blame, as if it was my fault he weighed hundreds of pounds more than a refrigerator.

Seconds ago he was a monster, but his awkward reaction had transformed him into a big baby before my eyes. I couldn't help but chuckle at his embarrassment.

He cowered at the sound of my voice. When he realized I was laughing instead of screaming, his jaw dropped with astonishment. "You are not frightened of me?" he asked.

"A little. Maybe. At first. Now I'm just…intrigued. You know they fly on the TV show."

"Who? What show?"

"*Gargoyles.*"

He scowled.

"Sorry. Grotesques. On *The Disney Afternoon* they perch on the top of buildings during the day and fly around at night."

"I do not have wings."

"I see that."

"If I did, I would be too heavy to go anywhere. I am stone."

"We've established that."

He pushed out a frustrated breath. "You talk a lot."

It was my turn to feel self-conscious.

A funny little chortle escaped him.

"So now you're laughing at me?" I tried to sound indignant.

"I apologize," he said through an expression that was trying to be a grin. "Yes. Like the drain pipes, I am made immobile by the sun's light. I often spend my days above the city. When the moon rises, I am free to roam."

"And be a Guardian, did you say?"

"Yes. We are appointed to aid you."

"Me?"

"The people of the world," he said, shyly.

"Oh. Right." I didn't really know how to react. On one hand, I was elated because my instincts were correct. He was, in a sense, a superhero. Congrats to me for believing that days ago. On the other hand, he was nothing at all like I'd imagined him to be. Every daydream I'd had about him was crushed under his hefty feet. He definitely wasn't a knight in shining armor or caped crusader. He was, for all intents and purposes, a monster.

Part of me wanted to simply turn around, go home, and pretend nothing, oh…completely insane, had ever happened. I'd be bruised for unknown reasons and haunted by stone grimaces for years as I continually denied our encounters. Mental illness ran in my family. My Guardian could expedite the process. My days could be spent lounging in gauzy white hospital robes in a moderately clean institutional setting. Well. At least I could quit catering.

Even though Discovery Channel taught me he shouldn't exist, he did. According to fairy tales, humans weren't supposed to be exposed to that side of life. It supposedly didn't even exist. But it did, and I'd been exposed to it, touched by it—literally—more than once.

I felt calm when he was near. Most people would be running for the hills, but I was laughing with him. Surely those were reasons to embrace the situation, right?

Belief in the impossible shaped our world.

I decided that the existence of the impossible could shape my life.

"I want to know more."

He cocked his head and looked at me queerly.

"I want to know all about Guardians and grotesques. About you."

"That is not for you to learn."

I ignored him. "I mean, are there others like you? Do you have magic powers? Can you read my mind? Do you have family? Friends? Have you always been this way?"

He turned away, placed his hand on the wall and heaved as if he was choking on a sob.

I softened my tone. "Can you cry?"

He shook his head, no.

"You weren't always like this, were you?"

Again, he shook his head.

It started to fall into place in my head. "So…you're not supposed to be made of stone, but you are." I stepped closer to him. "Right? Just like I wasn't supposed to be a complete failure at everything, working a shitty job, and getting beat up on New Year's Eve." I paused. "But that's exactly what happened."

He turned around and his face was dry. He was right, he couldn't cry.

"Unexpected things have happened to both of us."

"Unexpected things happen to many people," he said.

"Yeah, but you're the only one who knows what's happened to me," I snapped. Like him, I wanted to cry but couldn't. I was more angry than sad. Why had I refrained from sharing my problems with the people in my life? Why were my issues reserved for a stone beast? What could this talking gargoyle do for me that real, hot-bodied, caring humans couldn't?

The answer seemed to be everything.

Friends. Family. Trained professionals. None of them would have any idea how to tackle the eccentricities of my problems, my feelings. I had the irrational sense that the strange creature in front of me would be better at handling my life than even I was. I held up my index and middle fingers. "Two attacks. Both times rescued by you. Doesn't that just scream fate to you?" I searched his face. "Unless of course you've been following me."

"That is ridiculous" He coughed. "I have not been following you."

"Well maybe you should. Or at least check up on me."

He turned, and his laughter mocked me.

"We're supposed to know each other," I insisted. "And frankly I'm afraid of what will happen if we don't. You said you're a Guardian."

"So?"

"So, obviously if you don't guard me, something terrible will happen."

That shut him up. He stared me down and then spoke under his breath. "Are you threatening me, human?"

Was I? I was. "Yes, because everything is a threat to me!" I sounded completely off my rocker, I know. I hoped he didn't possess a modern enough sensibility of social graces to recognize that I had exactly *none*.

The Guardian's eyes avoided mine. His gaze settled at the dirty place where the floor met the wall. "I do not agree with that. But I understand your fear."

"Do you?" I challenged.

"Yes." He struggled with his next thought.

"And yet, you're just going to leave me here?" I spread my arms and let them drop. "Under the street?"

"It would be against my nature to leave you feeling so... vulnerable."

"Which means what?"

His recommendation seemed difficult for him to utter. "We can...meet. Once or twice a week. Just to check in."

I opened my mouth to speak, but he held up one hand to stop me.

"But you must live your life in the meantime. Like a normal human."

"Who says I'm a normal human?" I asked in a flippant tone.

"You must promise me," he said, his tone urgent, serious enough to subdue me.

"I promise."

"I will be near if harm comes to you."

And there it was. We were bound.

We stood silently in front of each other, not really knowing how to proceed. The fear that had latched itself to my bones melted away. I stood a little taller knowing he'd officially be on my side. "Do you have a name?" I eventually asked.

His head tilted to the side, questioning.

"If we're going to hang out, I should at least know your name."

"Garth," he said. "The Guardian."

"Yes, I'm clear on that last part. Thank you, Garth. I'm—"

"Jeremy," he said softly. "I know."

2. The Origins of Stone

Our first scheduled meeting was probably a real exercise in patience for Garth. I did most of the talking, so the majority of what I said wandered into the typical "woe is me" outlook that New Yorkers enjoy falling victim to.

"Well, if you are so miserable, change things until you are not," he said.

I snorted. "Okay, that'll be so easy."

He didn't take my bait, adding in a soft tone, "Believe me, human life is short. Make something of it."

Now, he could've drawn that conclusion based on voyeurism and the occasional conversation with (lucky/odd/unsuspecting) people like myself, but I had a feeling it was more personal than that.

I narrowed my gaze. "I've been doing all the talking. You need to tell me your story."

"How can you be so certain I have one?"

"Seriously?" I asked, in a droll tone. "You're a rock."

"Precisely."

"You're a *talking* rock. Which requires an interesting history." I leaned back, crossing my arms.

"You make a good point," he muttered.

"So? Start talking." Hopefully I could pick up a thing or two from him. Isn't that how life lessons are learned? One must listen to the horrors of the less fortunate to realize how precious existence truly is? Being that Garth was a stone monster, forced to sleep when the sun came out, it was safe to say that he was less fortunate than I.

His story began much like the beginning of our relationship had, with him waking up in an unexpected place after a less than pleasant experience. From the looks of him, he'd had a lot of unpleasant experiences, but the one I'm talking about was the first. Maybe the worst. In any case, it got the ball rolling for all of the others.

He was, he told me, born human and lived a normal human life. Well, it was normal for the time, which was very, very long ago.

"How long?"

"I can't remember. Long enough to see man rise and fall time and again."

"So, longer than a year?" I joked. I just wanted to keep him talking.

"Humans of history were smarter than you know," he said. "But, being humans, they've always found a way to—"

"Screw things up?" I interjected.

"I suppose you could say that."

He launched into a tale that took hours while I sat mesmerized. War had ruined the great ancient cities—cities whose knowledge rivaled that of today. Memories of their glory faded into legends and legends faded into obscurity as new beliefs swept through the land. Powerful men adopted those beliefs and forced them on their people, settling them into simple lives in simple towns.

It was a dark time.

Garth's village had to join the revolt, part of the Great War that challenged the King's authority. Even though the little town had barely seen how evil the King was rumored to have been, they fought with their countrymen in opposition to their ruler. A dangerous move but they were confident in their beliefs. As was the law back then, every available man was sent out, including the human Garth…

"I apologize for crying. It probably is not making you feel any better," said Garth to his mother. His father had died years before, leaving him to care for her and his sister, Evie. The thought of leaving them alone, potentially forever, tore him apart.

"Garth, you will not be gone for long. The latest news is good. Our forces are making progress," said his mother. Her attempt at comforting him didn't work.

"They are not our forces," he said in a bitter tone. "We have no association with the effort. There is no reason for our involvement."

She stilled him with a touch. "If your sister or I were victims, would you act?"

"Of course. You are my family."

"Well, think of your countrymen as extended family. If things are bad for one of us, they are bad for all of us," his mother scolded gently. He was too old to think her right all the time, but she was.

"I am just...afraid, that is all. What happened to simple times?" he asked.

"Times were never simple, child. Not for a moment. The former Kings might have wanted you to think their rule was the best, the most simple, but the Way of Things is much more complicated."

"It doesn't have to be."

"Life is more interesting when turned upside down. You might find out something about yourself."

Garth burst into tears and crawled into her embrace, like he'd done as a child. He was much larger now, but felt just as small. "I will miss you."

"I know, love. And we will miss you. You will be back soon. I know it."

Evie wandered into the room, carrying Garth's giant traveling sack on her back. "This bag is *huge*. I could never carry it! Good thing you're big," she said.

He scooped her up and twirled her in the air. She was a happy girl. Being away from her would hurt.

All too soon, Garth's friend, Francis, stood at the door, packed and ready to meet the others in town. He and Francis had grown up together, done everything together, so it was fitting that they should go to war together. The two comrades wobbled down the darkened roads to meet their new family and leave their old ones behind.

Garth never looked back but he wished he had.

He was left with no image of his home—the place where he'd never get to grow old, marry a wife, or raise a family...

"Was that the last you saw of them?" I asked. He said nothing. "Is this too difficult for you?" On that night, we were on top of an apartment complex in the West Village, where things are rather quaint…for Manhattan, at least. He looked through the naked branches of a tree lined street and sighed.

"It is difficult. But it is good. I have not talked about this in a long time. I used to recall my human life quite often, as a way to hold onto it. I've probably forgotten a lot," he said somberly, almost in a hum. "Yes. That was the last time I saw them."

I waited out Garth's mourning silence for a moment, and before long, he carried on with the tale…

It had taken several years and countless lives for the war to come to a head. Garth spent much of his deployment performing mundane support tasks, as it turned out he wasn't much use on the field. Francis was a more capable fighter but did his best to hide those traits to stay with Garth. One of their longest stints was on funeral duty, during which they picked up bodies (what was left of them) and burnt them on a pyre. If Garth wasn't already afraid of battle, hearing the crackle and hiss of the carcasses of fallen friends made him even more so.

When the final showdown was at hand, the rebel forces had been badly depleted. Every man needed to be thrust into battle, even scrawny Garth and awkward Francis. The armor they once cleaned was fitted for them after its original owners had been slain. The stench of war and death on the gear sickened them as they walked out onto the field.

Knowing full well what blades could do, the two friends spent every effort during the battle avoiding them. As their fellow soldiers were annihilated one by one, Garth and Francis hid in trees and played dead.

Cowards? Yes.

Stupid? No.

They were, after all, fighting for freedom. What good was freedom if they were dead? Dreams of victory had been crushed; their only hope was to slip away unharmed.

Eventually, hiding places grew scarce and fatigue set in. Before long, one of the King's men was upon them. These brutes were huge in stature, pumped full of secret concoctions to amp up their natural bodies. Francis and Garth were not slain in the ensuing battle, but were certainly immobilized. They lay side-by-side on the frosted plain, atop heaps of dying men, with their consciousness slipping. Sleep came quickly, like it or not.

After being scraped off the field, Garth woke up with aches far worse than those on harvest mornings, but alive. Relatively well, so far as he could tell. Most of his companions weren't so lucky. Piled around him in a cage, like bundles of twigs waiting to be tossed into a flame, were abbreviated men: some without limbs and even one without a face. If they weren't moaning, they were probably dead. Better off. Dirt, rust, and blood painted their twisted bodies brown.

It came to him all at once. "Francis!" he gasped as he jolted upright.

"Over here!" replied a little voice.

Garth scanned the men, each one worse off than the last. He spotted his friend clinging to one of the iron bars of their entrapment. "I'm coming," he yelled over death's groans. In the confusion of seeing the once brave men in such a horrific condition, Garth failed to realize his own. His right leg had been completely crushed and folded like an accordion beneath him.

After some necessary screaming and a sick stomach, Garth pulled himself together and dragged himself over to his friend's side. Francis's body was broken so badly he needed to be propped up to keep from suffocating himself.

"Thank the heavens for these bars. They may enslave us, but they are saving my life," Francis said. He was always trying to lighten even the darkest of times.

Garth examined their prison, terror blossoming through him. An enormous cage surrounded them, as if they were animals in a traveling show. This spectacle was set up in the King's base camp as a type of amusement for his victorious soldiers, who laughed and cursed at their opponents' misfortune.

Soon the rowdy men were hushed, and a robed man approached the bars with golden props and bejeweled scepters. He began to pray.

"That language isn't ours," Garth said.

"It isn't the King's either, he just prays in it," said Francis.

"Is it true they pray for our souls?"

"Yes." His eyes met Garth's. "It will make them feel better about killing us later."

Garth looked once more at the other prisoners clustered together behind the same iron bars. "They did not pray for our men they killed in the field."

"Maybe he doesn't want us dead. Maybe we are being recruited," said Francis.

"No. I'd rather die."

"This is the time for bravery, friend. More so than in battle." He patted Garth's knee, a small gesture of comfort. "You know, there is humor in this."

"I doubt that," Garth whispered.

"There is humor in everything. If that King is hoping to recruit the best soldiers, he's wrong. They are already dead. That's what happens to the brave."

Garth couldn't help but crack a smile.

"There was no winning this war," said Francis, calmer than he should be given the circumstances. "Our only options were to fight and get slaughtered or avoid it and get tortured. That isn't fair."

"Maybe he'll just whip us and then send us on our way. We'll go home and scare the town into never revolting again. At least we'll be alive."

He looked at Garth with a raised eyebrow and said, "You have the strangest sense of optimism."

A horn blew, commanding everyone's attention. Torches led a procession through the camp toward the cage. The King's soldiers bowed their heads as he made his way to the prisoners. It was a sin to look upon him, as he claimed to be of divine lineage.

"I bet none of them have ever seen his face," whispered Garth.

"They could be fighting for a scarecrow for all they know," replied Francis. One of the thugs nearby glared in their direction, demanding silence.

"Traitors!" screamed the King, toward the caged soldiers.

"Traitors!" echoed his men, before settling into a seething, charged silence.

"As inhabitants of my kingdom, you are my people. Your rallying against me is a sign of ungratefulness for the fruits I bestow upon you."

Would that be it, then? Garth wondered. A lecture?

"You are a monster!" exclaimed one of the caged men. "They obey you out of fear, not loyalty."

Garth cringed. What kind of fool would insult the man who decided their fate?

The King approached the confine and grasped two of its bars. "I...am a monster?" he asked. His voice crept into Garth's ears and rung his spine. "You offend me." He turned to his men. "He offends me. He offends God!" The men roared in agreement. "These traitors think that I am unjust. They do not believe in my appointment to the throne. Shall I prove them wrong?"

Clubs beat against the ground and shields met helmets, rattling the cage.

"No, no!" said the King, waving his hands to quiet the rabble. "I am a just and fair man. Any judgment is left to God above." His hands rose to reference the sky where his new god was said to reside. "Feed them and give them drink." The crowd was clearly taken aback but didn't dare make a sound of displeasure.

Guards rushed food into the cage. The ravenous prisoners barely chewed, just devoured whatever came before them like beggars in a garbage pit. The King's soldiers silently watched.

When the supply was depleted and the men were satisfied, they lay strewn on the ground of the cage like their dead countrymen on the field. The King looked on from a golden throne without a care. The sun was setting and night's first chilly breeze rolled down the cliff sides.

Queasiness overtook Garth. Looking around, he could see that the others felt the same. One man began to groan and soon that groan turned into an agonizing scream. Possibly gas? The result of eating too quickly? Garth waited for the symptoms that seemed to be running rampant and when they hit, he knew it was more than bad food.

The entire cage seized as the men convulsed and thrashed against its bars. The sounds coming from within were no longer from men. Skin ripped, bones twisted, and bodies bubbled.

"Men without God are not men at all!" cried the King. "Now, who is the monster?" The crowd howled as agony tore Garth into a deep, silent blackness...

"That was the beginning of my new life," Garth said.

I couldn't help it, I stared at his leg, the one he'd claimed had been crushed in the battle.

"It grew back that night. Along with this hump and these horns."

"And a sleek, new skin made of granite."

He ignored my attempt at positivity. "No. I was not yet stone. Just a monster. Unfortunately."

I swallowed past my embarrassment. "So this...transformation... was some sort of torture?"

"Not so much torture as security. If a slave is disfigured, he's less likely to leave his master."

I balked. "That would give me more reason to run away. Didn't you hate him even more?"

"I despised the man. But it is hard to flee when you look like this." He referenced his own, weird form. "Monsters always stand out among men. And where would we go if we did escape? We were unrecognizable to our families." He appeared to choke up, even without anything to choke up on. After a moment, he gathered himself and continued, "There is no use killing a soldier if he can be resourced in another way. The King was practical when it came to those things."

"So what did he have you do?"

"I'm getting to that," he said through a half-grimace, half-glimmer. He seemed almost...happy that I found his story so enticing. "We became a sort of police force."

"You had to protect him?" I gasped.

"Yes, but also the capitol city and the people there."

"*His* people," I said with disgust.

"Innocents," he corrected. "They just happened to have a terrible ruler."

"That's still pretty shitty."

Garth chuckled to himself. "Yes. Yes, it was. We were not so easily swayed, though. We were still serving the man we had risked our lives trying to topple. Obviously, there was resentment." Garth grabbed his head as he tried to search for something. He found a somber thought that moved him forward. "I can not remember his name. The other Guardian...two syllables." He looked at me sadly, "Forgive me, I haven't—"

"It's fine. I understand."

"One of us, another Guardian, could not bear his position and he left the palace. He did not get very far, though. Some townspeople believed he was a demon and killed him. It took about twelve men to bring him down, but they got him. Then they burnt the body in the square to ward off further evil. People were very superstitious back then."

"Maybe it was better to be dead?"

Garth shook his head in distress. "The King went a step further."

"Further than turning you into slave creatures?"

"Yes. A week later, he returned with the head of the runaway's wife. Not only were we at risk if we betrayed him, so were our families."

"What a tricky bastard," I said under my breath.

"As my mother said, I was at war for family. She was right. So we bit our lips and lived to protect the King. We hoped our lives would pass quickly and that our souls would be reunited with our loved ones, long after all of our passing."

For the first time in hearing his story, I rolled my eyes. For some reason the idea of black magic, monsters, and Garth's very existence to begin with was understandable, but the fluffy soul business I just couldn't ingest.

"You think it is funny. The souls," he said.

"No, not funny. I just...when it comes to religion, I just...don't have one."

"It has nothing to do with religion. Humans have souls. It is a fact. As far as you know, I should not even exist, right? Magic?"

"I know. My reasoning of what's real and what's not...it's stupid. Magic versus science...and all." I had no clue what I was talking about. A few short days ago, I was scared of devil children in the medicine cabinet. I certainly had no right not believing in ghosts.

"Science is magic and magic is science, Jeremy," he said bluntly. "You humans think you've discovered everything there is to know. You thought you had it all figured out in medieval times, then one hundred years ago, and then fifty years ago. But you always prove yourselves wrong. One day you will find that there is more to the world than atoms and cells and mathematic equations."

"Something divine?" I asked, with a hint of sarcasm.

"Something you simply have not figured out yet," he said. "You will, in due time. Until then, I will just have fun watching you speak so convincingly about all that you humanly know."

❖

The local mall of my childhood town was a tiny thing. It had all of the usual suspects lined in rows, begging for business. But thirty miles west of my little beachside city was the Mecca of South Jersey shopping: the Freehold Mall. About three times a year, Mom and her girlfriends would pack us kids in the car and pilgrimage to the shopping center that made ours look like a five and dime. We'd haunt the halls of that two-story behemoth until the recycled air made us sick, but we'd eventually leave feeling like the satisfied consumers we were bred to be.

In time, my friends and I reached an age when we could wander around without parents, as long as we agreed to meet them at a specific time and place at the end of our collective sprees. Even though we were only a bunch of meager fifth graders, venturing into the mall without the 'rents was a turning point. The glimmers of growing up were upon us and soon we'd be "whatever"-ing our way through life, just like Cher and Dionne in *Clueless*. Our weekly allowances were spent on soft pretzels and milkshakes before we hit up the very best teen stores. Soon our interest in clothes would fade and we'd make our way to the dork stores. If there was a pile of plush animals, cartoon characters suspended from wires, dinosaur dig sets, rainforests in boxes, or castle dioramas, we were there. Hell, I still eat that shit up. It was in one of those shops that I met Dedo, a little stone creature much like Garth…only pint sized and mass-produced.

I laid eyes on him and immediately needed to take him home. I don't remember what went through my head at the time but I felt like he was alive, waiting for a caring soul like myself to scoop him up for $15.99. It was my duty to rescue him from the plastic shelving and constant sound of children playing with rain sticks. After much begging, Mom agreed, and he was packed in a tiny box made of recycled material. I carefully transferred the bag containing the box home like it contained my sister's liver. I was super excited about my new friend and promptly showed him off to my father, whom I knew would be thrilled that I wasn't bringing home a My Little Pony.

Dad's library was filled with sacred texts, occult conspiracies and crumbling editions of everyone's favorite fantasy novels. Some dads have books on cars; mine had the Egyptian Book of the Dead. He didn't attend any secret midnight meetings, as the books were just the result of a passing fad, like the time he started collecting accordions or listened to strictly Cajun music for three months. However, his general interest in the subject matter had staying power, mostly manifesting in his very specific taste in movies. I was a spiteful child, so any recommendation from an authority figure caused me to do the polar opposite. "Jeremy, come watch this movie with me. You'd like it," he'd holler from the other room. I'd obligatorily stomp over to the couch and pretend to be interested. Despite my pissing and moaning, I usually liked what he was showing. I refused to watch *Clash of the Titans* about seven times but eventually caved, and I'm very glad that I did.

Dedo's arrival launched Dad into research mode. He pulled information out of giant books as if he were a grand wizard. "The gargoyle's grotesque form is used to scare away evil spirits, hence their popularity as decoration on sacred buildings through most of the civilized world," he read from some encyclopedia of magic-goblin-wackadoo-craziness.

"Of course," I thought to myself. Bringing Dedo home had been my subconscious way of taking control of a situation that had plagued me for years: nightmares.

My mother had become an old pro at coming up with tactics to rid me of bad dreams. First she tried opening the window every night and asking the monsters to leave. Then the bad dream gate was installed. It was meant to keep trolls and whatnot out of my personal space…but it was really just a childproof gate in the doorway, imprisoning me in my bedroom and keeping me from crawling into theirs. Dream catchers, bedtime prayers and other mental trickeries were deployed in the war against boogies and for the most part, they worked. Purchasing Dedo was my (almost) grown up self's last effort to purge myself of an affliction that I was too old to be suffering from.

I swiftly unwrapped my gargoyle and gave him a prominent spot on my dresser so that he could monitor me throughout the night. As with the rest of my family, I affectionately kissed Dedo goodnight and greeted him every morning. Just as compulsively as I used to ask God to grant me sweet dreams, I would wish Dedo good luck on his nightly prowl.

In high school, my world shattered—along with Dedo—the result of a routine room cleaning. My over-zealous dusting killed him. I lost it. At seventeen I was inconsolable by having broken what most people would consider a toy. The kitchen counter became a trauma unit as I frantically gathered up the pieces and glued them together. Thankfully I was home alone and didn't have to face anyone with the embarrassment of going crazy over a smashed knick-knack. But, to me, he was more than that. That's why I couldn't stand looking at his haphazardly reassembled head and his chipped shoulders. He once guarded me with pride but I'd reduced him to an unsightly arts and crafts project. Could he even see out of his hot glue-glazed eyes?

Finally, I conceded defeat. I said goodbye to my stalwart friend, buried him in the woods behind my house, and braved the nights alone.

For my sanity, I had to believe that everything in my life was a product of coincidence. Upon meeting Garth, I tried wiping Dedo from memory. The pebble that kept me sane years ago had no connection with the boulder that had kept me alive on New Year's Eve. The tiniest thought of the two in correlation with each other forced my mind into drawing strange conclusions that I couldn't begin to understand.

That I didn't want to understand….

❖

Our meetings were brief because I'm a normal person of the world and sleep primarily when it's dark outside. Garth did the opposite. "So, is your species related to vampires or something?" I asked at our next encounter.

"Oh, this evening-meeting situation," he laughed. "Yes, I suppose we are similar. Except those Night Creatures are made of flesh and blood."

"And so were you when we left off."

Garth easily tired of playing storyteller. The effort required recalling his past and the baggage that came with it exhausted him. "Yes, that changed rather quickly," he said as he ran his hand down his arm. "I can not feel this. Well, I feel some sensation of contact. If I had absolutely no sense of feeling, I would not be able to do anything. The details in touch that most take for granted are lost to me." His finger grazed my jacket. "Nothing. Contact, but nothing more. I know it should be soft. Sometimes I fool myself into feeling it, but that is only when I remember back to my human days. This jacket probably feels much like a scarf that my sister had. I think of that and I know what this should feel like. But those days, those memories, are getting further and further away."

He pulled away and I ran my fingers over the fabric. It had a sleek, almost wet feeling. It was synthetic. Probably nothing like his sister would have had but I didn't say anything.

"I am sure you can imagine what I must have looked like when I had skin. Take away the stone and put something else ugly in its place," he said.

I tried my best. It took me awhile to get over the CGI, video game image that my brain automatically created after years of pixels attacking my eyes, but soon it came. For a fraction of a second my mind saw him how he once was. My breath stopped.

"My skin was blotchy. Boils and bumps, coarse hair and sharp nails. I was revolting."

He was right. Gross.

"Then, I could feel it all. I tried my best to avoid reflections, to forget what I looked like. But it was hard not to catch a glimpse of my feet as I walked or feel the rough skin on my fingers when my hand closed. Even breath blew through my new lungs differently, like a fat dog or a dying horse. Every moment was excruciating." His hands clenched into a fist. He held them so tightly that the tiniest sprinkle of dust fell through his palm.

I instinctually grabbed him, trying to set him at ease. It was the first time that I'd voluntarily touched him. We both flinched and his hand released. "I'm sorry," I said. "Were you remembering?"

He nodded. "When I was turned to stone, it was a blessing to lose those sensations. I became completely removed from my body. This is just a shell that I live inside of."

From the way he was acting, it seemed like the night was going to be cut short. I'd barely been with him for five minutes and he was over it. "Do you want to continue?" I asked.

"Yes." A pause. "After that first escape, the King realized that we were simply too strange to be out in the open. His new religion was budding. Real demons, as we were called, guarding the King brought up many questions. We had to be kept secret. There were more than enough men already working to police the streets throughout the day. We were used exclusively at night, after the lamps had all been put out. He turned us to stone and hid us high above the city on the towers of his palace."

"And that was the beginning of grotesques and gargoyles?" I asked with a bit too much wonder.

"No. Strange creatures have been carved into stone throughout history, which is what made us blend in so easily."

"But he didn't have to make you stone. You could have just lived as monsters above the city, right?"

"It is not easy to sleep soundly *like* a statue with the sun beating down on you during the day without actually *being* a statue. With this stone curse of day sleep, we were the perfect Guardians. The sun rose and we were forced to rest. Townspeople looking up at the tower would see nothing out of the ordinary. If we were caught patrolling at night, we could easily stand still and be mistaken for decoration. We did not need to be fed because stone does not eat. Stone is harder to destruct, is more deadly in a brawl, and most importantly, doesn't die. The King had made us Immortal."

To me, his condition was interpreted as a type of übermensch—a superman. "Immortality. That's kind of cool, right?"

"Nothing is 'cool' if you are not given a choice. I would have never chosen this life," he growled. "I am separated from everyone I have ever loved."

"Garth, I—"

"I can not die! I can be destroyed but I can not die and pass on like the rest of you." He turned away and walked into the darkness cast by a nearby building. "Immortality is for those who were born Immortal. I was not meant to be this way. I was born with a soul, like you. When he changed me, that soul left because I had no use for it. Because I am not meant to die."

"Immortals don't have souls?" I tentatively asked, afraid that he'd snap again.

He quietly shook his head and then mumbled, "Souls shouldn't be wasted on beings like us."

Whoa, that was a lot.

We were tired.

Well, I was tired and he was tired of me.

Without too many more words, we called it a night and I headed home.

I walked to an inconvenient subway. Sometimes in New York, nighttime and an iPod are all a person needs to clear his head. I knew Garth was probably trailing me or at least within proximity, just a scream away. Knowing that, I mustered some courage to walk past the scene of the crime. I wanted to face my fears and remind myself that Twenty Sixth Street wasn't a lava-filled wasteland inhabited by Orcs and goblins, but just a normal city block. It was simply a place where an unlucky guy encountered sad people, hell bent on ruining somebody else's night.

That neighborhood bustled with people during the day but the business-free evenings made humans scarce. The sidewalk was new, probably laid in autumn, and scaffolding clung to the buildings like parasites. The freshness of the surroundings made the stains more evident. By now, about a week later, the blood was brown and looked like any other city juice, but I knew what it really was. I expected to see just a few speckles but I found a wash that covered an entire slab of concrete.

The realization stunned me. If I had lost that much blood, I'd have died.

More than just *my* blood had stained the sidewalk that night.

Apparently Garth was right. He was very deadly in a brawl.

3. Enjoy *Your* View.

Every weekday at approximately 10:55 a.m., I'd bolt out of bed and head for the coffee pot to do the brewing of my morning potion. Then my roommate, Meg, and I would nestle ourselves onto our broken couch for the commencement of *The View*. Sure the current affairs covered on that show were skewed by bad jokes, obvious segues, failed understanding of issues, and Elizabeth's general, mind-numbing conservatism...but we ate it up. That was also the only time that the two of us had to check in with each other.

"I can't believe you stayed at home for so long. Most of the world got back from vacation last week, before the New Year," I said. "I doubt whatever you did with your family in Bayville compared to the possibilities that awaited you here." My "New York is superior" complex was in full swing.

"Says the boy who hates New Year's," she argued. "Besides, New Year's Eve is expensive and we're too poor to do anything really fabulous."

"Don't use that word. This isn't the Flamingo Club."

"Ew. I'm sorry. You only had fun because you got free drinks at your lady-friend's bar," she said with a restoration air. "*That's* what you did, right? You went to that weird Texas *joint*?"

"Yes."

"Naturally. Anything of note happen?"

Obviously the prescription of her glasses was weaker than her contacts. If it were later in the day and her "eyes were in," she'd have noticed the remainders of my injuries. Because she was one of my best friends, I debated what concoction of truths and lies I could rattle off. There could definitely be no mention of stone men. The whole hate-crime thing needed to be left out, too. I was still too embarrassed. Talking about it would just bring up all of my suppressed feelings of hatred towards the human species and intense violation of personal space. She'd feel obligated to tell every living soul about the incident, resulting in the assignment of an escort to constantly haunt my wake. Besides, if she couldn't tell that anything was wrong with me, there was no point bringing it up.

"No, nothing," I said. "Oh, I did kiss some random man, though. I think he may have had Bell's Palsy because half of his face was kind of dead. Of course that could have been the whiskey…"

She grimaced. "Did you go home with him?"

I grimaced. "No, sir. I got the spins and had to leave. I didn't want to have another *Charlie Incident*." Charlie was a boy I dated for a hot second after college. We got absolutely tanked one night and I threw up on him and all his earthly possessions. Mortifying. To this day I make myself feel better by telling people that he was into it. That way I don't look like the tragic one.

"What about Robbie? What's going on with that handsome fellow?"

My face went as dead as the man's I had just described.

"He was with his boyfriend, wasn't he?" she asked, semi-sympathetically. "You probably shouldn't get too hung on him."

"I'm not hung up." Lies. Besides gargoyles and hate crimes, Robbie was all I could think about.

"Do you daydream about the day he breaks up with Nick?"

"Shut up."

"Do you come up with different scenarios for your first kiss?"

"I'm going to pour hot coffee on your lap."

"Will you hide your love affair from your co-workers or will you hold hands while you pass mini-cheeseburgers at wedding receptions?"

"Really. I'm going to rip your face off."

"You're not angry. You love this attention."

She was right. I did. If I talked about liking Robbie enough, maybe a romance would manifest itself into existence. "I know, I know!" I laughed. "I like him and I feel like a crazy person because of it!"

We shared a laugh at my misfortune before she became awkwardly silently. The only time she got like that was when she had something to say but was afraid to say it because she knew I'd bite off her head. "What?" I asked.

"You know I hate to pry, but one of your *other* friends messaged me while I was at home."

Suddenly I was a teenage girl. People were talking about me behind my back. They knew something...no, had opinions about me that I wasn't aware of. More than most injustices on Earth, I hate being out of the loop about issues pertaining to Jeremy King. "Who? Asher? Dan?" I was mentally murdering them both.

"The gay one." She smirked. "Anyway, he said that you took quite a stumble on your way home and have been acting strangely ever since."

"Define strangely."

"Nervous, anxious, generally kind of manic. Something about throwing a pan at his head."

Damn him. Dan. Couldn't a person have a slight mental break without it being shared with the world? "It was a plate. It was an accident. He crept up on me. I'm going to kill him."

"You're being so violent."

"Hyperbole. I'm angry. Have we met?"

"Regardless, he was just giving me a heads up in case we need to call the men in white or something." She took a sip of coffee and kept her eyes on me. "But you're acting perfectly normal right now. Must have just been a phase."

Ugh. *She* was patronizing *me*. It's supposed to be the other way around. I'd give her this one opportunity. Only because I didn't have the energy to do otherwise. "That's exactly what is was. You know how I get at this time of year. It's depressing."

"*Exactly* what I said. I know how you hate to discuss feelings so we'll push this all from our minds. I was just doing the obligatory roommate thing by inquiring." She knighted each of my shoulders with her Bahamas souvenir mug. "I deem you mentally sound. Now, I have to take my morning constitutional."

She got up and waddled to the bathroom, leaving me alone to bring my boiling rage at Dan down to a simmer. How dare he go behind my back like that! Sure it was a nice gesture to be concerned for my welfare, but my mental state is *my* mental state. No one else's. I couldn't help but be pleased with myself, just below my anger, though. To Meg, I appeared relatively fine. My being around Garth must have worked. Just as I predicted!

"False alarm!" Meg wailed as she walked back into the room. "I just need more coffee." She took a seat just in time for a commercial break.

"Two bodies found crushed and hidden in a Chelsea storm sewer. Today, at noon," said Lori Stokes, local newswoman.

That word. *Chelsea.* Every time it was uttered, it lit up my mind like a flare. Hearing it attached to violence was the equivalent of a punch to the gut.

"Dear god, that's terrible," Meg moaned. She took a dainty sip of coffee and toasted. "Happy New Year."

I needed her to shut up, stop making light of the situation, and let Lori do her job. I lunged forward to absorb the rest of the Channel 7 teaser. The last shot was of the location where the corpses were found. As I feared, it was Twenty Sixth Street—my personal ground zero. Only one person could have physically done it, and that person wasn't a person at all. Garth.

The blood retreated from my face. I shuttered.

"Jer, are you okay? You look positively sickly. I didn't mean to get you all self-conscious earlier."

"It's not that. Just the thought of those men in the sewer…it's unsettling." Even more disturbing was the knowledge that Garth did the damage. Throwing someone into an electrified rail is one thing, but pulverizing two men into burger meat was a whole other realm of disturbing.

"It's not nearly as bad as when those kids lit that homeless man on fire down the street. Now that was really wild. New York is rough!"

I finished watching the show in a haze and anxiously waited for the news to announce more details. After multiple segments about recessions and store closings, I got the dish on Garth's victims: Someone complained to the city about a smell coming from the sewer. When an official finally checked it out, two bodies were found. They had been brutally beaten—almost pulverized, until the bodies could be stuffed through the sewer grate.

The air had been pretty frigid on the evening I'd walked by the scene, which probably suppressed the smell. But, that explained the gruesome stains on the sidewalk…

I'd been instructed to walk into Central Park and find Garth in the Conservatory Gardens. That uptown portion of the park rarely sees foot traffic because tourists think that Manhattan terminates at Sixtieth Street. A few brave souls sometimes venture up to the reservoir on Ninetieth Street, but then they turn around at the first sight of a black person. The thought of Harlem turns most white people whiter—fine by me because I lived on East 102nd Street, which might as well be Afghanistan to a person from the Midwest. My Central Park was positively libraric compared to the hustle and bustle of Bethesda Terrace and The Mall. I could find solace just two avenues away, past the projects and Mt. Sinai Hospital's varying types of eyesores/architecture. However, on one issue I still sided with the tourists: nighttime = no park.

"Are you trying to get me killed?" I rasped, as I entered Conservatory Gardens and caught a glimpse of Garth. "Walking around in here in the middle of the night is like wearing a glow in the dark 'rape me' shirt."

"If I remember correctly, you were walking down a street in Chelsea when you were attacked. It looks like you made it here without a scratch. You might want to re-think what you consider to be dangerous," he replied, proud of himself for being a smartass.

I frowned. "Speaking of Chelsea, your…*handiwork* made the news today."

He just grunted.

"You didn't tell me that you killed those men."

"You did not ask."

I flailed a bit, raised my voice. "You didn't have to do that, Garth. Jesus! You could have just…scared them…or pushed them around a bit."

"Do you think that is what they wanted to do to you?" He elevated his to a quiet boom. "Do you think they would have stopped beating you up after you were appropriately scared?"

"I…don't know."

"And you never will." Garth paced, brooding. "Those men had dark hearts. If they had lived long lives and died natural deaths, they would still be guilty when judgment came. I just brought them there sooner and hopefully saved others from being…scared in the meantime."

Apparently I had a vigilante on my hands, and not just the knock 'em, sock 'em kind, either. I didn't know what to think about that. My mind whirled. "Do you kill often?" I asked, in the same tone one might ask, "Are you new here?"

"No!" he said. Then added, in a subdued timbre, "No. But if it is necessary to protect the innocent, I will."

I blew out a breath, forked shaking fingers through my hair, and kept my hand clutching the back of my neck.

"Long ago, penalties were much harsher for crimes much smaller. Your modern justice system prevents that—"

"Which is a good thing," I said.

"Sometimes. Criminals don't always deserve another chance, especially ones who commit such hateful acts."

He had a point. But still…murder.

He looked at me from inside his usual shadowy corner. I stood in the open, bathed the moon's bright light. "Something about this is unsettlingly familiar, Jeremy."

I had no idea what he was talking about. I certainly didn't have a history of relationships with statues.

"I suppose that is part of why I have sought a friendship with you. You are reminiscent of…" He fell into silence. I was losing him in a difficult memory. "You remind me of my friends. My old friends."

Friends.

Yeah, I remembered having those.

I hadn't seen my friends in a while. I couldn't help but question my sanity level for sneaking off into the night to meet with the vigilante grotesque instead of doing normal things like go on dates with humans or drink gin and tonics on a friend's couch while watching YouTube clips of Britney Spears. I'd even begun making up excuses to people about my whereabouts. Sometimes I'd say that I got cast in something and had rehearsal, then other times I pretended to have developed a smoking habit.

"How many cigarettes did you have? You were gone for an hour," Meg would ask. I'd tell her I took a walk or met a friend on the street. Looking back, that seems equally sketchy. Everyone must have thought I was crazy even without the part about the gargoyle.

Garth laughed when I told him that. "Francis and I had a friend like that, one that we would sneak away to meet. We used to tell her stories like I do to you. It might be her that you remind me of."

I assumed that she was my quirky medieval equivalent. Maybe the local call girl who made midnight deals in stable stalls and alleyways. It turns out that I was wrong…the polar opposite, even. Their friend was another statue in town named Helena, and she was the most innocent thing for miles. She stood untouched in the middle of a pink marble fountain in the town square. Unlike the grotesques, Helena wasn't a former soldier or another one of the King's experiments. She was simply an enchanted statue, sharing the monsters' affinity for moonlight. Garth and Francis stumbled upon her on one of their nights patrolling the city.

Life as Guardians had become long and monotonous. Many began to forget the Great War, the King's cruelty and even their former lives. All that existed was life as grotesques: sleeping during the day and standing sentinel at night. Garth and Francis worked tirelessly to hold on to their memories by sharing them with Helena. She had none of her own because she'd never really lived. Her thirst for everything human bordered on obsession. They were often sucked into hours and hours of describing the tiniest details of how snow is both wet and cold or what it felt like to have hair. As they schooled her on life they managed to feel just a little bit human.

Over the years, Garth noticed that his friend had developed a particular fondness for Helena. Francis was somewhat of a flirt back in the village and it was nice to see those human traits begin to shine through again. Garth never developed those skills or a particular urge to prowl. He'd always been content as the sidekick. Even in the presence of such a beautiful specimen like Helena, his goblin-y appearance killed any urge to love. Francis didn't share similar sentiments, which Garth viewed with a heavy heart, knowing his friend didn't have a chance with something so lovely.

Love and lust aside, they often spent evenings perched on the side of her fountain reminiscing days gone by:

"Then there was that time you fell through the ice!" Garth laughed.

"That was awful," said Francis.

"We were just walking on the ice—"

"A bad idea to begin with."

"And all of the sudden he was gone. His foot fell through and sucked his whole body in with him."

"It was terrifying."

"Very scary."

"You laughed."

"Well, it was funny. Just imagine—"

Helena wasn't in on the joke. "The cold could have done what exactly?" she began to wonder.

"It could have been deadly," replied Garth.

She gasped. "You could have died?"

The boys briefly looked at each other. Yes, he could have. "Humans aren't built like us. Exposure to extreme heat or cold can kill them," Francis said.

Helena put her hand up to find a breeze. She rubbed her fingers together. Nothing.

"Thankfully, we were close to home," added Garth, "We got him near a fire. He was lucky."

"And Garth was nice enough to wrap himself around me and keep my body warm," Francis teased.

"Body heat helps. And, you're welcome for saving your life."

"No, no! I'm very thankful! Even if it did make me look like an effeminate."

"What's that?" asked Helena.

Francis and Garth let out a laugh. "You know, a man that…acts feminine," Francis explained.

"Like a woman?"

"Yes," he continued, and then he paused to search for an example. "Like the Prince in the palace over there."

"Our Prince?"

"Yes."

"How so?"

Francis regretted opening that door but he was forced to step through. "The Prince, they say, he's…what would you call it, Garth?"

"I'm not getting into this, Francis."

"Oh, come on! The Prince, well, he dresses…and acts…"

Garth begrudgingly tried to help him. "He's a…"

"What would you call him?"

"I really don't know."

"A deviant?" suggested Francis.

Garth thought on it for a second and then agreed. "Yes, that sounds right. A deviant."

"So they say."

"Yes, so they say."

Helena was still confused. "How do you know? Have you seen the Prince?" she asked.

The two looked back and forth, waiting for the other to speak first. "No, we haven't," said Garth. "Not many people have. He doesn't go out much. From what I know, he's quite odd."

For the first time, Helena looked at Garth like he was the ignorant one. "So he's odd because he is like a woman? Does that make me odd?"

They hurriedly backpedaled, "No, no, no. You're supposed to be," Francis said, tripping over words. "You're supposed to be… womanly."

"I don't think I know what that means," she said.

"Forget about it. It's fine. You are just fine," said Garth, trying to move on.

She looked down at her perfectly carved curves and her flowing gown and wondered if that was what made her a woman. "Does that mean he loves men?" she finally asked.

The awkwardness was suffocating. "I suppose, Helena," said Francis, wanting to put an end to the conversation. "It doesn't really matter."

"Actually, it does," she said. "He's being mistreated, yes?"

Garth and Francis shook their heads.

"And you're laughing at him."

They would have turned red if they could.

"Don't you think that it's wrong that he can't be the way he is without ridicule? We should all be able to—" she was becoming upset "—act and…love any way we want. Even if it is different." She looked at Francis for too long.

Garth saw her identify with the Prince that nobody had ever met.

Like him, she loved something different.

It was Francis, the grotesque.

❖

"Do you ever think about what they called gay people back in the day?" I asked Asher over dinner in NYC's twenty-something gayborhood, Hell's Kitchen. I hadn't seen him since Gluttonfest and had to show face before he started to think I was a hysterical homo and had me committed, like Blanche Dubois in *A Streetcar Named Desire*. His concepts of human psychology were developed strictly based on the plays he read in our college Theatre History classes.

"They called them fags," he said, caustically.

"Is that a thing now? Are we reclaiming that word like the blacks did with nigger?"

He shushed me, "Don't say that."

I rolled my eyes and continued, "Really, though, homosexual and gay and fag are relatively new. I mean before there was the norm of heterosexuality, before Sodom, when people could 'eff' whomever they wanted without scrutiny."

"Like ancient Greece."

"Sure. Like how would they refer to two male lovers? I thought 'deviant.' But I don't know because that infers that it was bad. When did it become deviant?"

"Are you taking a gay studies class or something?"

"No. Just curious." Garth's story about the little 'mo Prince got me thinking. I began to wonder when being gay had become an issue. If Garth was as old as he claimed to be, it seems gays have had it hard for a really long time.

"I think it was that messed up religion of yours," Asher said as he stuffed a turkey burger into his face.

"Uh, my family had no religious stance." Thanks to my mother's family's Bible thumping background, she felt obliged to at least *expose* me to God. Of course, I was much more interested in watching *The Wizard of Oz* on a loop on Sunday mornings. My father slept in, having received a lifetime's worth of Jesus H. Christ from twelve years of Catholic school. I took a cue from him and usually pretended to have a stomachache. I employed the same technique for getting out of swimming lessons and soccer practice. Needless to say, I'm a hedonist who can't dive or block a goal.

Mom did manage to get me into the sanctuary (a few times) without my skin igniting upon entry and I did (somehow) retain a general knowledge of the good book. I mean, how could I enjoy a Cecil B. DeMille film without it?

Anyway...

"I guess the big guy did us in," I said. "Your people helped, though. You Jews share half of our Bible."

"Who cares? All I believe in is brunch and Broadway," he sang as my eyes rolled so far into my head I could see my brain. "Oh, speaking of Bible stories, I got this great adaptation of Fairy Tales—"

"Nice," I deadpanned.

"Some of the humor is really weird and dry, much like the shit in the Bi—"

"Asher, I'm not even religious and I feel like lightning's going to strike me." I edged away from him, stealing glances to the tables around us.

"Whatever. I'll let you borrow it when I'm done. The Fairy Tales, not the Bible."

"Blue cover?"

"Yeah."

I rolled my eyes again. "I've been trying to lend you that book for months."

"I thought that was the yellow one."

"No, that one just has nice pictures."

Because all unsuccessful actors have to try their hand at writing before settling on becoming teachers, Asher and I were batting around the idea of creating something based on the life of Hans Christian Anderson. Most people don't realize it, but he was as secretly gay and tortured as anybody who wrote about mermaids and fairies would have been in nineteenth century Denmark. Asher decided Hans's story could really "sing." That's gayspeak for "let's make that a musical." In the days before Garth, we'd have writing sessions while listening to *Wicked* or another fantastical, soaring cast recording. But my preoccupation with a boulder man forced my attention elsewhere. Sometimes I'd convince myself that I was doing research by reading a few bedtime stories on the subway. That's *totally* not creepy or anything.

"Oh! Speaking of gays and Biblical justice, not that we were, did you see those photos on the *Times* website today?" he asked, even though I had repeatedly told him I never read the news. "They actually had shots of those sewer men."

I almost pooped my heart out. "No. I don't think I want to see that, thanks."

"Fine, but it turns out those men had a history of gay bashing in three states. One of their victims is still in a coma from an incident two years ago," he said, volume raised for dramatic effect.

"That's crazy." I pretended to be surprised.

"And in addition to their blood all over the place, they found traces of blood from a third party! Looks like a hate crime went down right in the our back yard—"

"Holy shit—"

"And, obviously, those idiots messed with the wrong queen. That bitch must have been fierce." He looked awkward saying that word.

Vomit heaved into my throat but I managed to keep it down. Asher blinked, noticing something was awry.

"Pee break" I lied, darting toward the toilet. Each single-occupancy restroom at that restaurant had different recording artist-inspired decor. I thought Dolly Parton would be the most soothing for a near-puke experience. A twangy anthem blasted from hidden speakers as I tried to organize my thoughts about that evening: I was attacked. I was knocked to the ground. I was bleeding when I woke up. Therefore part of me was strewn on Twenty Sixth Street, making me the third party.

I didn't kill those men.

They tried to kill me!

I almost began to pray for my wrongly accused soul. Then I realized I didn't want to waste a perfectly good fifteen seconds talking to myself.

Nothing was reported, so nothing was on file. I was never on Twenty Sixth Street. My bruises were the result of too much tequila and a one-inch heel on my boots. This boy was completely removed from the situation. Nothing to worry about.

Right?

With my face freshly splashed with water and hair lightly coiffed, I went back to the table. I couldn't even look at the rest of my meatloaf sandwich. That was the first time I'd ever lost my appetite.

"Welcome back. If you're not going to eat, at least finish that margarita. These things aren't cheap," Asher scolded. "Anyway, before you got the shits, I was getting somewhere with that gay bashing thing."

Please no.

"I didn't have the shits."

He ignored me. "Apparently similar cases with smashed bodies have shown up before."

What?

What?!

"Asher, people are crazy," I said, trying to shut this conversation down.

"Yeah, but after doing background checks on the corpses, police found that all of the men had committed some kind of hate crime prior to being pulverized." He squealed with excitement. "Do I smell a gay vigilante screenplay after Hans?"

The sick feeling came back.

That time I couldn't keep it down.

❖

"Garth, I need to talk to you," I feebly announced when I met him in the garden outside the Cathedral of St. John the Divine on West 110th Street.

"Of course you do. That is why we are meeting," he said. "Come on, get on my back. We are going up."

My acrophobia blocked out his words. "No, we need to talk. It's important."

"Not as important as this view." Without pause, he picked me up and slung me on his back. Even with me on board, he scaled the cathedral with the grace of a spider. He'd had centuries of practice.

St. John's is immense, one of the largest churches in the world. Even in its unfinished state, its vastness in conjunction with the views of the city almost knocked me out. Of course that could have been the altitude. When we reached the front bell tower, Garth gently set me down. My stomach still roiled from the dinner conversation, so it took me a second to gather my wits.

"I know what—"

"This view is incredible. It reminds me of the palace," he said.

I found his happiness about a place that had imprisoned him for so long strange.

He noticed my confusion. "I hated it there, do not get me wrong. But there was no denying its beauty. You would have loved it. These behemoths never cease to amaze me. So much effort poured into one building." He patted the floor as if it was a dog.

I took in the vista for a moment, but my mind wasn't on the view. "I know what you're doing. This whole superhero thing. I know," I said, pointing a finger.

"What do you mean? I told you already that I cannot fly."

"The really good ones can't. And stop avoiding the subject."

He stared at me long and hard.

Why I was berating him? He'd saved my life and probably the lives of many others. The courts slapped bigots on the wrist and simply hoped they'd change their ways. With Garth around, the riff raff were taken care of for good.

Then again…for *good.*

I gulped.

"What is the problem with eliminating people who lead lives full of so much hate? They are in the wrong. They are lost causes. The human species has no time for such stupidity. It stunts you all." He waved a hand. "I am doing everyone a favor by killing them off." Garth was as sincere as he was angry.

I softened my tone to placate him. "But isn't that what they think of me? That I'm in the wrong? That I'm the lost cause?" I didn't necessarily believe or agree with the bigots' opinion of me, but vigilante murder cried out for some sort of a rebuttal.

"Do not say that!"

"It's what they think, Garth!"

"Faith and morals are choices, opinions." He reached out to literally shake some sense into me, as if he and I didn't share this viewpoint. "Instincts and love are not."

"I know—"

"Being yourself, the way you are meant to live, is not stubbornness, Jeremy. And do not let anyone tell you differently."

"Garth! I agree with you. Please!"

He seemed to realize how forceful he'd been. When he let go I could actually feel my arms redden beneath my jacket.

"Just tell me…how many people have you killed in this effort of yours?" I asked, rubbing my arms.

He growled, ducked his head, and stalked away.

"I'm sorry," I cried out after him. "I just don't know if killing people is the answer."

"They could have killed you!" he screamed as his massive fist bashed a cornice off the wall. "Would that have been a better option? Getting beaten to a pulp because two idiots did not like the way that you walked or dressed?"

"But that's the point!"

"I may come from a barbaric time, but if there is one idea that I will hold onto it is that we should not tolerate people who wish harm on the innocent."

His words echoed into the night. I said nothing; I didn't disagree.

"No court or prison can rid those people of their dark thoughts," Garth said, his tone as serious as I'd ever heard it. A tear didn't fall, his breath didn't shorten, but his body heaved, his face clenched and a soft moan came from inside. "They would have killed you. I could not let that happen. Not again."

His words struck me like a gong, and he launched out of my sight before I could go to him.

Just like that.

I stood alone on top of the cathedral, allowing him time to compose himself somewhere nearby. Several minutes passed and I began to get nervous, so I sat in a decorative nook, hoping my silhouette would be lost among the carved stone figures instead of alerting those below to a potential suicide jumper.

Several minutes passed. Still no Garth.

My legs were beginning to cramp.

"Fine," I yelled, "if you want to act like this, I'll go home."

"How will you get down?" he asked from behind me.

I didn't know. I searched for some kind of trap door that lead to a hunchback's lair or the secret meeting place of the knights' templar or the Ark of the Covenant or something…*anything* but where I was. With a sigh, I stood and wandered between the saints to find my way out, but their gaunt faces frightened me more than the potential of falling to an untimely death. Garth took hold of my arm and guided me to a safer spot.

"Stay," he said. "I will tell you. Forgive me."

I studied his face for a moment, then sat.

He settled against one of the lifeless statues. "A memory lingers with me. It forces me to do what I do now."

"Why?" I whispered.

His rough features looked almost tender. "You are not unlike those who first moved me to be a Guardian of great causes. I have seen true evil and lost much to it."

4. The Garden Incident

The Devil is always watching," said mothers to their children while tucking them into straw mattresses. The King instilled fear into them, and so they did the same to their families. Prayers needed to be said, devotions needed to be paid, or the Devil would come. Most people had never actually seen a demon, but there was always someone who knew someone who knew someone else who had. And that person had merely seen a Guardian. The strategic exposure of the elite agents kept peace throughout the King's land. Their stone grimaces scared the townsfolk into kindness. Cruel, lewd, and dishonest acts became things of the past.

Soon the Guardians grew bored. Garth spent most evenings roaming the grounds or lying about like a lion, waiting for something exciting to happen, and he'd developed a fondness for a certain tower at the back of the palace, one that overlooked a gigantic garden. Because the greens were forbidden to anyone but royalty, the General of their fleet felt it unnecessary to post Guardians there. Its emptiness made it an ideal place to become Garth's secret resting spot.

While Garth lounged and admired the view, the reclusive Prince left his chambers, walked onto the large terrace, and descended into the oasis. From above, Garth jerked to attention and stared at the rare sighting. The young heir was always hidden from view, leaving the grotesques wondering if he suffered from a strange sickness or deformity. Garth felt lucky to behold him, a lithe and elusive shadow wandering in between trees. He wasn't a leper or a hunchback, but a normal young man. At least, that's how he seemed.

Far in the distance, he saw the Prince approach a pond. The perimeter of the water was lined with elegant willows, except for a clearing laid with slate the color of jewels. The centerpiece of the patio was an exquisite statue of an Egyptian Queen on her throne. The Prince ran to her and climbed into her arms, almost mimicking the Pieta on the steps of the King's church nearby. He lay there for several minutes and cried. Garth felt strange about watching that private moment, but he couldn't tear his eyes away. Eventually the Prince recovered and sat in her lap, like her throne was his own. He stayed there for hours and gazed out over the water, at their invisible empires.

From then on, when he wasn't on duty or stealing away to Helena's fountain, Garth tried to observe the Prince again. He witnessed the same occurrence just a handful of times, each one more desperate than the one before.

On one particular evening, Garth grew tired of waiting and decided on a nap...

Although Garth had lost much of his humanity, he could still dream. For that, he often feared what sleep would bring. What excruciating detail from his past would his mind recall? What unlikely scenario could be conjured to make him even more remorseful of his stone exterior? A birthday? A wedding? A child?

His decision to rest was masochistic, but in a life already filled with so much heartache, why not add more pain? He thought that sorrow would eventually crush him, that the weight of all his troubles could actually smash him to pieces. So he napped, waiting for madness and death's good graces...

The peapod he'd found in the garden as a child.

His father's dirty hands holding it out for young Garth to open, to discover the surprises that nature had wrapped inside.

"Go on, open it," Father said.

Garth slit open the side of the pod.

It screamed.

Garth wrenched awake to a shriek from below.

He looked for a fellow Guardian to report to, but he was still alone. The vast garden, acres of perfection, lay completely vulnerable.

"Hello?" he called. No answer came except echoes from the hollows of the palace beneath him. He cautiously moved to look over the edge of his tower, like a child afraid of looking under his bed. He waited for another sound.

It was just a dream. It was all in my head.

Another scream confirmed his fears and his sense of urgency surged. Could it be the Prince?

It had been years since he'd had to interfere with the humans. And when he did step in, he usually had Francis with him. He didn't want to go in alone. It was off limits. He needed approval from the General. But the scream was—he heard it again—it was definitely one of distress.

He remembered the Great War, where the cries of endangered men were ever present. Then, he was helpless. He couldn't do anything to save them. Now, he was strong. Nothing could stand in his way. "Be bold," he said to himself as he plunged down. He leapt from ledge to ledge, convincing himself that he had courage. He swung from balconies and sills, ornaments and pillars until he reached the high, stately terrace.

The screaming continued. It snaked its way to his ears from deep within the garden, on the far end of the grounds. He sprinted over the intricate cobblestone pathways and splashed through the delicate reflecting pools. Still, the cries were too far away. The ordinary paths were useless. Then he noticed a thin, meandering dirt trail weaving its way into a dark thicket. Traversing through the patch of unruly forest instead was a shortcut, providing he didn't get insanely lost along the way. This Ramble, as it was called, was notorious for twisting people's direction.

There wasn't much time for strategy. Every second wasted was another punch, stab, or tear at the victim he was trying to save. He'd have to brave the Ramble. Just one step inside and it immediately swallowed him.

Having lived in high places for so long, Garth had become moderately acrobatic. The forest was, in theory, a prefect place to use that skill. He could swing like a jungle animal from branch to branch, just as he'd done on the palace's cornices.

Less like a lemur, more like a gorilla, Garth underestimated his weight on the fragile trees. The first one proved to be extremely dissimilar to stone pillars, sending him to the darkened forest floor with a great thud.

He lay in a heap of leaves and listened for another scream, another clue as to where to go next. He heard the snap of twigs and desperate panting behind him. A similar sound ricocheted passed his right ear. How many people were nearby? Before he could investigate, something barreled into him. His cumbrous body was lifted and tossed to the side as if it were nothing more than a branch blocking a trail.

Whatever-it-was had little interest in Garth.

Garth recovered and cannonballed through the trees to escape, feeling a pang of sadness for all that he was unwillingly decimating on his way. After what seemed like forever, the Ramble spat him out into the airy clearing beside the pond. Actually within it instead of above it, Garth understood why the Prince enjoyed it. It was a peaceful place, the kind of spot where he could easily lose an hour or two, were he not on the prowl for the source of the screams, dangerous or not.

Garth brushed himself off and marveled over the perfectly overgrown vines and the ornately laid slate floor. The purples, grays, and blues of the flat stones were stained an uncharacteristic red. Upon closer inspection of the crimson wash, Garth realized it was actually a river of dried blood. He followed its trail to the pink marble throne, which was somehow missing its Queen.

Half a gasp escaped him when the heard the humans approach. The prospect of being seen immediately drained the valor from his system. The King's twin nephews ran onto the patio, gasping for breath. Before either party could be disclosed by the moon's fresh light, Garth dove behind the throne to hide. He listened.

"I think we're safe," said one.

Garth heard the other's teeth chatter before he spoke. "I don't know, brother. What...what is that?"

"What?"

"Your mouth. It's just...*gushing* blood."

One of them coughed, followed by the sound of something wet splatter on the ground. "Oh, God. Oh, God!"

"Help!"

"Help us!"

Another seemingly bloody cough.

Garth couldn't hear anymore. He had to step in, even if it meant exposing himself and his trespass into forbidden territory. He hurled his body over the back of the throne and into their view.

The twins screamed.

"Another!"

"The stories are true!"

"No, no," said Garth. "I'm not going to hur—"

Before he could explain, another stone-being drove into the twins, tackling them to the ground. It was the marble Queen.

Garth leapt for her, but he wasn't quite fast enough. She pinned one of the men to the floor and smashed his head like a vase full of wine.

The other twin hollered in terror as he watched his brother's features drown in burgundy.

"You killed him!" Garth yelled. He wrestled her away. The living twin tried to hobble away, motivating her to emerge more forcefully from under Garth's body.

She grabbed the man by the collar before he could escape. "Because they killed *him*," said the Queen, bitterly. She tightened her hold on the shirt, forcing a choke from her captive's throat.

Again, Garth tried to intercept, but she kicked him. He launched backwards into the throne. "Who did they kill?" he gasped.

Her eyes widened and lips quivered before releasing a growl. "You don't know?" she asked.

"No. I heard screaming, I came to help, I saw blood, I—"

"The *Prince*!" she roared. "They murdered the Prince! Last night!" Her voice lapsed into an impassioned rasp. "I was there for the whole thing. I was his favorite. He came to me for comfort after they had their way with him." Her speech took effort, as if the slightest inflection would send her into tears, even though as a statue like him, she was incapable of shedding any.

"I…I didn't know."

She looked at him in shock. "How? How do you, a Guardian, not know?"

"I wasn't—"

"I've seen you, I've seen you watching us from your tower." Her eyes narrowed on him. "Are you in on the plot to change succession?" She surged forward, restraining him once again on her former chair. Her face met his with only a few inches between them.

"No." He trembled. "I'm here to help. I was in the square last night with—"

She wouldn't hear any more. She let out a great, guttural roar. The crisp night air allowed it to blast clearly through the garden like an alchemy explosion. Then she turned her attention to the surviving twin. "Where is his body?" She shook him. "Where is...my Prince's body? Why are there no funerary flags? Were there no rites?" She furiously wept into his face.

The man's eyeballs rolled around in his head before finding some semblance of focus on her. "He doesn't deserve any," he said. And then he spat blood at her.

Her crying ceased and her despair turned to a violent rage. She raised her arm and threw him into a nearby tree trunk. His fall was accompanied by several cracks and he was left groaning on the ground.

"Please," said Garth. "You *must* stop."

The wild Queen was deaf to his pleading. She picked up the dead twin and slung him over her shoulder dragging the other one by the leg across the stone floor, back toward the Ramble.

"No...you can't!" pleaded Garth. He was stuck. He didn't know what to do. He still sat jumbled on the throne because his feet couldn't agree with his mind.

Before disappearing into shadow, she halted and found a thought. "I don't believe the stories, you know."

Was she really going to engage in conversation at a time like this? "What stories?"

She looked back at him. "They say the grotesques on the palace are demons. I know that's untrue. The real demons are in my hands. And I will destroy them."

Garth watched her vanish into the thicket. As he did, his body relaxed. If he moved quickly, he could have made it to her in time to save the remaining twin. But he didn't want to. The reason wasn't completely clear, but he sensed she was right. She had been modeled after Cleopatra, a legendary leader whose influence toppled even the mightiest of men. The stone version of the queen seemed to have the same abilities. He sat in her seat of power and hoped to absorb her aptitude. If only he could be so stalwart, so strong.

The cries coming from the Ramble weren't of terror like the ones that lured Garth into the garden moments before; they were the savage, guttural screams of the dying. War had taught him the difference, and that time, he didn't feel sorrow.

Those men deserve it.

Dawn came to find a garden of death. The blood of three men stained its grounds and the royal robes of the Queen, who sat happily on her throne. As Garth slept on his tower, two bodies were discovered at the bottom of a stairwell. The King ordered that funerary flags be flown. The kingdom was in mourning for its favorite twins.

5. Climate Change

I've managed to convince myself that the slightest variation on traditional weather is a result of Global Warming. Al Gore has told us time and again that Earth is going through hell, so my tolerance for cold is decreasing. Every January, I find myself asking the sky why it's snowing. "This doesn't feel like atmospheric depletion to me!" I say with a shaking fist. I yearn for an eighty-degree day in March. I want to praise fossil fuels for their warming effects and buy aerosol hair spray to continue their work. I prematurely reach for iced coffees and short shorts, booze-fueled nights and regrettable mornings. Ten hours later the warm front leaves and I'm left shivering in an unseasonably light coat. Winter is like the unbearable trailer before the movie I paid to see. If I had money, I'd escape those treacherous four minutes and run to the concession stand, but I just have to deal. I tried to explain the erratic weather to Garth because without humanity's gluttonous ways, I wouldn't be able to repeatedly stand on rooftops in the middle of winter.

Garth has told me my tendency to make light of tragic and/or scary things, like the destruction of our planet, helps me tear focus away from the true horror of most situations. He calls it a "mask for complacency." Possibly, but the volume of our problems is almost too great to bother fixing. The general shittiness of the human species cancels out the compassion. There are too many of us and we're all too selfish. Maybe we need a celestial Dr. Kevorkian to put us out of our misery.

I wondered if Urban Outfitters had a "misanthrope" T-shirt.
I'd look great in it.

"You don't recognize the great opportunities you have," Garth said. "This world belongs to you. It is yours to enjoy but it also yours to protect."

I rolled my eyes at what I'd heard so many times in yoga classes and documentaries. And given the conversation, our view was far from ideal. We stood on an abandoned factory off Eleventh Avenue overlooking the West Side Rail Yard. It was an almost anti-environmental site, a large ditch littered with skeletons of trains and trash. The gaping hole in the earth looked more like man's first attempt to penetrate hell than a functional place to park out of service trains. "Don't preach to me," I said. "Tell the people ruining this island with things like that."

"I'm not trying to preach to you, Jeremy. What I am saying is not only common sense; it is the Way of Things. This idea is written into the fabric of time. It is the meaning of your life."

If it was so important why hadn't an official announcement from Jesus-Easter Bunny-Mohammed-Allah been broadcast on the giant TV screens in Times Square? Call me crazy, but if there's a meaning to life it should be public.

Then Garth rolled his eyes. "You have a house, you take care of it. Maybe humans are as simple as you claim they are if they can't figure that out."

"Please." I snorted.

"What's being done to the world is the equivalent of you pouring gasoline all over your apartment. You might not light a flame, but the potential for destruction is there. And it smells terrible in the meantime."

I walked away from the edge, found a chimney to rest against, and kicked back for a lecture. "Well, enlighten me about the rules of the universe, Garth, since I, and a few billion others seem to be in the dark."

"This is the only home you have. There are many, many worlds out there but this is the only one for you. Your relationship with the air, the water, the sunshine and moonlight are specific and unique to this planet and to this planet alone. You mortals are this world's finest achievement."

"True in my case," I quipped.

He ignored me, true to form. "More than any creature, you humans hold the most promising capabilities for advancement, the greatest capacities for emotions, and the highest complexities of thought. These traits, these billions of years of perfecting and evolving from the tiniest speck of stardust have made you the guardians of this earthly plane."

"It's a lot of pressure, Garth." I uncomfortably drummed my fingers against the metal roof beneath me.

"It's truth. The human race's sole purpose is that of a caretaker." Garth paused, watching me to make sure that I was receiving his valuable information.

I rolled my hand like, "Go on."

"Then there are the Immortals, like myself," he said. "We are here to protect the mortals. We are forces of nature, manifested in various forms, or in my case, we are the products of those who know how to manipulate it."

"Now that would be some skill."

"Our order is beyond ancient, began by rogues from other worlds who have been enlightened by discoveries and destructions." Garth came closer as if to guard his words from eavesdroppers, despite our hundred-foot advantage. "There is a third link in this chain, a very mysterious side of existence, the lack thereof: Death."

"I thought we were all reincarnated into goats and bunnies, or whatever." *Again* with masking my complacency. Truthfully, I wanted to know if I was going to come back with a fluffy white tail and bad karma.

"The souls of deceased mortals are indebted to my kind for protecting them in life. They observe from afar and assist when they need to. But being Immortals, we rarely need help. So the souls enjoy a relatively easy afterlife, hence your ideas of heaven. They aren't far off."

"That seems simple enough," I said, not wanting to admit that I was impressed. Overwhelmed but impressed. "But why don't *we* know this?"

"Some do, but as they say, 'knowledge is power.' It's been twisted and corrupted over the centuries. Most people are left with variations on a theme." He shrugged one massive shoulder. "This has made the Way of Things unbalanced. The mortals have become carried away with progress."

"Isn't progress a good thing? Are we supposed to stay dumb?"

"I did not say that. Progress is wonderful. Necessary. But progress is not without consequence. Your kind's thoughtlessness is why we Immortals don't interact as often as we used to. Some of us have lost the adoration that we once held for your kind." I couldn't help but feel insulted. It wasn't my fault. "Do not think of this as a strictly modern problem, though. Back in my human days, the balance was breaking. This deterioration has taken thousands of years. Now the Way of Things and the Immortals are all but forgotten."

"We've taken your jobs away," I said.

"In some cases."

I stood and ran to the center of the roof, raising my hands to the sky like a Baptist. "Maybe you should become a prophet. Go tell everyone about this," I said, half-joking. "Or maybe I should. After all, I can stay up past 6 a.m. You'll be the superpower that sends visions and I'll be the mouthpiece. We could make a great living, you know."

He shook his head and chuckled. "No. Prophets and Gods are too often just distractions from the truth. Tell whom you please. If you end up dying from a heat wave or a nuclear bomb, you will at least die knowing the truth."

For someone who was part of a dying race, he sure had a good sense of humor about it all.

❖

That evening I was revisited by the nightmares I thought I'd buried with Dedo.

I was walking through Union Square on my favorite day of the year—the day spring finally shows its face. Smiling people debuted light jackets, bounces in their steps, and the trees revealed neon buds from their seemingly dead branches. The leaves created a pointillist painting above me. Thousands of chartreuse dots caused my eyes to cross, blending the world into a beautiful blur. I closed them and opened my other senses to the weather. Notes of wet dirt and pollen filled my sinuses. I couldn't get enough of the childlike memories they evoked, so I stole another inhalation.

The second whiff sizzled capillaries and invaded my lungs with the dry fumes of a bonfire. Through teary eyes I looked up to see violent orange flames consume all that was green.

Fire poured onto the people below the canopy. I narrowly escaped the blaze before it began chasing me uptown, its heat threatening to melt my backside along the way. I didn't dare turn around for fear my eyes would boil out of their sockets from the inferno at my heels. The rancid tang of burning flesh accompanied me on my panicked sprint up Broadway.

Manhattan transformed into a dream world. Avenues twisted under my feet and skyscrapers stretched hundreds of floors beyond their roofs. Every time I tried to turn down a side street, dense hedges would sprout to block my way. I became lost in the Queen of Heart's maze. No choice was given between this way or that, because the devastation had followed me in, forcing me deeper and deeper into the labyrinth. When I reached its center, a twisted sign for Twenty Sixth Street greeted me. But this version of that infamous road didn't end at the West Side Highway, it dead-ended in a chain link fence like a frame from a comic book. Two futures awaited me: imminent death or an unexpected rescue. I waited for Garth to come for me. I closed my eyes and listened for the thump of his stone feet against the asphalt.

Silence. Even the roaring flames came to a halt. From the shadows of the nearby buildings, I heard footsteps. Two ghastly figures emerged. They were patchwork humans, with broken limbs re-sewn to the places they'd been torn. I tried to show courage by facing my enemies with a confident scowl and a puffed out chest, but meeting their eyes crumbled my nerves. They were my eyes attached to my face and my body. Zombie versions of myself approached with smirks that reveled in the trouble they were about to create.

After weeks of asking for the details of my attack, they were shown to me in a twisted snuff version of *The Parent Trap*. I became the voyeur of my almost-death. I sat in a torture device with my eyes pinned open, forced to watch. The camera moved from shot A to B to C, crossing the line and ignoring the rules of Filmmaking 101.

Based on my height and weight, I posses about four quarts of blood. That four quarts looked more like four gallons as it cartoonishly spewed from my body. I was beat so quickly, so violently, that I could actually see it race from blue to red as it escaped my arms, legs, face, torso…

❖

Garth awoke to pandemonium among the Guardians. The air was thick with theories about what had happened in the garden. The two murders had been so gruesome, they surely must have been the work of a madman.

"They put up a fight, that is for sure," said one of the grotesques. "I heard they were beaten beyond recognition."

"The twins. Why would anyone go after them? They are of little use. Third and fourth in line, if I remember correctly," said another.

"Whoever did it should have started at the top with the King. That would have been the smart thing to do."

"But that's why the twins killed off the Prince," interrupted Garth. "So that they would be next in line."

The Guardians looked at him with puzzled faces. "Garth, what are you talking about?"

One more Guardian pounced into the conversation. "Who said anything about the Prince? We speak of the King's nephews. They were found dead this morning," it said.

"I know," said Garth, "But the Prince was found dead, also. Yes?"

Garth had always been the smartest of the lot, but it seemed as if his fellow grotesques were beginning to doubt that.

"Don't you think we'd know if the heir to the throne had been murdered?" one asked, laughing.

"Well, maybe not *that* Prince. He hasn't been out of the palace in years. I almost forgot he even existed!" They cackled in Garth's face.

At that point he began to filter out their antagonizing remarks. Was the Prince still alive? A body hadn't been found, forcing him to doubt the Queen's story. But there'd been so much blood near the pond. Where did it come from? He suddenly felt in the middle of something very complicated. He had to tell someone. Francis would surely be with Helena, so he darted to the town square to meet them.

They sat giggling at the fountain, unaware of the conspiracies swirling around them. Francis played the usual role of storyteller. He was recounting a time in their youth when they'd stolen a boat from the boathouse and rowed into the middle of a lake for no particular reason.

"A boat?" she asked. "I've never seen one of those."

"You wouldn't have. They float in water, like the leaves that fall in your fountain. Only larger and made for people to sit in," Francis explained.

"And you took this...boat and just...floated around?" she inquired.

"Yes. We were looking for something to do one night and it seemed easy enough. Only when we finally got in, we realized we had nowhere to go. We just paddled in circles and enjoyed being burglars."

Garth leapt up from behind. "Yes. I recall being very nervous that we'd be spotted. Of course, Francis had no fear. My stomach was in knots the entire time."

Helena's eyes widened and a smile grew across her smooth face. "Oh, that sounds so exciting," she squealed. "I can't imagine what that feels like."

"It would be like wandering around in broad daylight," Francis suggested.

"Maybe not that extreme," Garth said. He turned to Helena. "Maybe it'd be like stepping off your fountain for a while and into someone's bed chamber."

They laughed a bit and then Garth turned the subject to a more serious note. He told them about the scream and venturing into the garden and all of the other subsequent gory events. The whole time Helena stood silently, listening in horror. When he was finished she asked, "Does it hurt when you die?"

"I don't know," Garth said. " Some people die on their own, like in their sleep. Others meet more unnatural ends. What the Queen did to those men probably hurt."

She nodded her head, trying to understand.

"But what they did to the Prince must have hurt," she replied, beginning to comprehend.

Francis paid no mind to their conversation and instead sat thinking on Garth's story. "Well, I don't think we should say anything unless we're asked," he eventually said. "We swore to protect the town from outside forces. If that family wants to tear itself apart, that's fine with me. That old King deserves whatever tragedies befall him. I hope they all kill one another. Then maybe we'd be free."

The grotesques swore allegiance to the King out of fear, but resentment ran deep. Francis was always more outspoken about his distain than the rest of the Guardians.

"What about that statue in the garden? Do you think she's a threat?" Garth asked.

"Maybe she killed the Prince, too!" Helena interjected.

"Perhaps she'll get the King next," Francis said, gleefully.

"Oh! What if she was lying to you? Maybe the whole palace is at risk. Maybe the Prince isn't dead, at all," proposed Helena, excited by her ability to connect the pieces.

"That passed through my mind, also," Garth said.

"Do you really believe a filthy garden statue is systematically taking out the entire royal bloodline? For what? To usurp the throne? Something tells me the people of this kingdom won't take to a block of stone as their monarch," said Francis in the most sarcastic tone possible.

"Maybe I'm right. There could be an evil spirit trapped inside her," Helena said. "I've heard that spirits can haunt practically anything."

Francis was tired of the conversation. He jumped from the fountain and onto the dusty ground. "Then I'd like to meet her. Evil or not, we stone things need to stick together."

"It might be nice to have another woman around," Helena sighed. With that, Francis looked at Garth as if to say, "That one can be yours."

On one Friday night, I was bored. Garth had left the city to pursue something secretive. I assumed that he needed to go bash another gay basher. Or he was at a conference of griffins or participating in an alien investigation workshop. I was at the point where nothing fazed me, especially from my enchanted stone superhero. Robbie was busy, too. He was being couple-y with Nick. Even though I had other friends to choose from, I found myself restless for Garth's and Robbie's company. I missed them…but they were such odd people to be missing. Why did I yearn to be with them, the two men who made my life stranger than it already was?

I began meeting up with Garth out of necessity. I actually couldn't function without him. He hung around because he was concerned I could end up in a sewer or cooked medium-well on the subway track, from someone else's—or my own—doing. Knowing he was invested in my life made me feel safe. As he told me more about the Way, the scary stuff my mind concocted began to disappear. What went bump in the night was common knowledge to me, so I didn't have to make it up anymore. His stories were becoming as addictive as his watchful eyes. To think I was the first one to hear him out since Helena was both intimidating and incredible. I was like a therapists specializing in faerie, and like all shrinks are to their patients, I became important. Never had I been so frank with someone. Never had another been so trusting of me. It was a nice feeling…a foreign one. Our meetings were brief, so each date left me wanting more. That's what they were I suppose…dates. Of course my goal wasn't to get him in the sack, but that wasn't my goal with Robbie, either.

I genuinely enjoyed being around Robbie. An intensely intellectual brain inside a person who could talk for hours about peak oil and twentieth century Berlin contrasted his childlike interest in finger puppets and dinosaurs. He was unconcerned with what people thought of him, unafraid of being himself. He often got flack for having dropped out of college to which he'd say, "I don't know what I want to be yet. Why would I waste all of that money until I know?" His carefree approach to life was addicting. It was exactly what I needed. In a way, he had the same effect on me that Garth did. Both of them were able to make the same keen observation: I needed to chill out. I could hear them congruently say, "Try living your life instead of worrying about it."

So why, out of the millions of people in New York, was I constantly thinking about two unattainable someones? Why did fate have to be such a bitch and make one of them in a relationship and the other a vengeful stone monster? I didn't love Garth. He was a fucking gargoyle. But maybe I was able to see into him, into the human part. I didn't know if I loved Robbie, either. Could I have been confusing our friendship for romance?

When we worked a shift together, we were inseparable. There was always a joke to be laughed at, an idea to be discussed. If we went out, typically with a larger group, we'd let our drunkenness be an excuse to be touchier than usual. My hand would lie on his shoulder for a beat too long. My lips would graze his ear on accident when leaning in to speak at a loud bar. On more than one occasion a friend would lean in and whisper, "You know he has a boyfriend, right?" Embarrassed by my blatant display of attempted adultery, I would then sink into a quiet depression for the rest of the evening.

Things got complicated on an early March day when I went over to Robbie's place to watch some TV with friends. The friends ended up bailing and we were left alone.

Both of our heads were turned in the direction of the television but I wasn't watching it. I was looking at him. I became absorbed in the angles of his face, the slope of his nose, the oiliness of his forehead, and the slightly chapped pink on his lips. I imagined myself a blind person, only able to see him with my fingers. How would they feel while grazing over such differing territories? Because I had sight, I would never find out. They were sensations that only his lover would know.

"What?" he asked.

He'd caught me.

"Nothing," I said. My head went back in the direction of *American Idol*. I felt his eyes on me. "What?"

He shook his head. Nothing.

"Do you ever feel like—" I started to say. It just sort of drooled out of my mouth. I couldn't bring myself to finish the thought. I turned back to the TV.

His breathing was deep and quivery. I hoped that he was trying to find a cute way to complete my sentence. Instead he'd probe and prompt me to be the bigger man. "Ever feel like what?" he asked.

I couldn't acknowledge him. If I acknowledged him, I'd inadvertently speak. Words would spew from my mouth and I'd have no control over their meanings. I think that's what he was looking for, though. I had to be the one to monologue about my love for him. That way he didn't look like a cheater. In college, I was stuck in a similar situation with a now-ex-friend. I confessed my feelings and it blew up in my face. I didn't want to take the same risk with Robbie. With tightly closed eyes, my mouth searched for something in my empty word closet.

"Look at me," he said.

Fine. I did. Magnetism locked all four of our eyes on one another. We became caught in a pre-kiss moment, the kind where each party silently negotiates who will make the first move. I'd been there with plenty of men, but my time with Robbie was a standstill. A face off. We were stuck. Attraction's tractor beam pulled us together but we resisted.

I broke free. "I should go," I said as I got up from the couch and began the hunt for my cell phone, keys, and jacket. I cursed under my breath for allowing myself to get that close to Loverdom with him. "Fuck, fuck, fuck, fuck. Asshole, stupid, stupid, asshole…"

Just as I was about to reach for the door, he caught my arm. "Wait!"

Crushes come and go but once a kiss is placed on lips, a chapter is written. Three feet from the front door, in the blue light of the television, we opened the floodgates, exchanged pheromones, and set our story into motion.

"But what about Nick?" I asked when I finally pulled away.

He got frazzled. "I don't know. Things haven't been great. He was supposed to come over tonight but I haven't heard from him."

"So I'm the rebound? The second string?"

His hand grasped mine. "No. You're not. Getting to know you has made me realize that I don't like him. It made me realize that—"

"That you deserve to be with someone who is crazy about you."

His eyes lit up and the corners of his mouth rose. "Are you crazy about me?"

"Yeah. I think I am."

His phone lit up on the coffee table. Nick had been sending texts but silent mode had kept Robbie from hearing them. I'm sure the lip smacking contributed to his deaf ears, too.

"He's coming over. Maybe you should—"

"Yeah, I know."

On my way out of his apartment I felt like slamming my head into the broken tiled floor. How did I get myself into situations like this? It was irresponsible of me to be around him. I'd already been beaten unconscious on the street once. I didn't need another enemy in his boyfriend. I should have just placed myself in solitary confinement until I was too old to date or until some decent hate crime legislation was passed.

While muttering obscenities to myself, I ran into just the person I'd been thinking of. All I managed to say to Nick was a quick, "Excuse me," as I slipped by him in the hallway. I hoped he couldn't put the pieces together. But dating in the twenty-first century not only involves two people; it includes a network of friends on websites that display a person's every move. Nick had looked me up when he heard murmurs of Robbie's new "buddy." He knew my face, my sign, my favorite movies and what I'd dressed up as on Halloween for the past three years.

❖

"I think spring is finally on its way," I said to Garth. We were back in Central Park, perched on a rock overlooking the water. The air had lost its icy bite and was replaced with a chill-less breeze.

"Did you skip down the street like you'd hoped?" he asked.

"I did, I did." I took in a deep breath through my nose. "I can even smell it. I don't know how people can live in places with only one season. The changes mark time. Each season gives us a chance to start again."

Garth smiled at me then looked back out at the water. "I do miss seeing the vibrant colors of spring. They are much different against the moon. Duller. Those treetops must be stunning midday."

I told him of my dream about exploding trees. It had come to me on several occasions. I began to fear that it had meaning, like the dreams in a Shakespearean heroine's soliloquy. When those ladies dream something, shit goes down.

Garth explained that my dreams shouldn't be taken lightly. "Often, dreams are the only communication we have with our subconscious. They bring secrets to the surface. Some believe dreams are like letters between mortals and the souls of mortals passed. Do you have a dead relative who may be trying to speak to you?"

I couldn't think of a soul. The only close relatives I'd lost were my grandparents. Surely there was no unfinished business between us because I was only a child when they passed away. "Shouldn't those souls be speaking to you, anyway? Isn't that breaking the chain of command? You're my Guardian, not my Papa," I argued.

Garth laughed. For a second he looked human. "That is true but sometimes they can't help stepping in. After all, they loved you long before we did," he said. The reference to love made him slightly uncomfortable the moment it settled.

When Garth arrived back at the tower, the General was quietly leaning over a wall, keeping watch. As a human, he'd been a big, brute of a man and his stone form reflected that. His features were severe, much more fear-inducing than the other grotesques. He'd been the leader of the Guardians since their transformation and was the only liaison between them and the King.

The General seemed to sense a visitor and whipped around. "Garth," he grumbled.

"I apologize for sneaking up on you, sir," Garth said nervously.

"No matter. I heard you caused quite a stir with the others this evening. Something about the Prince?"

Garth told him everything.

The General was attentive without letting a single word register on his face. He was as stoic as ever. Garth supposed it was an old army trick. By the end of his account, he waited for a "congratulations" or a "well done, my boy."

"I'm going to condense and repeat what you just told me. You let me know if it sounds a bit…well, just listen," said the General, condescendingly. "You heard suspicious activity below and, instead of reporting it, wandered into the garden alone. A decorative statue told you that the Prince was dead. Without proof, I'll add. Then you watched said statue slaughter members of the royal family and didn't even try to stop it. Now you wait until nearly morning to say anything. Is that right?"

Garth immediately regretted going to him. Looking back, it was naive. "But I didn't know, sir. There was blood everywhere. I believed her when she said it was the Prince's."

"Exactly what she wanted."

"Well, is the Prince alive?"

"That's not the issue here, Garth."

"It's not?"

"No. The issue is that you were an accomplice in the murder of the King's nephews, the heirs to the throne."

"The Prince is the heir. Where is he?"

"You are a criminal, Garth."

"You're not listening. Why would the Queen kill in cold blood? You need to go speak to her. Or find the Prince. If he's alive, she was lying. If not—"

"That statue is possessed," roared the General. "It is a demon, killing without reason, attempting to infiltrate the palace, tearing it apart with death, sorrow, and fear. And now it's trapped you in its web."

Garth felt as if he were talking to a wall. Yes, his actions had been stupid. He should have stopped the Queen and taken things up with the law, but half of his story was being completely brushed aside. The General was difficult under normal circumstances, but he was being uncharacteristically so when faced with Garth's questions.

"You're not acting like yourself, Brogan. What are you hiding?" Garth asked.

The General lunged at him, pinning him down against the wooden slats of the floor. "You will address me as your superior, Guardian. Is that clear?"

"I'll address you as a superior when you act like one. You can't get angry about my lack of protocol when you are ignoring all of the facts. What is happening in the palace?" They may not have liked one another, but their experiences bound all of the Guardians as family. It was no longer a matter of codes and procedures, but of friends and trust.

Brogan bore down on him. His massive hand pressed onto Garth's chest. The floor let out a crackle. "I hope that you aren't suggesting I had anything to do with the incidents in the garden."

"Incidents?" Garth asked with an emphasis on the plural. The Queen was right. Something else happened there, something that would prompt her to seek vengeance. "What else has happened? *Sir.*"

Brogan uttered a frustrated grunt and pressed Garth harder. "It is the devil at work," he roared. If they could have, his eyes would have likely flared red and burnt holes into Garth's head. A bird's chirp interrupted his rigor. Brogan's expression softened. He rose and composed himself. "It's nearly morning. Forget everything that you have seen. The twins' passing is tragic and should be acknowledged appropriately. You may spend your evening in mourning tomorrow, if you'd like."

Garth was so disturbed by his leader's erratic behavior, not a word escaped him.

"Get up!" bellowed the General. "The sun will rise shortly. To your post." Garth scrambled to his feet. "And Garth, you will never refer to a block of marble as a Queen. There is only one Queen and she is sleeping in the palace below. May she be blessed."

Garth made it back to his post just in time for the new day's light to dissolve the moon. Francis perched nearby, already in his usual spot. He stretched before striking his final, frightening pose. He smiled at Garth then said, "I'm growing tired of this game. Let's run away soon." He chuckled, then peered below and bore his fangs.

Garth tried to do the same, and with the same level of humor, but he didn't have it in him. What was the point of scaring off evil when it had already found its way inside? He hoped the Queen was safe. He had a bad feeling about what would happen if she were found out. There wasn't anything he could do, though. The sun would soon rise and he'd be forced to sleep. He folded into himself, hugged his legs, and hoped to dream of something pleasant...

I asked Garth what he dreamt about that night.

"Francis. I dreamt of Francis. We didn't get along when we first met back in the village. It took months but somehow we became the best of friends. Life is funny like that. You can grow to love just about anyone," he said. His face was sadder than I'd ever seen it. I asked him to continue but he'd had enough reminiscing for one evening.

I couldn't follow up with Robbie because I didn't want to come across as desperate. Reaching out became off limits. I couldn't reveal that our kiss meant as much as it did. For him it may have been just a kiss, but to me it was the crowning achievement of a ton of hard work. From the moment I met him, I obsessed over how I could let him know I liked him without explicitly saying anything. How could I look both cute and hot, but not look too done-up? Which compliment toed the line between a friendly admiration and a sex-fueled come-on? What clever quip implied that other men thought I was a catch without the implication of sounding like a whore? Secretly loving someone with a boyfriend was a tough job. Getting that someone to break up with his boyfriend was even tougher.

About a week passed and I hadn't heard from him. At that point I basically started scratching notches into the wall like a prisoner as I counted the days until he contacted me. I even began to think Nick had brutally murdered Robbie after I passed him in the hallway. Why else would I be left in the dark?

Nine and a half days later (or about two hundred thirty five hours if you're bonkers), I finally saw him at work. By that point I was borderline irate with how he'd handled the situation. I spent the entire subway ride to my shift practicing the ways in which I could show him how insulted I was. I contemplated giving him the cold shoulder, belittling him in front of our coworkers, or giving a lecture sprinkled with references he wouldn't understand.

We were working a sit-down dinner at some bank's corporate office. I got him alone in a hallway outside the handicapped bathroom and then proceeded to word-vomit all over him. "So this is how it's going to be now?" I said. "It's like you invited me into your house but you locked the screen door."

"What?"

"You know I can still see through the screen door. And I can hear through it. I could also easily tear through a screen door and raid you of all your earthly possessions, but I'm not a crazy person. Instead, I've been waiting quietly outside for you to greet me…even though it's rude for you to make me wait like that. When you invite someone over to your house, you should have all of the doors open and you should be waiting for them in the foyer. With food. And a drink."

He looked at me queerly, like I was an escapee from Bellevue Hospital's mental ward. I don't blame him. I was wearing an ill-fitting catering tuxedo and yelling about screen doors.

"What movie is that from?" he asked.

"Huh?"

"It's from like a romantic comedy or something, right?"

"What?"

"Isn't that something that one girl says in that movie?"

"That's the vaguest thing I've ever heard."

He smiled and shrugged his shoulders. He was trying to be cute. I couldn't let him.

"No. It was an original metaphor, thank you." I said.

"Well then, it was the most convoluted thing I've ever heard."

"I just want to know what's going on between us," I snapped. Anger had raised my volume. I'm sure that I had a crazy Jack Nicholson in *The Shining* look in my eye too. All of the care I'd taken in not letting him know how much he meant to me had flown out the window and landed fifty-seven floors below on Park Avenue.

"I'm sorry," he whispered. "I've just been letting this whole Nick thing settle."

"Settle? You either want to be with him or you don't. You either want to be with me or you don't."

"I really like you. You know that, Jerm. I'm just concerned that I'm rushing into this."

I should have known. The dumbest thing a person can do is break up with one partner and then immediately jump into a relationship with another. There's a grieving process that needs to take place. Ugh. If Robbie started dating me, I'd be his rebound. I had too many feelings invested in him to be that. But I also didn't want him running around with every other cater waiter in NYC until he was ready.

An outsider would be quick to point out that I was being led on. Robbie was keeping me on a short string that he could easily yank in his direction when he decided he was ready for love. I didn't deserve that. Unfortunately I was on the inside of the situation, up to my eyeballs in mixed feelings. Nothing was clear. I was fine being on-call for when he changed his tune.

6. No Turning Back

U pon moving to the city, most people reconsider their must-haves in a living space. Suburbanites yearn for corner bedrooms; we just ask for a simple hole in the wall for an air conditioner. They want back yards large enough for a swing set and a swimming pool; we want a fire escape. Oh, the hours I've spent precariously perched on a rickety iron structure while looking at the stars. Okay, pretending to look at stars. I swear they exist somewhere beyond the light pollution.

Unfortunately, paranoia forces many windows leading to fire escapes to be dressed in metal gates, like the ones used to keep the steerage folks below when the Titanic split in two and subsequently sank. My window had such a gate. One time, Meg closed the gate while I was out there. When I rattled it to get back in, she shouted, "Stay back…or I'll shoot you all like dogs!" Now typically I applaud any use of *Titanic* quotes inserted into pedestrian conversation, but that particular scene prompted me to have the gate removed and accept the risk of having someone from steerage crawl in and steal my computer while I was at work.

I shouldn't give Spanish Harlem a bad rap. While it wasn't the safest neighborhood in the world, it wasn't the most dangerous either. I'm not dumb. I wouldn't have moved there if I thought I'd have my face scarred by a gang member. The Upper East Side was crawling further north by the minute. Soon I would be arguing with rich Jewish women at a smoothie bar.

Then a certain economic downturn caused the gentrification to change from a rapid fire to a flickering flame. Everyone stopped caring about the neighborhood and crime had a slight upturn. Mystery men began breaking into the buildings on my block. Thankfully, nobody had been hurt. Oddly, nothing had been stolen. The police blamed it on "bored kids." That may have been true because who would go through the trouble of breaking into an apartment without raping the place of its Macs and Toshibas? Even with their semi-valuable possessions still intact, the renters of the neighborhood were scared shitless.

My little boy nightmares made a reprisal, followed by anxiety about sleeping. The moment I pulled up the covers, my legs began twitching and my stomach twisted into knots. Falling asleep required me to be either dead-tired or inebriated. So one night, I may or may not have borrowed some sleeping pills from a spinning-out-of-control coworker to help me pass out. He instructed me to take them at the end of my shift so I'd be ready to pass out by the time I got home. Bad idea. I don't even remember the twenty block walk home, let alone finding my bed. Miraculously, I ended up there.

I think dreams have a surreal quality to prevent us from tweaking out (i.e., wetting the bed, sleepwalking, *really* murdering your boss). When they get too crazy, we're usually aware that we're dreaming and wake up. The same goes for when they get too good. That's why I never end up making out with Leonardo DiCaprio.

But that night my dream was absolutely real. There was no sense of fantasy, no third-person P.O.V., no animals in human clothes, and no melting clocks. My bedroom was as normal as ever. The light coming in from the window was as bright as the streetlights had always made it. It poured in and splashed all over my face because I was too stoned to close the curtain. I groggily turned over in bed to remedy the situation, but froze. The silhouette of a figure on the fire escape outside watched me sleep. I was so terrified, my body locked up. All I could do was watch it watch me. After peering at me for several minutes, the figure opened the window and stepped in.

I woke up, gasping and sweating.

I reached for my glasses and found the room appropriately dim. The real version of Jeremy had managed to pull the curtain closed before hitting the pillow. All was well. I shook off the dream and curled up with a blanket over my head, the proper post-nightmare position. Still shaken, my blood rushed and my breath shallowed. I waited for sleep to take me away but my body resisted.

The draft coming from my leaky window wasn't helping, either. I often tucked a pillow into the corner to provide insulation, so I reached over and pulled back the curtain enough to throw one into place. I tossed it without looking, my head still covered. I waited for the soft thud that should have followed but I didn't hear anything. The pillow had flown right out the window, which was half open.

Fear paralyzed me. I do a lot of stupid things but I would never sleep next to an open window in cool weather. Someone else had opened it. Meg had no reason to come in my room. Who was it? If there was an intruder, my sheets surely weren't going to provide any real protection. I had to venture out. I uncovered my head and saw my room in a kind of darkness I'd never seen before. The bright lights outside my window had been blown out. As my eyes adjusted, all I could make out were shadows. My bookshelf stood tall in front of me. The dresser drawers were pulled open and messy, just like I'd left them. A pile of laundry stacked high on my desk chair, waiting to be put away.

Then the laundry loomed forward, in a most un-laundry-like way.

Terrors confirmed. Someone was in my room and he was coming at me.

I tried to scream but nothing came out. My eyes closed and I waited to feel pain.

Suddenly, the window blew in as if I'd been living next door to a landmine. Something flew by me like a boulder from a Roman catapult. My cowardly instincts were activated and I once again threw the covers over my head, protecting myself from the rain of glass and broken wall. The energy vacated my room as the intruders rumbled down the hall. When I finally poked my head out of its cocoon, the place looked more like a war zone than the bedroom of a homosexual with good taste.

I gathered some courage and bolted into the living room to investigate, ignoring the pain underneath as debris pierced the soles of my feet. I left a trail of blood from one end of the apartment to the other. My run came to an abrupt stop when I reached the end of the hall. I discovered a pile of undecipherable body parts and pieces of demolished furniture. The puddle of blood underneath it snaked its way to the one under mine, re-staining the hardwood a deep red.

Only one thing could have done that kind of damage. Garth. And he was huddled in a dark corner, covered in the same mess that I stood in.

I took a step toward him. My bare foot landed on something chunky that wasn't once part of my now destroyed coffee table. It was organic and slimy. That made the violence real—the death of a person where I usually watch TV was real. Vomit hurled into my throat but I coughed it down. The floor had seen enough splatters.

"What…what happened?" I whispered, somehow thinking that I could prevent waking Meg.

"Are you alright?" he asked.

What kind of question…NO, I wasn't alright. There were pieces of a stranger strewn around my living room like freaking puzzle pieces. I erupted. "I'm…" I pointed to the chunks of drywall behind me. "What did…?" I pointed to the chunks of human below me. "Who was that?"

He rushed forward. "Are you alright?" He reached for me.

"No," I said as I backed away, stepping on another squishy thing that I didn't dare think about. Still, I yelped.

I heard poor Meg tear open her door and stomp down the hall. "Jerm?" she cried with a tired voice.

Garth looked at me sorrowfully and mouthed the words, "I'm sorry." Then leapt from the crime scene and through the window.

The following moments were a blur. I think Meg screamed when she entered the room. That scream turned into hysterics. I recall trying to cry, to have a normal reaction like she'd had, but I was numb. I looked back at the hole in my wall where the window had once been. My life was just as gaping, as vulnerable. Anyone was capable of breaking in and trampling on me. The feeling was too horrifying to process. Of course I couldn't cry about it.

Meg and I were left in our ramshackle apartment with the remnants of a person neither of us knew.

❖

Garth was stirring under the newly-nighted sky. The Guardians began to mill about, readying themselves for another evening patrol. In the early moments of darkness, it was polite to keep the noise down. The humans were still awake. Only the shuffling of stone feet on stone floor could be heard.

But a voice quivered through the archways of the tower, "No…" The General stood behind Garth with his eyes digging into his back. "This can't be. It was supposed to be you," he hissed.

Garth jolted to attention. "Sir?"

"He got it wrong. It was supposed to be you," the General said. His shaking finger pointed to the empty space near Garth.

Garth's eyes followed to the spot. It was where Francis had perched just hours before. Where could he have gone? Possibly to Helena's fountain, but Francis would never wander off without first telling Garth. Did someone steal him away during the day, while they were immobile? That wasn't fair. They were defenseless in that state. Garth let out a growl. "Where is he?" he asked.

The General was unable to say.

"Where is Francis?"

"Look down, Garth."

He did. It was difficult to see at first, but soon his eyes attuned to a pile of rubble at the base of the palace. Garth's hand slid over to the empty space. He patted the spot as if his friend would materialize from underneath the massive bricks. "Francis," he whispered, his eyes still on the ground. Then he called down, "Francis! Francis!"

No answer.

His hysterical voice echoed down the streets and through the cavernous palace, attracting the attention of the other Guardians. One grabbed his arm in an attempt to calm him, but Garth threw him back towards the General, who crept wide-eyed into a shadow.

Garth met the General's gaze before he could escape. "You pushed him."

"I didn't…I—"

"You didn't even give him the chance to fight, you coward."

"Don't be a fool," barked Brogan. "I was asleep just like him. Just like you. I didn't do anything."

Garth rushed toward his cowering superior and cornered him between two massive pillars. "*You* are the demon, not that old decoration in the garden!" The other Guardians watched silently. They had never seen Garth filled with so much rage.

"It was a mistake. We can discuss this in private," said Brogan, trying to appease the monster in front of him.

"It was supposed to be me. You were trying to silence me."

"I wasn't trying to do anything, my boy. I told the King. I had to. What he did next was his prerogative."

"But you knew what he'd do. You set this up, which is just as bad."

Garth had seen men do extraordinary things on the battlefield. Soldiers would come at each other in fits of rage so intense that when they finally met, the earth itself seemed to shudder. That same power came over him as he went for Brogan's neck and threw the General's massive body to the ground. The General looked to his soldiers for mercy but found none. Maybe they were finally tired of their servitude or maybe they sensed the King's wickedness seeping into their now submissive leader. Whatever the reason, they turned their backs. He struggled, but Garth's hold was pointed and strong.

It was over just as quickly as it began. Garth hurled the General towards the street to meet the same fate as Francis.

Garth roared like the monster he was trying not to become. The soulless pile of rubble on the ground was just a pile of rubble on the ground. Francis' death was permanent and Garth was responsible. Finally, he felt as ugly on the inside as he was on the outside.

Police lines were drawn, photographs were taken, and evidence was catalogued. Meg and I tried to answer the detective's questions but we were both too shaken to think coherently. Discovering a room full of human remains wasn't an easy event to process. Normal folks like us shouldn't encounter such grisly scenes.

I'd finagled my way out of having my face shown on the nightly news, claiming trauma and shyness. In truth, I didn't want my family tuning in for the weather only to find that a vicious murder had taken place in my living room.

My lack of communication with the parental units wasn't right. I thought of calling them but I panicked after thinking about how the conversation would go. Dad would answer the phone with a hearty, "Ye-ello!" His greetings always crescendo to a sharp point, letting you know he's excited to hear from you. At that point, I'd choke. I wouldn't be able to tell him. My mother would cry too hard to even bother. To drop such a catastrophic bomb would ruin everyone's day. They'd whisk me home faster than Garth had come barreling through my window. I'd need accompaniment from the National Guard to take a simple trip to the grocery store.

Hiding the attack from my friends was going to be the greater challenge. The fates already allowed me to keep them in the dark about getting hate-crimed on New Year's Eve, thrown into the subway track a few days later, and continuously rendezvousing with Quasimodo's best friend. I'd reached the total allotment of secrets a person is allowed in one lifetime. Everything after that, including a vigilante rocketing through my window and murdering a person in my living room, would be forced into the open. Meg's witnessing of the post-Garth scene didn't help either. As good as I was about sealing my lips, she was equally good at letting hers fly. I asked for discretion but she was in therapy and believed that communication was the solution to all of life's problems.

Our temporary homelessness during the cleanup process added to my difficulties with staying on the down low. The following week turned into a tour de New York as I slept on couches all over the city. I was surprised at how little time I'd spent at my friends' various apartments prior to the break in, especially the ones in far off lands like Brooklyn and Queens. We watched movies and ate popcorn and rotted in front of reality television. Luckily, most everyone tiptoed around the events that had made me their guest. I was happy to play dumb. Conversations tended to wander into the typical, "So, how are thiiings?" to which I'd reply, "Same ol', same ol'." That answer was both lighthearted and vague, tricking the asker into believing my life, well my life outside of the murder investigation, was just as boring, uninteresting, and depressing as always.

The only people who didn't let me off the hook were Asher and Robbie. Asher possessed a large Jewish nose (by his own confession) that loved being in other people's business. Because he was my best friend, he was under the impression that he had permission to be direct with me about the whole ordeal.

Robbie was doing this faux-boyfriend thing that I found incredibly irritating. My near death experience was his "wake up call," as he put it. Since he could potentially lose me at any minute, he wanted to spend every single one of them in my presence. Obviously that was taxing, especially with the new resentments that I harbored toward him. I hated that I had to be on the brink of death in order to gain some attention. Would future advancement in our relationship require events as major to prompt them? If I wanted us to move in together, would I have to walk into a day care wearing a vest made of dynamite?

Still, he was being sincere. He seemed genuinely sorry about the course that we'd had to take in order to get where we were. His interest in my well-being had spiked, too. Robbie felt entitled to real answers. For a split second I contemplated telling him some version of the truth (with the omission of the supernatural, of course), but then I remembered it had taken him months to become truthful with me. He'd have to earn that information out of me.

"There were two break-ins and a murder," I said, not *technically* lying.

"Yes, we gathered that," Robbie said, exchanging a look with Asher. Dinner had been cleared, leaving my mouth completely available to talk instead of chew. I contemplated dessert.

"Person number one broke into my room. Person number two noticed and bashed through my window to save me from person number one. Then person number two broke person number one into many pieces. Police came." That was my story and I was sticking to it. Asher looked at me, waiting for me to say what he already knew. I half-heartedly reported, "And based on person number two's killing style, authorities believe that he is the same person who dumped bodies in a Chelsea sewer on New Year's Day."

"I told you he knew," Asher said to Robbie.

"So you know the other part, right?" Robbie tentatively asked.

"The guy…the guy all over my living room, had a record for assaulting some gay men last year," I said, defeated by what was apparently public knowledge. "A detective told me the other day at my one-millionth interrogation. How do you know this stuff?"

"Blogs," Asher said. "That's all I do at work."

Well apparently his blogs (as well as the NYPD) failed to realize the connection to the fried man on the Eighth Street subway track. I suppose if Garth had taken the time to pulverize *that* body in the same way, it'd be added to his growing list of accomplishments. Thankfully he just left that victim where he'd died, framing bashed basher number two as a suicide jumper. I sighed with relief.

"You have a gay superhero looking out for you," Robbie sang as he tickled my stomach. I quickly swatted him away out of irritation and because I feared puking in public, yet again.

Asher was pleased as punch. "Maybe we should scrap this Hans musical altogether and write that vigilante movie. You actually *had* an encounter. There's no way it wouldn't sell," he said.

"I'm too close to the events."

"Fine, we'll give it some time. Since you have no feelings, you'll be over it by Friday. It's really a no-brainer."

"It's not a bad idea. You could use the money, Jerm," Robbie chimed in. "You should at least sell your story to a magazine."

"There is no story," I assured them. "It all went down in like fifteen seconds. The fact that it happened to me is completely random. It would be like a unicorn walking through the front door and licking your face with its magic sparkle-tongue. People would ask why it chose you and you'd have absolutely nothing to say." Weird analogy, I know. And with my recent experiences, a unicorn would just be the norm.

"Actually, I'd have to tell the truth and say that I wash my face exclusively in milk and honey, which is a unicorn's favorite," Robbie said.

He was really cute sometimes.

"I hope they can identify him. The superman's blood has to be somewhere, right? He busted through a freaking window," Asher said, getting louder and louder with each word for emphasis. "It's impossible that he got through a pane of glass without a scratch."

I found it strangely charming, how little they really knew.

"What would that do? DNA doesn't prove anything if it isn't catalogued someplace. If Supergay has a clean slate, he's not going to show up anywhere," Robbie said. He'd argue with Asher about the color of table salt just to annoy him.

"Maybe it will match the random blood from the scene in Chelsea. There was third-party DNA there, remember?" Asher smartly replied.

"That doesn't give you a name. It just confirms what everyone already believes: that the same guy is smashing gay bashers to smithereens all over the city."

As they fought over the discovery of Garth's non-existent blood, I began to break down. The mystery blood in Chelsea was mine…so was the yet-to-be-detected blood in my apartment. My feet were still wrapped in bandages from all the glass on the floor. I was present at both crime scenes despite my best efforts to pretend that none of it had ever happened. It was only a matter of time before I would be called in for blood samples and get linked to both crimes and arrested as a serial killer and put on trial and sent to jail and raped in the shower and murdered for coke and I couldn't do anything to help myself because I was trapped at dinner with fucking Sherlock Holmes and Doctor Watson.

I needed Garth.

With my vagabond status, my routine was upset. I hadn't seen him in days. We didn't even know where to find each other.

"Damn, I have a voicemail," I said as I pulled out my phone. My screen said absolutely nothing but I pretended to access a message anyway. I had twenty seconds to come up with an excuse. "That play I auditioned for is having a last minute callback tonight and they want me to come in."

"It's eight o'clock," Asher said.

"It's some off-off-Broadway thing, they don't keep industry hours," I said, which was actually true in some cases.

"Do you want us to come?" asked Robbie.

"No, no…finish up here. I'll meet you in like an hour or so."

"Are you sure you're okay?"

"Listen," I said, "if I'm constantly monitored, how will I ever re-adjust? I'll just be a bit, promise." I smiled and rubbed the back of his neck in an attempt to reassure him.

"Okay. Be careful. And call me," he said before a quick hug.

"Just don't get killed, homo," barked Asher, in his backward way of showing concern.

Even after multiple attempts on my life and coming face to face with a serial-killing-demon-statue, I'd managed to keep my eyes relatively dry. But as I walked out the door of that restaurant I had a Meryl Streep-in-*The Hours*-style break down. For the first time in days, I was alone. I'd been escorted from restaurant, to bar, to apartment, to subway, to other apartment, to lunch, to *everywhere*, every minute of the day. Now, I felt too vulnerable. All the progress I'd made shattered, like the shards of glass connecting me to Garth's crimes. Yet that grotesque was still the only thing that made me feel safe. Would I ever be able to function without his constant watch? Maybe it was entirely my fault. The law of attraction would have agreed that, because trouble was constantly on my mind, it was bound to follow me. I was so scared of evil, evil would present itself whenever it could. Garth would be stuck with me because I'd never stop needing his assistance. My paranoia was ruining both of our lives.

I walked through Hell's Kitchen, a neighborhood where gays should definitely not show emotion, with tears streaming down my face. I walked west without dignity, without care, and without cruising. I was a magnet for danger and I secretly hoped it would finally succeed at what it'd been trying to do since New Year's.

The West Side Highway's lights flashed nearby. Beyond that, the river sat darker than the night sky. Warehouses and glass condos towered over me. I was at the crossroads of the wealthy and the destitute. Eleventh and Twelfth Avenues were infested with the city's underbelly. My head crowded with thoughts of hobos and crackheads lurking in the nooks and crannies of abandoned lofts and half-finished luxuries. Even if they weren't there, I saw them lumbering for me.

They asked for coins and called me names and touched me with their dirty, crusted fingers—a stylized version of regular homelessness. The people in my mind were better suited for a Dickens novel. They had blackened teeth, knitted shawls, and quivering voices. Their hands wore fingerless gloves and tried to reach for my shoulder and pulled me off the sidewalk and into their shanty village under the street.

I was relieved to feel Garth's strong hand pull me aside. My face lit up before I fell to pieces on his freezing shoulder. His hand clumsily ran through my hair as I sobbed. His touch was too heavy to be comforting, but I pressed myself into it just to ensure myself of his presence.

Garth feverishly looked through the garden for the Queen. Any judgment he'd passed on her gruesome actions had disappeared. Now that he'd lost a friend, he understood her anger. He reached the pond and found the courtyard demolished, her throne in ruins. Even the twisted willows had been torn from overhead and bobbed sadly in the murky water. He searched through the rubble hoping that he wouldn't find a piece of her.

"Guardian!" cried a voice from within the woods. The Queen pounded over the broken stones and wrapped him in her arms. The impact of their two bodies shook the ground. Garth stood in her entwinement, unable to recall what to do in an embrace.

"What are you doing back here?" she asked, finally letting go.

"I needed to find you. I knew you'd be in danger."

"I sensed that, too. I've been hiding elsewhere."

"I believe you. I believe everything you said."

The Queen smiled and touched his face. He flinched.

"Everything was plotted," he continued. "I told Brogan about the Prince's murder. He wouldn't hear it. He said you made it up. He was protecting someone. I think it was the King."

"I saw the *twins* kill the Prince! It couldn't have been the King," she insisted.

• 110 •

"But it was. Behind the twins, it was. There was a plan to change succession. I know too much so he tried to destroy me," Garth's train of thought wandered but he found it again. "He failed. He assassinated another instead, a friend of mine."

She stared out at the water, her lip quivering with the beginnings of what seemed like an uneasy emotion. Garth waited for a reply but she instead bolted towards the palace. Before she was out of sight, she turned to him and said, "I'm sorry about your friend."

Garth called after her but his voice was muffled by the denseness of the woods, which swallowed her in one dark gulp.

Like the night they'd met, Garth pursued her through the garden. "What will you do? Kill the King? He's heavily guarded! He's powerful!"

"I won't rest until I find vengeance, Guardian," she barked.

"Wait!" He caught up, reached for her arm, and swung her backwards. "My name is Garth. I guard no man. Not anymore. Especially not the King." The proclamation seemed to lift a million pounds from his shoulders. For the first time in years, he stood a little taller. "But he will destroy you. I can't let you do that to yourself."

She turned to him. "Then help me."

The weight came back. He hunched again. "No. Absolutely not. I told you, I—"

"You are a Guardian of justice now." She stared at him to make sure he absorbed what she'd said. "The King has ruined you, has he not?"

Garth was silent. He looked at his feet—his stone, misshapen feet. "He trapped me in this form," he quietly said.

"He what?"

"He did this to me."

"What else?"

"Tore me from my family."

"Yes, yes…"

"Enslaved me and…"

"Say it Garth. What else did the King do to you?"

"He killed my best friend!" he roared. "He killed my only friend."

She grabbed his hand. "Now I am your friend. Together, we will end his reign of terror. You will be free."

A mixture of inspiration and fury filled the crevice where Garth's heart used to be. It coursed through cracks like blood through veins until it reached his head and blinded him to nothing but her calling. The King needed to die.

They raced through the palace, demolishing everything in their path. Nothing could stop them on their blood mission. Garth was the first to meet interference: a guard. Before the ironclad man could raise his sword, he was trampled. The sounds of cracking skulls and breaking doors soon filled the sleepy halls. Stone proved more destructive than metal that night.

The Queen arrived at the revered bedchamber before Garth. When he entered, he discovered her standing over the King's bed, staring down at him as if he was a baby in a crib.

"What are you waiting for? Do it, already!" Garth cried.

She didn't move.

A newfound fury sent Garth towards her. "If you don't, I will!" he screamed.

"The old fool," she said, her voice full of sick. "Passed out on spirits. Sleeping through everything, even his own death." Her speech was faint, lost somewhere beyond the large room. Her sentiment didn't last long. Her fists raised and fell upon the old King's head, bursting his brain like a ripe cherry. "Come, Garth. There's still more life in him. We will do this together."

Garth approached the bed-turned-altar. Their brand of holy wine spouted towards the ceiling, granting them the same solace the King had pretended to find in god. His menacing eyes stared up at them, registering their faces. The stone ones were gladdened by it. It would have been a shame for him to die while sleeping. Such a luxury is not afforded to men like that.

The palace soon fell silent and they sauntered back through its halls, drunk on retribution. The Queen's marble was stained with nearly the whole royal family: father, son, and cousins. The statues adorned that war paint as a constant reminder of what they'd done and for whom they'd done it.

"What are you thinking?" asked the Queen.

"I've never killed anything before," he said.

"Never? But you were a warrior."

"I couldn't even kill a bird for dinner, let alone a person. I was terrible in battle."

She laughed softly. "It's not over, I'm afraid."

Garth quickened his pace.

"Where are you going? It's not safe in the tower. You'll be smashed to pieces come daylight," the Queen said, still strolling behind him.

"I need to get Francis. I won't let him be swept away with the morning trash. There must be a way to help him pass on."

She came to his side. "What do you mean?"

"I wasn't always like this. I was human once, with a human soul…but this is an Immortal form."

The Queen looked confused.

"As Immortals, we don't have souls because we don't need them. We don't grow old and die. When an Immortal is killed, it just ceases to exist. That's what happened to Francis. I need to help him. This can't be the end. He deserves to be…" Garth's voice cracked. Hopelessness began to take over. "He deserves to pass on. The dead need to be…wherever they need to be." He sobered up then broke down again.

The Queen caught his fall and cradled him until his heaving lulled. "I know how to help," she whispered. "The Prince died in my arms. I saw the Angel visit him."

Garth sat up, feeling a glimmer of hope in that word: Angel.

She went on, "The Angel of Death, it comes to everyone. I had always thought the Angel came to collect souls, but it doesn't. It comes to give them guidance."

"But Francis, he doesn't have one. The Angel didn't visit!"

"True, but I heard the Angel's counsel. It told the Prince what to do. The beginning of the journey is the same for all souls. It will probably be coming to the King soon."

"He doesn't deserve it! It can't possibly come to wicked souls," Garth interrupted.

"It does, it comes to everyone. The Angel is blindfolded, so as not to pass judgment on the good or the evil. There are others who decide that."

"I don't understand."

"There are tests a soul must take on its journey to Heaven. The tests determine whether the soul is worthy of passing on. If they don't pass the tests they are claimed by the Underworld."

"What if the soul doesn't go on this journey? What if it refuses the tests?"

"That happens, especially if a soul knows it's guilty of sin. It will stay and haunt the living to avoid the odyssey."

"I'm sure that's what the King will do."

"So we must guarantee that the guilty are where they need to be, instead of staying here," said the Queen with a confidence she hoped would creep its way into Garth. "We will use the Angel's guidance."

"Did it mention specifically how to seek vengeance?"

"No, but it told the Prince he must first find a witch. She gives the next set of directions. Surely, she'll be able to help us. We'll secure the King's fate and help Francis. Maybe you, too."

Garth had believed himself to be a Guardian for as long as his body was intact, but at that moment, for the first time, he saw a glimmer of possibility. He could have another chance at life. He could live and die like the rest of the world, like everyone he'd ever known and loved. It'd been countless years since he'd last seen them, his human family. Surely they were all long gone. Even so, he was comforted in knowing that their greatest adventures awaited them after death. Evie had always been such a fan of faerie stories. Her journey must have been just like one. How delighted she must have been when she died…

"You're not going without me," protested Helena. After collecting the pieces of Francis, they stopped by her fountain to say goodbye. Garth held their friend in a large burlap sack that she grasped with all her strength, trying to connect their earlier discussion about death with what was in front of her. It was her first experience with loss, not just of a friend, of anything. "I want to help. The two of you are the only friends I have and now he's gone and you probably won't return."

She was right. Garth couldn't come back. The palace was massacred and a manhunt would soon begin. Then again, the only people who knew the truth were dead and the other grotesques certainly weren't going to go after them. He wondered what they'd do with their newfound freedom.

"Garth, it will be hard enough for the two of us. We're limited to the night, so we must move swiftly. It's not out of the ordinary to see statues in the city, but in the country, two stone ladies and a monster with a sack on his back will be a bit odd," insisted the Queen.

Helena stepped off her fountain and confronted her. "I don't know you, but I do know that you're being very insensitive. Just because you were a decoration in the palace doesn't make you royalty. I'm coming with you and if that means we'll have to try a bit harder to stay hidden, so be it. I will not stay on this wretched fountain just to decay and think of the friends I once had."

The Queen silently agreed to let her come.

The group darted through the town's narrow streets toward the country. They needed to flee the capitol before sunrise, before rumors of stone monsters invading the palace emerged. They sought shelter from the daylight hours in a small grove of fruit trees outside the city walls. The whole kingdom would be in mourning, so they'd be safe from curious farmhands.

As the sun began to rise, they settled down to rest. Garth curled up, guarding his shattered friend. Helena laid her head on the lumpy bag. For the first time, she slept next to the man she loved, even though he was just a pile of rubble beneath her. The Queen settled slightly off to the side, granting them time with the bag and each other. Before the first rays of sunlight hit Garth's face, he secretly turned his head to catch a glimpse of her. To his surprise, he caught her equally secret glance at him.

"I did not mean for this to happen," Garth said to me. "This is all my fault."

I couldn't argue with him. He murdered a man in my apartment. He'd put me in a pretty tough situation.

But he'd also saved my life…again. I was a constant target for danger and I didn't know why. Deep down I wanted to believe that the three attacks on my life were connected, but the more I thought about it, the more confused and afraid I became. Investigating that topic forced me to confront every choice I'd made and every person I'd met. Who could I have ticked off so greatly that they would send multiple assassins for my insignificant and harmless self? Someone *big* had a vendetta out for me, like a god or the President of the United States or a student loan corporation. How could I possibly battle against enemies like that?

"Garth, I'm just glad you were watching out for me." I put my head on his shoulder and had the strangest feeling. Something deep down within me confirmed my fears. "Have you always known I was in danger?"

Garth had trouble searching for words, like he had suddenly reverted back to some European tongue. "I…it is not very clear…but I had a sense that I should…be more invested in you. More than just a friend whom I tell stories to."

The tears stopped and I looked at him with a scrutiny only few have seen.

"I need to be Guardian to you for reasons other than those you originally asked me."

"I don't know what you mean. Why? Is it because of the blood?"

"What blood?"

I was about ready to walk in front of a bus. What blood? The most pressing issue of my entire life was completely unknown to him. Apparently he knew something more detrimental? Fantastic! "My blood is at *your* crime scenes, Garth. It's pretty bad. The cops are going to think I'm the one smashing men into pudding and stuffing them in drainpipes. What exactly are *you* talking about?" I asked like I was speaking to a child.

"Yes, that is also…pretty bad. We need to get you some help." He was in as much shock as I was. He grabbed my arm and started leading me back to the street.

"No," I yelled. I tried to take his hand off me but it didn't budge. "What are you keeping from me?"

"Something is…I think…I do not think that these attacks have been coincidences," he confessed.

"That's becoming obvious. Who is trying to kill me?"

"I do not know," he roared. "I've been trying to find out."

"Is that why you keep leaving town? You're looking for a long lost crystal ball or psychic to tell you?

"No, actually I've been looking for a witch," he snarled.

"Holy Hell, Garth! You can't just spring this stuff on me!"

"I need to take you to Rita."

My phone began to ring. It was Robbie. "Garth, wait!"

"She can help us, I promise."

My phone made another sound. I had a text message. "I'm on a time constraint."

He stopped pulling at me and turned around. "Yes, you are. If we do not do something, you are going to either be dead or in jail. Your date can wait."

"I'm sorry I have to face real, living, breathing people in my life," I spat out like dragon fire.

He pulled away. A rebuttal was on the tip of his tongue but he held back.

"I'm sorry," I said. "I didn't mean to hurt your—"

"Stop." His hand came up, trembling. It touched my cheek. He brushed a stray curl from my face. "Those people cannot help you. Come with me."

7. Stumped

The Angel's instructions weren't terribly specific," said the Queen as they rose from their first day outside city walls. "It told the Prince to go into the forest and seek out a Horse. It would lead him to the witch."

"Do horses run wild? I've only seen them in town," Helena asked.

"They're rare," answered Garth. "Mother used to make us carry oats in our pockets on long trips through the woods, just in case we came across one. They're bad omens. She was very superstitious." He smirked at the wacky memory, as if feeding a bad omen would somehow make it less bad.

Without any real directions, they were left to wander aimlessly through the woods and hope to encounter the Horse. They ventured to primeval places where the trees were ancient and the likelihood of crossing paths with the spirit world was great. Believed to be haunted, humans rarely ventured to that part of the forest, extinguishing the stone ones' fears of being discovered. Helena was delighted by practically everything along the way and kept her companions busy with question after question after question.

But nights of meandering grew tiresome. Garth was especially weary as the bearer of Francis' broken body. The physical heft of the bag and the emotional weight of Francis' death brought up feelings he hadn't known in years. On one particular evening, the load became too great. He stumbled upon an old tree stump, the perfect place to rest. He swung Francis from his shoulder, gently placed him on the ground, and took a seat on it. The rotting wood cracked beneath him.

"Excuse me!" screamed a voice.

"Pardon?" Garth said, startled by the unexpected sound.

"Stand up, you fool!" cried the voice again. Garth obliged and circled the area in search of the unfortunate creature he'd accidentally squashed.

"Garth, look!" cried Helena with a pointed finger towards the stump.

He turned around and saw a most unusual site: A bark-covered face, just as if someone had carved it into the side of that old tree. Through the wooden skin Garth could see that the face was young, around the age he'd been before being turned to stone.

"I'm sorry," Garth said.

"No worry. You didn't know." The stump replied.

"Are you enchanted?" asked Helena. She was more thrilled than she'd been about the last ninety-nine things she'd passed along the way.

"No, are you?"

"Yes, in some way or another, all three of us are," said Garth. "Are you a tree spirit then?"

"Not that either. This tree died many years before I moved in. That's how I was able to inhabit it," grumbled the stump. Helena's head cocked to the side. "I'm a ghost. Died in battle many years ago. Joseph is my name."

Garth assumed he'd died in the same Great War, but he decided not to probe. "Good to meet you, Joseph. My apologies for sitting on you."

"Not a worry, not a worry. You shouldn't feel a bit guilty for sitting on a stump. I'm just biding my time. Pay no mind to me," Joseph said as he uncomfortably glanced from side to side.

The Queen nudged Garth as if to say, "Ask him."

"Joseph, may I ask you a question?"

"Yes but do be quick about it. The lot of you are making my disguise rather obvious."

"Are you *haunting* this tree?"

The look in his wooden eyes was etched with disdain. He nodded. "Were you once looking for the Horse, Joseph?"

The stump filled with terror. "Please don't speak too loudly. It'll hear you! I should hope you aren't in search of it, yourselves. No, no, no. Tell me, did you speak with that deceitful Angel?"

Helena and Garth looked at the Queen to do the explaining but she appeared as spooked as the dead tree before her. "Yes," she finally replied. "I witnessed the Angel direct a soul on his journey. We are seeking out a witch. I understand the Horse is meant to bring us to her."

Joseph laughed a malicious laugh. "The Angel didn't tell you the Horse is a Judge, did he? You won't be getting on its back to ride to her door, no. You see, not all souls go to the same place. The Horse, it begins choosing who's worthy."

The Queen fell to the ground, grabbed the old tree, and shook its thick lichen bark to the ground. "What do you mean, you old stump? Why would an Angel lead souls into a trap? That Horse could drag us straight to Hell!"

"Yes!" Joseph hissed. "How else would guilty souls be judged? Nobody would willingly face such a gamble. If all souls knew the trials were avoidable, this world would be brimming with spirits. All biding their time like I do."

"How do you know this? Why haven't you been judged?" asked Garth. He wasn't sure if they should trust a cut of wood. Then again, a block of stone shouldn't feel ill will for something equally inanimate. He felt silly for thinking anything at all.

"Because I refuse to be," Joseph sang through a kind of grin that made Garth uneasy. "I died with many others. A whole generation of boys was lost. A whole generation of boys was on the same journey to the other side. If you could view with a soul's eyes, you would have seen more ghosts than trees here. Every one of us searched for a steed and nearly every one succeeded. But not me. See, I saw what really happens. I thought war was a nightmare. But it was nothing compared to that animal. That Horse. I wouldn't even call it a horse. It's a monster, it is. As soon as it looks at you, it knows. It knows if you were doing untrue things when you died. If you weren't, it offers you passage to the witch. If you were, it drags you down to the Underworld. I saw it happen." The stump twitched, trying to shake the memory. "I didn't give it a chance to judge me. I fled. Hide in dead things. Been doing it for years. The others gave up and said, 'Horse! Come for me!' Not me. Here I am."

The storytelling caused sap-tears to pour from his bark. Garth felt pity for the stump. He wondered if they'd ever locked eyes on the battlefield.

"But why are you afraid?" asked Helena. "Did you die with a clear conscious?"

Joseph stopped his weeping and looked to her with despair. "That's just it. I don't know. I believed in what I fought for. But who's to say what's right and what's wrong in war? Every soldier thinks he's doing the right thing. Now I doubt my actions. What if I was doing the devil's work? I will not be punished for being led astray!"

The Queen stroked his rough cheek. "There are many, many horrible leaders. *They* mislead their people. Our King was an evil man. The wars he waged were in vain and *he* will pay in the end. The men he *forced* into battle will not face that fate."

"But I saw," interrupted Joseph. "My countrymen, many of them, dragged into fire. I heard their screams from below the earth!"

"Then they enjoyed the kill," she asserted. "They bled other men to conquer. The clouds of influence are thick but not inescapable. If you died knowing what was right, then you are a safe man." She pet his rough bark like it was hair on a child's head.

The sap stopped running and the Queen lifted her hands. Joseph was gone.

"Did he go after the Horse?" asked Helena.

"I don't think he ever will. He was confused when he was alive and is even more confused in death," the Queen replied.

"If I were him, I'd do the same thing. Why would anyone want to leave this world?" Helena wondered.

The Queen shuttered. "Some people are done with this world. Let's move on." Her walls were always built high, but in the hours following their encounter with Joseph, they proved impermeable. She barely said a word after their encounter.

Helena made the first effort to lighten the mood. "Tell me about yourself," she said, a little too cheerfully.

The Queen answered with a puzzled look.

"I mean, how did you come to be? Are you enchanted like me, cursed like Garth, or some kind of rogue spirit like Joseph back there?"

"Do I look like a rogue?" asked the Queen, clearly not wanting any further discussion.

Garth answered for her. "She's an enchantment."

Helena's eyes widened and a smile spread from ear to ear. "So am I! Do you remember yours?"

"No," said the Queen. She looked at Helena who obviously wanted to divulge more information. "Do you remember yours?" she asked with little interest.

"I'm not completely certain but I do remember hearing stories around the fountain. Sometimes, late at night, lovers would wander into the square and sit by me. I was awake but I had to be very still so they wouldn't notice. They'd admire me and talk about a sculptor who chiseled the image of his long-lost love into marble. It turned out so beautifully that it was put in the middle of the town. The constant reminder of her made him so distraught, he killed himself."

"And that brought you to life?" asked the Queen, shocked that such an innocent thing like Helena could be the result of something so morbid.

"Yes! Have you heard this before?"

"That sounds like a story too tragic for lovers to tell at your fountain."

"Oh, it is. It's very tragic but also very beautiful. Life must end to create a new one. Like how grass dies and turns to dirt which grows a flower." She proudly looked to Garth with a smile as big as the forest.

He congratulated her on her analogy with a nod.

"That's...a very nice way of looking at things, Helena," said the Queen.

Garth agreed, "And you are, in a way, keeping the memory of their love alive."

"You're right! Many, many people came to the fountain and told that story. I hope it's remembered for years to come," Helena said.

"Actually," the Queen began, "I have heard of you. The Prince occasionally went to your fountain. He would throw devotions into its waters. To remember doomed love affairs, I suppose. He was very dramatic about love. I'm sure you're deeply missed by the romantics."

Helena stopped walking and tried to cry. "I'm so selfish. I shouldn't have come!"

"You came for Francis. That's not selfish at all," said Garth.

"Yes, but the Queen is right. I'm leaving all those people alone. They came to my fountain to be inspired. I've abandoned them."

Garth went to her and rested his heavy hand on her shoulder. "Let people seek out their dreams instead of being distracted by idols and love stories. Humans spend too much time doing that. You've freed them."

"He says, as if there is something wrong with being a dreamer," the Queen scolded. "The Prince came to me for that reason. He dreamed by me, he could escape with me. That's why I'm here. That's why we're all here. When he looked at me he saw a beautiful, strong leader who wasn't ashamed of being who she was. He saw things in me that he wished he could see in himself. That's why statues exist. We encourage dreams. We are distractions. The world is full of terror but we provide refuge. We are reminders of better, different things."

She turned to Helena, "I'm sure there will be many who are disappointed with your disappearance, there's no doubt. And it's nice to know that when the Prince came to you, you were listening." She quickly glanced to Garth with sorrowful eyes that silently apologized for her tone. "But I'm also sure that if the Prince knew you were alive, he wouldn't want you stuck on a pedestal, listening to pathetic love poems all day. You've never experienced life, just overheard it. You've freed yourself."

The Queen kept a quick pace that left them in her wake. As she bounded ahead, they could see why the Prince enjoyed her company: she was beautiful, strong, and unashamed of whom she was.

❖

I avoided a hclicopter-searchlight-S.W.A.T.-situation by calling Robbie before we set out for Rita.

"I was worried," he said.

"Don't be. I'm fine." I tried to sound reassuring.

"That's the dumbest thing I've ever heard you say."

"What?"

"Telling me not to worry"

"Well, you shouldn't. I'm fine. I just got to the audition."

"Jerm, someone tried to…" He avoided saying what I knew he wanted to say, like the words would trigger an episode. "I thought you'd at least text me when you got there."

I felt like a tenth grade version of myself, checking in with mom upon my arrival to the movie theatre. "I'm going to be a while. They're running behind."

"Should I come?"

"Now *that's* the dumbest thing I've ever heard. I can't bring friends to an audition," I snapped.

Quiet.

Garth was giving me the "get on with it" glare. "Listen, I'll call you when I'm done."

"Are you okay? If you don't want me around, say it," I could tell the question was more to push my buttons that illicit sympathy.

"At this moment, no I don't. I've been under constant surveillance and I'd like a few minutes to myself, thank you very much." That shouldn't have come as a surprise to him. I really, truly needed everyone, especially him, to get off my back. My text message inbox was full of questions about how I was doing and whom I was with and when I'd be around. Was he concerned about me or concerned about me doing to him what he did to Nick? Without thinking, I blurted it out. "And before your mind even wanders there, I'm not off hooking up with some theatre district dancing queen."

Quiet again. I was right.

"That's what you thought," I said. "You thought I was out with someone else."

"No."

"Yes, you did." My mind almost reverted to making embarrassing *Sex and the City* references about cheater's paranoia. I quickly moved on before I made one out aloud. "Are you serious? You of all people should not be the one pointing fingers."

"That's not fair. I told you that I'm done with Nick. I want to be with you," he whined.

I couldn't help but wonder if he'd been saying the exact same thing to Nick about me.

Then again, our relationship wasn't that serious. The whole "boyfriend" term, complete with all of its baggage, hadn't been used to describe anyone, Nick or myself. We were all floating in gay limbo. It was hard to get especially angry about the situation because I didn't know what the situation was. If he was fake-seeing me and fake-seeing Nick, there *technically* wasn't a problem. Even if I did have the opportunity to be a true-blue "other man," I didn't have time for it. I was focused on more pressing matters, like witches, ghosts, and not being continually gay bashed as I went about my day.

I couldn't process the many facets of my life's dilemmas. I didn't have the time or the mental capacity. So I just got *generally* angry, spitting venom in whatever direction would alleviate pressure. Since he was my immediate irritation, he would be the first recipient. "Pick one, Robbie. Him or me."

"I care about you! I can't stand being around him anymore. He makes me feel bad about myself," he whimpered. Something in his voice was sincere. Maybe he was stuck, like smoking a cigarette to satiate an oral fixation when all that's really needed is a piece of gum. Cancer sticks can get you kind of buzzed for a minute, but they ultimately make you feel like shit. And they kill you. Gum cleans your teeth, freshens your breath, and sometimes even whitens your teeth. That man needed some gum!

Unfortunately I didn't have the time to commit to a healthy exploration of our feelings. Robbie was great and all…but not being accused of murder was greater. When your ass is on the line, the relationship bullshit we create is just that: bullshit. I had to keep pushing and get rid of him.

"Good. You should feel bad about yourself because you're doing bad things. You don't have any business keeping tabs on me. After months of leading me on, you can't decide we're exclusive just because you almost lost me. Maybe you should pretend we never happened. You can't have us both, you selfish dick."

I hung up and immediately regretted the last twenty seconds. I gagged out a few sobs. It felt fantastic. Having an emotion unattached to a crime scene was welcome no matter how terrible the emotion was. I reveled in my sorrow like a college freshman listening to Dashboard Confessional in an illegally candle-lit dorm room.

Garth gave me a minute before pulling me from my sad haze. "Rita's this way."

❖

When she wasn't being an avid student, Helena helped pass the time by entertaining her fellow travelers with stories from the fountain. She had a tendency to hold onto each encounter as a precious, beautiful memory. But most of them were relatively humorous.

"This one woman, she would come almost every day and float violets in the water. They were so pretty," Helena sighed. "But she didn't leave them there for very long because she'd eventually gather them up...and eat them!" The Queen and Garth erupted in laughter. "She thought they'd give her luck in love! Of course, violets don't grow year round so she'd have to find alternatives, like—"

The laughing stopped when they heard a clacking. The Horse appeared on the top of a rocky slope.

Their eyes fixed to it without catching its glance. Garth had seen warhorses tower over men but the one before him was more enormous, more dazzling than any he could recall. Its metallic color changed from silver, to grey, to blue depending on the angle it caught the moonlight. With every move of its bulging muscles, the three became more unnerved. Eventually its two beady eyes landed on their corner of the forest.

Helena shook as its eyes grazed her. "Don't worry," Garth said. "We have no souls to be judged. It's just curious."

After inspecting Helena, its eyes moved onto her companions. As the Horse sniffed and snorted, the Queen grabbed for Garth's hand. "I'm scared," she whispered.

The mighty stead surged forward, leaping from the rock and onto the ground in front of them. With one toss of its mammoth head, it threw Garth and Helena to the side. The Queen was left to face the beast alone. Its eyes narrowed and seemed to peer beneath her stone skin.

"No!" she hollered.

The Horse reared and let out a neigh that shook autumn's leaves from the surrounding branches. Its body rushed toward her, forcing Helena and Garth to shield their eyes from watching their new friend get pummeled by its heavy hooves.

"We just want passage to the witch. You and I both know that no judgment needs to be made here," asserted the Queen.

Helena and Garth opened their eyes and saw her standing defiantly as the Horse knelt down and invited her aboard.

8. Old Ladies and their Gifts

It definitely wasn't an ordinary horse. An ordinary horse would have buckled under the weight of a solid marble Queen. Even if it were an extraordinary horse, there was no way that Garth, Helena, *and* a sack full of Francis could fit on its back. Garth panicked while thinking about the possible scenarios. Would it invite him aboard? Would each of them go alone? How far was the journey? Would it really take them to the witch or would it plunge them into a fiery pit like Joseph said? His fretting was interrupted by Helena's giggles. He gave her a stern look for not taking the situation seriously.

Soon the Queen was just as amused. "It's amazing!" she laughed.

Garth looked at the Horse beneath her. Its four legs clicked the earth and with every stomp, it doubled in size to receive more passengers. When it was appropriately large, it bowed its head and allowed the rest of them to board.

Its trot through the forest eventually turned into a gallop that morphed into an impossibly fast sprint. As they accelerated, the trees, ground, and sky became mere blurs. A soft pink began to infiltrate the muted colors around them as the sun's cursed light flirted with touching the Horse's hind legs.

In the distance, Garth saw a clearing. The surrounding growth abruptly stopped at its edge, which was enclosed by a circle of smooth pebbles. The Horse and the sun simultaneously jumped into the ring and onto a patch of manicured grass.

Light washed over their stone bodies, forcing them to reside themselves to hibernation. They would have to wait another day. Garth closed his eyes and waited for the sudden onset of sleep. He hoped for happy dreams that would quickly escort him into the following night. But the blackness that he usually saw inside his eyelids ignited into a blazing red. The sun was overhead and he was still awake.

Unsure of the brightness above, Helena shielded her grinning face. "More magic!" she exclaimed. She jumped from the Horse and awkwardly wandered around the clearing, disoriented by the new colors and shapes. She stumbled towards the pebbled perimeter.

The Horse let out a roar-like neigh and galloped in front of her.

"I wouldn't pass over the stones if I were you" said a voice. "They're keeping you from your curse." The Horse led the Queen and Garth onto the ground where they met a very old, very crooked woman. Despite what appeared to be the wear and tear of hundreds of years, she was ornately adorned with beautiful robes and a meticulously painted face. After staring at her for a bit too long, they noticed she had lost all of her hair. In its place was a wig made of yarn, powdered and quaffed to perfection. "My name is older than this world, impossible for you to pronounce, so I won't bother telling you," she huffed. "I have been expecting you."

"You have?" asked Garth.

"These eyes saw you coming, yes. Usually I only meet with souls but I think I can make an exception for Immortals. It has been a long time since I've seen your kind, it has. You're a dying breed, they say."

The woman led them to the center of the clearing where she let out a piercing whistle from between her crinkled lips. The statues waited patiently for something fantastic to happen but their high hopes were left dangling in midair. The old crone became angry and whistled again, even louder than before.

The ground rumbled and the trees outside the magic barrier parted. A peculiar looking cottage peaked out from the foliage and walked toward them on four legs. The chelonia-resido entered the circle and began to dig. When it found a reasonable depth, it placed itself inside the hole and sat like a nesting bird.

While the exterior was certainly out of the ordinary, the interior was exactly what was expected of a witch. Dust and oddities filled the home to its brim, poking out of windows and chimney shoots. They followed closely behind the hag as she searched her shelves. "I've noticed you're missing souls, you are. I'll say you can't get to your final destination without them," she said as she picked up a jar and took a sniff. Her face contorted. She threw it on the ground and continued her hunt. "You must retrieve them. You must." Garth tried to interrupt with a question but he was met with an angry shushing.

"Patience. I'm telling you," she continued. "They are trapped in the birch grove, not far from here. You and only you will know which tree holds your soul. Chop down the tree and your spirit will be free. Simple." The directions rang from her lungs like a song she'd always known and expected them to know, too.

"Will we return to our former selves?" asked Garth.

She looked around and cocked her head at Francis. "The one in the bag, his soul's body is dead. Dead, dead. It will exist on its own. Just a soul, he'll be." She walked toward a locked door and paused. "Your body looks intact, Guardian. Your human soul will finally return your body to its mortal form." With that conversation ended, she unlocked the door and went in.

Before Garth had time to relish in the idea of becoming human again, the witch beckoned them to follow her. They descended a long staircase into a damp basement lit by an unusual light. The statues searched the room for a flickering candle, but one was nowhere to be seen. Instead, the clean glow of the night sky illuminated the sublevel room. Balls of light floated in the air like moons. When their eyes adjusted to the foreign sources, it became clear that the orbs were actually luminescent fruit hanging from vines. Their transparent skin allowed their pulps to be seen, which glistened with the colors of a lightning storm.

The crone plucked one from its home and inspected it for impurities. "These are a favorite of the Bridge Keeper. You will eventually cross paths and these will help you on your way. I will give you a basket, enough for all of you to pay him."

"Thank you," said the Queen. "But we have one more concern. There are others who have or will be seeking your counsel on their way to the other side. They are the reason we—" She stopped herself and reorganized her thoughts. "They have murdered innocent people. How can we be sure they will set out on this journey and eventually meet their true fates?"

The crone stared deeply at the Queen, scanning her motives for impurities like she had examined the glowing fruit for worms. "Yes. I understand," she said. "No need to worry about the twins. They were dragged down to the Underworld the moment my steed laid eyes on them. I heard their screams. Pitiful."

The Queen's face was contented.

The witch continued, "But the King, he revels in his wickedness. He waits to visit me. I'd throw him down to Hell myself if he walked through my door. Don't worry, though. There are agents at work. *They* gather the evil ones."

The Queen's face tensed and she yelled at the small woman, "But how long will that take? Is there any guarantee that he will be brought down?"

The witch blotted her forehead, sweaty and irritated from the makeshift wig. "Don't worry, my dear. These are not matters of ours. The Way of Things will sort it out. A new world awaits you now. The troubles of your life are soon to be gone." She carried on with the picking of fruits.

The unsatisfied Queen grabbed the old woman and pushed her against the wall. "What lies beyond this shack is of no interest to me. I want that man to get what he deserves. Even in death, he continues to pollute the earth with his wickedness. This is not the time for secrets, witch."

"You are a strong one," whispered the hag. "Hold up your hand." The Queen obliged. Her fingers were still stained with royal blood. The witch grabbed a finger and licked it.

"What did you do that for?" the Queen asked with distaste.

"I cannot pull answers out of thin air, child." She closed her eyes, smacked her lips, and let the blood search for the King. "He is familiar with the forbidden magic and will not leave this world without a fight. It is not likely he will ever rest." After her forecast, the hag's eyes flew open and pierced the Queen's like a spear. "Now kindly back away. We will speak civilized on these matters."

The Queen obeyed. The witch turned to Garth and Helena, "Out! Both of you! I'll deal with this one then I want you all on your way."

They scurried up the stairs and waited amongst the witch's strange collections. Helena perused moldy books and artifacts. Garth promptly scolded her, not wanting to further frustrate the old woman.

"You'd better be going. It's been longer than you think. The sun's been set for hours," bellowed the hag. The Queen solemnly walked up the stairs and made for the front door. The witch fiendishly searched for the key to the staircase in her bosom, purse and finally her hair. "I need my rest. I'm old as sin and know all the secrets of the world, but am very much mortal. I'm just gifted, employed by the Way to do its bidding. This body dies around me, as you can see. I will eventually meet you all on the other side."

As she locked the door, she began to lose balance. The witch staggered around and clutched a table to stay upright. Papers fell to the floor and kicked up a cloud of dust. When it settled, the statues saw her on her knees with her eyes rolled backwards. "Except one of you," she bellowed. "One of you will be lost to us forever."

When the vision seemed to have passed, her eyes went back to their proper spot as if nothing odd had happened at all. Her breath was slower to return. She wheezed and coughed on the residual dust and eventually had to motion to Garth for help getting back to her feet.

Helena broke into frenzy. "It won't be me, it can't be me!" she cried. "I will not be left to wander this earth in stone. Make me real! Give me a soul! I want to live life instead of hearing about it from ungrateful peasants or soldiers who've been stone for so long they can't remember what it feels like to feel." She tearlessly wept around the hag's feet and grabbed desperately at her ragged gown.

"Enough! Enough!" The old woman kicked her away. "No need to act like an animal. Ask and you shall receive. I yearn for visitors like you instead of the usual old ghosts that meander through. You keep my long life interesting." She walked over to some cluttered shelves and spoke to herself. "I daresay this has been the most exciting day I've had in decades." Her boney fingers dove into the mess and carelessly threw bottles and jars until she found what she was looking for. Soon she was holding a thin glass vial between her thumb and pointer finger. The light from the window shined right through the clear fluid inside. "Here it is. Tears."

"That's all it takes? Tears?" asked Helena.

"Not just any tears, my dear. These are the tears shed after a lover's death. They are tears of love lost. They are the tears you couldn't cry when Francis died."

Helena glanced uncomfortably at Garth, as if a great secret had just been let out of the bag. But Garth already knew. Even though Francis was a grotesque and Helena was unfamiliar with the feeling, they had loved each other.

"Your life will be full of love. Even though you have lost one, there will be more. Human life is all about love; the many kinds of love that exist and the many times it is encountered," continued the witch before she opened the vial. She drained every drop over Helena's head. The tears ran down her face and dried there, leaving a salty white residue on her pink marble skin. "You too must sacrifice a tree in the orchard. Then, in time, you will gain a soul and become human."

Helena thanked the crone to the point of embarrassment.

"But wait," the crone said, irritated at Helena's premature blubbering. "There is one condition. You must not follow Francis into Heaven. You must live your life."

I had this theory that once a New Yorker meets a certain age, they go crazy. Not necessarily institution-worthy, but in a general curmudgeonly, looneytoons kind of way that sweeps them off to Lala Land. Years of New York-specific neuroses build up on top of the expected effects of old age to create geriatrics unique to the city. Women are usually more affected than men, although there certainly are some moon-bat males out there. One can recognize these individuals by their general disregard for people and personal space, the presence of laundry carts, broaches, paying in change, offensively bright scarves, sequined baseball caps, sunglasses, loud voices, large breasts, an unearned sense of entitlement, an affinity for New York baseball teams contrary to how much baseball is actually watched, oddly colored hair or a backwards wig/hairpiece, strange pets (put a hundred bucks on a pussy cat, though), china-doll makeup, rent control and personal stories about nights out drinking with (or nearby) Judy or Liza or both. I should also mention that their faces fall into two categories: plastic or au natural—but both painted as if they were starring in the original production of *42nd Street*.

Basically, they are a dream come true.

Rita was the ultimate example of these women. She lived off Tenth Avenue in a building that would have been demolished to make way for condos if not for the sharp economic drop. Her apartment was on the top floor of a very wobbly walk-up, inhabited by more vermin than people. Judging by the deteriorating hoard of junk we met at the top of the staircase, it was clear she was the only living thing that ventured that far up.

The door was ajar (and by "ajar" I mean, there was only a beaded curtain in its place) so we crept in. Her apartment looked like the wall of an Applebee's, but the neighborhood knickknacks were replaced with relics of Broadway's glory days and props from long condemned theatres. "Why are you visiting this washed up old fool?" she asked from a back room. Cigarette smoke billowed out of the darkened doorway.

"Are you Rita?" Garth asked.

She sauntered into view, pointing to her clavicle that displayed a gold necklace that read, "Rita," in a gaudy script. "That's what it says, sugar. It's just like the one Carrie wears. I, myself, think I'm more of a Samantha but it was a gift from a friend, God rest his soul." I gasped at the sight of her.

Rita was the definition of an old queen. Her thinning hair was dyed Kool-Aid red and slicked back like a forties movie star. She wore black tights and a sequined top that *just* covered her lady parts. The heels on her shoes were higher than most drag queens' and her kimono, dramatically draped from her shoulders, was cartoonishly

Asian. It would have been fitting for her to descend a silver staircase and have a "With a Z" attached to her name. Sadly she had neither.

She looked at Garth again and grimaced. "Jesus, Mary and Joseph! Who the hell are you? I didn't know I had a grotesque in this city."

"I am sorry, Rita. I have been traveling," he said.

"You should always, *always* introduce yourself to the local witch. God forbid something cataclysmic happened. Then what would you do? Have you met Chester down in the Bowery? He's an Immortal, too."

"I have not but I will keep him in mind. Thank you."

"There aren't many of you around nowadays so you'd better get to it." She sniffed. "Maybe you're not in my district, that's why you didn't feel inclined to say hello. This city is getting bigger by the day so we've had to train more witches and believe me, some of them could use a few more lessons, if you know what I mean." She glared at me. "I hope you're not here to apply for a position. Just because you watch movies about magic, doesn't mean you have the calling. Here, let me see…" She grabbed my face with her cold hands and pried open my mouth. "Stick out your tongue."

I obeyed.

"Nope, not in the cards, honey. Head home."

"We are not here for that," Garth said.

"Are you the oldest witch in the city?" I asked. Garth was irritated that I wasn't moving on to business.

"Never ask a lady her age," she grunted. "No, I'm not. There's that hag down on Jane Street, she's one of the oldest, period. A couple hundred, at least, but she's pretty much just a pile of skin nowadays. Absolutely useless. I'm sure she'll be fading away within the year. That's why I'm so busy! I need to keep the door open to accommodate all these souls."

"We have come to you for counsel," Garth announced trying to rein in the old woman.

"We? You, okay…but not him. I don't lend counsel to mortals until they're dead so go slit your wrists or something," she spat. "*Then* we can have a real conversation."

Garth was nearly steaming. "We have not come to ask for counsel. We are demanding it. I am Garth, of the First Legion of Guardians, former protector of Helena the Pure, the Royal—"

"My stars," interrupted Rita. She propped herself against an overstuffed chair to keep from fainting. "My apologies, Guardian. Had I know you were coming I would have prepared myself more accordingly. Should I get out some incense…an offering perhaps?"

"Are you famous?" I blurted, staring at Garth.

"Not only is your companion an Immortal, an honor in itself, but he is an Immortal of legend. Here, let me show you," she said as she began to rummage through a pile of books and files.

"That's enough," Garth said. "We aren't here to reminisce the old days. There is little time."

Good thing for him because I was nearly forgetting my predicament. We hurriedly explained everything, the attacks, the dreams, the intruder, and the blood. Rita received the information without much surprise. I began to feel like Garth and Rita had some shared understanding of something. Like the government, their world was over my head but I trusted them to take care of me. For a moment I thought I heard them whisper in another language.

I heard them decide the most pressing matter was the chance of my blood being identified at both crime scenes. Even though I was physically incapable of crushing a human being to death, Garth's dirty work would look like mine. Thank you, science.

"Normally, I would have to consult my charts to see if this was fated, but the world is becoming different now," said Rita. "The Way of Things is changing and the natural balance upset. Progress has thrown everything out of our control."

"So you can't help me?"

"We need to properly diagnose the problem but signs point to this being more than I can handle." She paused, thinking. "I might be able to help with the immediate circumstances but there are other agents at work here, ones beyond my knowledge. I may be old but I'm still a new witch in the grand scheme."

"What about the hag downtown?" asked Garth. "Can she help?"

"Even she is too young. And her body is dying so all her energy is focused on that," explained Rita. She looked at Garth. "It is time to summon the ancient ones."

"Can we do that?"

"The Way has a few tricks up its sleeve, buddy."

"Then what can I do now?" I asked.

Rita held up her finger, asking for a moment to light a cigarette. Her lungs were probably hard with tar but it didn't seem to affect her like everyone else. "Let me think," she said with a scratch at her scalp. Her lacquered hair sprung from its proper spot but she calmed it with some spit and a gentle pat.

"A forgetting spell?" suggested Garth. "I have seen people under those before."

"That's an easy one to cast but an easier one to undo. All they need is to be reminded," she said. A thought came to her and she snapped her fingers. "I'll change you!" She looked at me with wild eyes.

Anyone could have foretold my reaction. "No way!" From Garth's stories, transformations were not promising. I wasn't going to live out my life as a dead tree or a statue.

"Oh, please! I'm not going to turn you into this guy," she squawked while referencing Garth. "I'll give you new blood. It will be untraceable." It sounded extreme but her voice conveyed that it was simpler than most alternatives...whatever they were. "At this point, it would be easiest to find a Night Creature. They can change your blood with little effort."

"That would be a worse sentence than jail, Rita," said Garth.

"Oh, don't you believe the rumors. You should know better," she snapped. "Night Creatures aren't all about blood lust and coffins. They can't even change into bats." She rifled through cookie jars and under cushions. The apartment was stuffed with scrolls, books, pamphlets, spells, charms, and idols. If she was looking for something, it wasn't going to be easy.

"Wait," I said. "What's a Night Creature? Is it some kind of vampire?"

"You could say that," said Rita. She looked to Garth as if she was uncomfortable with the conversation.

"Do not look to me for help, witch. This is your idea," he said.

She thought for a second and then continued. "They're a controversial group. For quite some time, they were considered an abomination. They've come into better graces in recent years."

"That isn't very helpful," I said.

"Fine. Call them vampires. I wouldn't say that to one of their faces because it's derogatory, but yes, vampires." She flung her hands in the air and went back to rummaging through the apartment. "The Night Creatures are an evolved race of beings, very similar to humans, but more powerful. They're actually a step above you on the food chain. No magic powers or any of the stuff you see in movies. Just advanced capabilities. And of course an allergy to sunlight. How's that?"

"That's a little more helpful but I don't want to become one of them!"

"You won't! A full Transformation is only possible through a blood exchange. Blood *permanently* changes blood. Other fluids merely *infect* the blood…like a cold. You'll temporarily behave like one of them. It will go away over time."

I was disgusted and horrified. "You want me to sleep with a vampire?"

"Why do you think the male vampire is always shown with a harem of women? He's fucking them. They're getting a taste for his lifestyle and competing for his blood, the blood that will make them like him. Until he shares himself, the women just suffer from an extreme STD."

I'd been sexually active for several years and had never contracted anything. There she was asking me to dirty my clean slate…to do the exact opposite of everything I'd learned in health class. Such a sacrifice had better deliver some major results. "So this will make my DNA unmatchable? For sure?"

"It will mutate your blood for the duration of the infection, yes. If your blood is tested during that time, it won't resemble anything they've seen before."

"So I'll be half vamp…Night Creature?" My body began to quiver with nervous energy.

"I think I've explained that already." She disappeared into the bathroom and tore through the medicine cabinet. She called out to us, "These guys are pretty reluctant about this kind of stuff. A lot of horrible shit went down in the Eighties that made them scared of spreading it. Before that, there was a ban on Transformations that lasted several hundred years. Consider this a rarity." The clanging continued. It sounded like a construction site in there. "But I have a friend. He's a real softy. If I explain your situation I bet he'd be game. I just can't remember where I put his phone number."

"Sounds like he's a real good friend," laughed Garth.

Rita poked her head out of the bathroom and looked at him seriously. "He left town for several years when his partner died. We fell out of touch." Her eyes swelled and her voice quivered. "This kid was like a son to me. I'd trust him with my life." Then she looked at me. "You'll be in good hands."

9. The Dark Ones

The marshlands flattened the scenery beyond the forest of the witch's dwelling. Against a grey strip of dense shrubbery and shallow pools, the sky looked one hundred miles deep—an ocean standing on its head. The roving statues were more exposed than ever under the watchful eyes of heavenly bodies and whoever else laid claim to the land, which sounded like a family of woodpeckers. Consistent knocking on wood cracked through the soggy plain like reverse thunder.

If the sounds coming from the bogs weren't intimidating enough, the idea of solid stone tromping through deep mud almost put a complete halt to the operation. Garth was the first to try crossing into the marsh but he sank quicker than an unmanned ship. After a rather elaborate rescue mission involving several sticks and some good, old-fashioned heave-ho, he was freed.

"If that's going to happen every time you take a step, those birches on the other side will have rotted by the time we cross this thing," the Queen said. Even though Garth's confidence was deflated, he managed to let out a chuckle.

"I guess we'll have to walk around it," said Helena, already scoping out the never-ending perimeter of the muck.

Garth's ears perked up. His head shifted towards the grass. "Did you hear that?" he asked. "There was a rustling."

"It's probably just the wind," said the Queen.

"There's no wind tonight. The air is still. Something's in there."

"Of course something is in there, Garth. Rodents, birds, you name it. Don't tell me you've forgotten about nature while on top of that palace." The Queen continued rattling the possible contents of the swamp as another wisp passed nearby. "That was a big rodent," she said. Her eyes widened and fixed on the marsh. "I saw something."

The air hung heavy with a humidity that suppressed any stray breezes, causing the grass to stand as still as its observers. They waited to see what the Queen had seen. The serenity of the vista was interrupted when ripples began to dart from one end of the marsh to the other. Soon three swells converged on a path heading straight for them. The statues let out a tiny shriek when the wave of cattails broke at their feet.

Three little creatures stood before them. "We heard the slurp," one said.

"You're much too bulky for here, you are," said another.

The third was silent and decided that sniffing their feet was more productive than speaking.

The odd little creatures could stand upright but used all four limbs for walking. Their small frames could be compacted and rolled across the ground with a speed that created something bordering on weightlessness—that's how they traveled so quickly across the bog.

"Amazing creatures," Garth said under his breath. His habit for thinking out loud was becoming irritating, especially since the little things seemed insulted by his remark.

"Creatures?" one said, "Speak for yourself."

"Indeed," said the other. "That's no way to talk to those who came here to help you."

"I'm sorry," Garth said. "What are you, if I may ask? I've never seen anything quite like you. Have you, Helena?"

She didn't want to further upset them, so she just shook her head.

"Who knows," one said. "Some call us trolls."

"Imps," said the other.

"Some call us 'disgusting swine.'"

"But we certainly aren't pigs."

"No, sir. Not pigs, at all."

"We work for the Seekers."

"We maintain the pass."

The third grunted in agreement.

The eccentricities of the spirit world were beginning to overwhelm Garth. "The Seekers?" he asked.

"These marshes are full of souls in hiding. Mostly the evil ones. They avoid the judgment here," said a creature.

"It can be a treacherous place," said the other.

"The Seekers patrol the land, collecting the wanderers. Their chariots are too heavy for the bogs so they use the wooden pass."

Garth looked out over the marsh for signs of a road.

"It's well disguised," observed the Queen.

"That's our job," the third one finally snorted. It pulled out a mallet and gazed at it like it was made of gold.

"We don't usually allow foreigners on our pass but word has traveled fast about you, Guardian."

Garth was perplexed by the workers' claim. He'd just left the hag's home barely a day prior. How could there already be a rumor? Of course, it wasn't every day that an Immortal challenged the Way of Things by seeking a soul and demanding the condemnation of an evil monarch. He supposed his plans were a tad noteworthy.

The pass was camouflaged from meandering souls by a messy overgrowth. Between and beside its planks, weeds thrived as high and as thick as the surrounding grasses. The trip across was tedious. It was hard to discern board from ditch. The creatures lead the way, babbling on about this and that but rarely divulging anything useful. The secrets of Immortals and angels and witches and ghosts were as mystifying to them as to anyone. They were ignorant and superstitious—the perfect workers.

The walk took longer than anticipated, almost the whole night. The moon was low in the sky when the Queen began to see something in the grass. "It was a faint glowing," she claimed.

"Can you see souls?" asked a creature.

"Don't be foolish. No soul would make themselves visible to us or to them," said the other.

"Are souls invisible?" wondered Helena.

"Yes. Unless they choose not to be," answered a creature.

"Or if you're special. Or dead." Grunted the strange one with the mallet.

"I noticed a glimmering in the distance. I thought it was fireflies," the Queen continued. "But the glow came closer. Wait…" She pushed her way to the edge of the planks. "I think I can even make out a form." She peered into the dark bog. Before anyone could speculate her sanity, the Queen flew from the boardwalk and into the muck.

She had indeed seen a soul. The most aggressive of all souls had been following them through the marsh, waiting to throw them off course: the King. He'd murdered her Prince and now his ghost was trying to do the same to her.

"Do something!" shouted Helena. Garth began toward the edge but one of the creatures stopped him.

"You won't stand a chance in there. That soul is stronger than you! The ground is soft!" it yelled.

"The alarm, the alarm!" yelled the other to the one that hardly spoke. It searched the end of its mallet, which conveniently acted as a horn as well as a hammer. When it blew into the handle, a sound beyond their ears' capacity bellowed across the field, swaying the grass like a sonic boom. Shortly after, they felt a vibration underneath. The boards rattled from the wheels of the Seekers' chariots.

"They're coming, they're coming! They're coming for you!" said a creature in the King's direction. The warning must have shaken the King's grasp. The Queen shot her head out of the mud and gasped for breath even though she didn't need to take one in.

"Garth! Help!" she choked as she reached in his direction.

"It's alright. I've almost got you," Garth said with an extended arm. His fingers reached for hers but something pulled her back, again. An agonizing scream escaped her mouth before the life escaped her body. She became just a piece of stone bobbing in swamp.

From where they stood, they were unable to distinguish her state. "What did he do to her?" cried Helena. She went over to the horned creature, "Did he kill her?"

Suddenly, the Queen's face sprang back to life. Another scream shot from her and into the night sky. She'd returned to her form but was slipping fast.

Two unhorsed chariots arrived, each bearing a tall Seeker grimly robed in black. As they dismounted, they draped their cloaks over their transports to reveal stealthily built frames. Each body was thin— all legs and arms that sleekly plunged into the marsh in search of the unruly soul.

An invisible battle took place before them. The King was nearly transparent and the Seekers looked like nothing more that reeds among reeds. "Where is she? Where is she?" cried Helena, leaning over the side but careful of not falling in, herself.

"Calm down, she can't drown," Garth said trying to keep her at ease. "The Seekers will get him." He wanted to believe that it was true but somewhere within himself, he knew he was lying.

"Our masters will get him," said a creature. "That soul is done for with the Seekers here. Nobody stands a chance against *those* Immortals." Garth couldn't decide if it was just excited or actually taking a jab at his inadequacies.

The Queen emerged from the sludge and clawed for the walkway. As Garth and Helena went to her aid, the Seekers fell out of favor on the field. One of their tiny round heads cried towards the heavens as what looked like a branch flew onto the planks. The long arm twitched three or four times before it died.

With his comrade injured, the other Seeker lunged forcefully towards the King, who was growing more and more visible as the fight went on. But its fervor was short lived. The King's hands were quick to lock its limbs in an inescapable grasp. Just before the Seeker was torn apart, it shouted ancient words to the creature with the horn. The mallet was raised and another silent call was sent through the marshes to bring more Seekers to the scene.

Three more appeared running over the grasses. Their slender legs stabbed the earth as they strode. One more arrived on horseback from further down the pass. Unfortunately, the rage the approaching Seekers carried for the murder of their brethren was never released. Just as quickly as he dismembered an Immortal, the ghost of the King was gone. Nobody heard an incantation or saw a magic relic in is hand. He simply disappeared.

The Queen lay on the boards, covered in mud. She looked at the dead arm of one of the Immortals who had tried to save her. "How did this happen?" she asked. "Mortal souls should not be this strong!"

One of the Seekers stepped forward. "That one is powerful. It knows a forbidden magic, a magic that even we do not know how to combat."

❖

The Night Creature opened the door to his downtown apartment with the swagger of a Craigslist trick. "You're cute," he said with a smirk.

"Thanks," I replied, unable to decide if I should return the compliment or just take it like a man (on the verge of a nervous breakdown). Technically, I was there for sex, so some flirty back and forth would have been appropriate. But I was hardly in the mood. The date was made for anything but pleasure, like in the olden days when copulation involved an exchange of cattle and mules before the quote-unquote fun began.

He was definitely sexy...sample size sexy. His slightly odd model face was expectedly pale and framed by wisps of maple hair that fell from a messy ponytail. His long limbs were attached to a perfect v-shaped torso, like the diagrams of ideal bodies in anatomy drawing books.

"I'm Bryant, by the way. I don't know if Rita told you that," he said.

No, she didn't. All she did was send me on my way and say that, out of respect, Garth couldn't come in. At first that made me panic to the point of almost passing out. Then I recognized that having him around during intimate acts was weirder than his existence in the first place. I'd have to face something on my own for once. "Please tell me you talked to her about my situation. The reiteration is just too awkward," I said.

He laughed and flashed his large, prefect teeth. They were by no means daggers but I suppose his canines were more pronounced than most. "I did, don't worry. Rita and I are old friends. If she asks for something, I know it's important. And you can come in now." I was still in the doorway, gripping the molding in the hallway. "I'm really not as scary as you want me to be. And if I were, you'd already be in danger. If I made a move right now, your Guardian wouldn't have a chance in Hell at making it to you in time. My poison works quickly."

My breath promptly stopped and my face became as pale as his. I flinched as he made his approach. Actually, flinching is an understatement. I full out twitched. Possibly even thrashed.

"Hey, hey, hey," he said laying his hand on my shoulder, his thumb stroking my neck. "I'm kidding. Relax."

The apartment was immaculate. Modern and classic blended eclectically with artistic, and sometimes campy, touches. Large, leaded windows were exposed from their roman blind enclosure and beige linen curtains reached towards crown molding covered in layer upon layer of paint. The walls were jewel-toned, the furniture light. There wasn't a hint of usual vampire fare like velvet or gilding or gothic revival. I was only disturbed by the taxidermy. Right inside the door, a dusty stuffed bird cocked its head at mine. A fox crawled across a bookshelf and a bat hung in the corner. "I've been collecting these animals for years. Except the bat, he's new. I just couldn't resist that one." He chuckled. "It's nice to capture things before they decay. Give them the appearance of life, don't you think?" He looked at me for affirmation. "I think so, anyway."

Two cat-sized dogs came romping into the living room and sniffed my feet. My crotch was two feet too high for their noses. One of them quickly lost interest. "That's Murphy Brown," he said. Then he pointed his toes at the tinier, shakier of the two, "And this is Corky Sherwood."

"So, the dogs...you're gay, right?" I said, half-joking.

"How typical, I know." He picked up Murphy and walked into the kitchen to pour me a glass of water. "I'm actually hyper-gay. This affliction heightens my natural instincts. The taste for flesh, quick reflexes, and the need to breed, are all intensified as a Night Creature." He laughed again. At least he had a sense of humor about his condition.

"You do this often? Breeding?"

"Bad word choice. The need to…be carnal."

"You mean, fuck."

"If you like sounding boorish."

"I do."

He leaned onto the counter towards me. "You're going to be fun. I can tell. Lemon?"

"Did you buy that just for me?"

"They don't just add flavor to water, you know." He cut and garnished a glass fit for Martha Stewart. "To answer your question; No, I don't breed often. It's reckless." He quietly wrapped the remaining lemon in plastic and put it in the refrigerator. I caught him relish in the new scent on his fingers. "Spreading this condition must be done with purpose."

"And what we're going to do is purposeful?"

"The act isn't. That's nature. As I said, my carnal urges are very prominent. Dogs don't hump legs to make puppies. They just like the way it feels." He stared at me for a moment to see if I'd react to his suggestive tone. I tried not to turn red. Then he continued. "To infect, or breed as we're calling it, is a conscious decision. In your case it's the only way to save you. That's why I have no qualms."

What little color he had in his face flushed away. His eyes grew distant. I got the impression that he had baggage related to spreading himself around, as it were. The sorrow in his expression made me wonder what about his Night Creature-ness was so terrible. The man in front of me was no monster.

"My condition isn't something that needs spreading around. I'm not always this put together, if that's what you're wondering."

"Can you read minds?" I asked, suddenly transporting myself into every other vampire scenario in popular culture.

"No, but the face you're making speaks volumes about your thoughts on the matter. That, or you need to use the bathroom." He squirted a fluid from an eyedropper into my glass. The oily stream danced around and fought with the lemon's acid. A swift stir blended the battling forces nicely. "There's that face again. It's not poison. Just some poppy, passionflower, and lavender. Helpers. You're anxious."

I took a deep inhalation to collect myself. Then I fixed my hair, which had become a parody of itself during the last frenzied hours. I tucked several unruly locks behind my ears but an escapee bounced back onto my forehead. Bryant abandoned the glass he'd just prepared and tousled the disobedient curl. His seduction brought on feelings that I'd lost since my life turned to the fantastic. My constant distractions with attackers, witches, superheroes, and pseudo-boyfriends made sex fall to the wayside. The red light that I'd hoped would be burning over my relationship with Robbie had dimmed. I simply wasn't available. Most nights I just wanted to be in bed with someone, curled up in the safety of another's embrace.

With Bryant I felt free. The strings were cut. If torrid histories existed, they didn't matter. There was no courtship, no need to take things slow or impress him. His peculiarities were laid out on the table. No probing necessary. Real life was nonexistent. It was just the two of us and whatever surface would hold our weight.

His lips grazed mine and his sweet breath moistened the tip of my nose. "Are you sure you want to do this?" he asked.

Him, yes.

The vampire thing, not so much.

But there wasn't a choice.

He was hesitant. Our brows leaned against each other, leaving barely an inch between lips. "Are *you* sure you want to do this?" I asked.

"What happens to you, it won't last long. I promise," he whispered. "Don't hate me tomorrow."

I kissed him softly before The Way of Things took its course…

Who knew a vampire could be so sweet?

The deed was done and it was great…fantastic, actually. Tricks of days gone by had been quick and to the point. Those intentions were selfish and any attempts at helping a partner feel something were made only to hear compliments in the aftermath on technique. The voices in my head were typically bickering about status:

"What are you doing?"

"What is *he* doing?"

"You could do better."

"Get it over with."

But coupling with Bryant switched off my human processes. It had the satisfaction of a booze-fueled fuck without the drowsiness and nausea. We acted on impulse, created a give and take that energized our experiment. Our satisfaction was earned only by cooperation. The encounter was fleeting and perfect, like the last minute of a dream before the alarm goes off.

The dogs hid under the bed and scratched at a mangled toy. A fish tank trickled next to us. "What's that?" I asked while looking at a large portrait on the opposite wall. He lay next to me, arms across my chest and face buried in my neck. "Are you going to bite me?"

His head rose. Through a curtain of hair he smiled and mouthed "No." His thumb stroked my brow and he said, "It's a portrait of Cate Blanchett."

A surprising answer, especially to a Cate worshipper like myself. I knew Cate when I saw Cate, and that wasn't Cate. My scrunched up face broadcast my feelings on the sketch. "I'm not the most literal artist," he said. "It started as just a generic face. But I felt cruel drawing a portrait and not giving it an identity. So I assigned it to her. I thought it fitting because she's the same way."

"A blank canvas?"

"Yes. She can be anyone, not just because of her talent. Her face is so malleable. Perfect for a performer."

"She can probably do anything. 'Play Nixon!' and she'd do it."

He sent me an agreeable smirk as he looked at her. Their gaze held like old friends. "Wouldn't it be great to have a life as versatile as her face?" he wondered.

I could tell he was about to fall into an unhappy place so I moved on. "You're an artist when you're not sucking blood?" I said.

"I am. I drew comics for quite some time. The money was great. Now I can afford to experiment in different mediums. Art is a solitary kind of work. It's easy to work around the sensitivity to light and strange urges."

I became anxious thinking of how I'd be affected. I found comfort in his promise that it wouldn't last long.

"Don't go falling in love with me, Jeremy," he blurted out. I hadn't noticed that I'd nestled myself safely beside, almost under him. "The post-coital chemicals are intensified here. This tenderness will pass."

But I didn't want it to. I'd never felt so warm before. He wasn't cold like the dead things of his fabricated ancestry. He was anything but dead. Life exuded from every pore, always trying to show itself. There was a remarkable man buried under the constraints of his condition. I found his lips and obsessively kissed them, like my kindness would heal him and make him mine.

But I wasn't in a typical faerie tale. Kisses didn't return life to the sleeping princess. It ignited her nightmares.

"Stop," he yelled. "The dosage needs to be controlled."

"It's already in me," I said like I was trying to justify another beer after having already finishing the keg.

"I've done enough. You'll be glad I'm putting an end to this," he scolded. "Tomorrow morning will be unbearable." His argument was halfhearted. I knew he wanted my love.

I needed to touch him. As I went for his arm, his face, his hair, his *anything*, he grabbed me. His large hands wrapped around my delicate wrists. I whimpered.

"I'm sorry," he said. But he still dominated me. He pinned me to the bed and began kissing and nibbling my body, dancing the line between agony and ecstasy.

Just as I began to feel a bruise form under his clenched hand, he jumped from me. "Get out," he barked.

"Bryant, I—"

"Please leave." He turned away from me and looked at Cate's portrait.

10. Transformations

The travelers saw the light before they saw a single tree. The moon reflected off the birches' white skin, casting a heavenly aura around the orchard. Its brightness muddled the space where trees ended and sky began. Birch trunks pierced the heavens like giants with long, lithe necks. Garth wished he could climb one and place Francis on a cloud instead of facing the trials at hand. The thought of encountering the King again sent flashes of terror through him. If that evil soul could tear a Seeker limb from limb, who knew what it could do to them. He hoped the Queen's secret plan would put an end to him once and for all.

"I trust your scheme doesn't involve a blood sacrifice of my body...when I get one," said Garth.

"No, not *your* body," replied the Queen, frightening her friends before she broke into laughter at her own joke. "Unless, of course, you bring down the wrong tree and turn into a rabbit or a goat. Then, it might be fitting."

Besides a few variations on the trees' widths and markings, they all looked fairly identical. Hundreds grew in different formations in a forest that stretched for miles along the marshes. Some thrived in long rows, some grew in haphazard clusters, and some stood in solitude. Was their placement in the grove a clue as to which soul was held in which tree? Was their particular shade of white a sign? Maybe the bands on their trunks matched scars on the soul's one-time body?

"It will take forever to assess every tree. Let's split up. If you find yours, call out and we'll all help with bringing it down," suggested the Queen.

Garth strolled through, unsure what he was looking for. Since their journey began, they'd been half in the dark about everything. This venture was no different. He didn't think any of the trees particularly looked like him or stood like him. He studied each one for significance but quickly grew frustrated. He was beginning to forget what he'd looked like as a man, so finding the tree version of himself seemed next to impossible. He meandered, trusting fate to bring him and his soul together. He closed his eyes and stumbled through like a child on new legs, his hands grazing bark as he passed.

A cool sensation numbed his fingertips. Garth hadn't felt hot or cold or wet or dry or any other sensation since he was turned to stone. If he had any doubts that souls were in those trees, they were vanquished by those feelings. He touched each tree, trying to decode their significance. They played with his senses; some used temperature, others scent. Others used his emotions. One tree made him anxious, another angry. Whose soul was trapped in each tree to prompt such feelings?

After experiencing a vast range of feelings, something deep inside him began to flutter. The place where his soul would have been began to ache, like it was near something long forgotten. He drifted between the trees, aiming for the locale where he felt it most. He brushed a certain tree that caused an explosion inside of him, forcing him to fall upon it and cry. For years, if he cried, his tearless sobs felt inadequate. As he embraced that tree, hot, salty, *real* tears poured from his eyes. His stone face was frigid from the cold night air, freezing the tears into crystal shards as they flooded down his rough cheeks.

"I found it!" he cried. "It's here!"

The women came running in his direction with an excitement matching his own. Helena pranced about, unable to contain herself. "It's real, Garth! The witch was right! Soon we'll all be free!" She twirled around, stumbling on roots and slipping on leaves. As she began to fall, she caught hold of a nearby tree and pulled herself up again "This is him," she gasped. "This is Francis!"

Garth and Francis' trees stood next to one another, just as they'd been perched atop the castle.

"Helena, which tree will you have?" asked the Queen.

Helena frantically looked around for one to connect with. She felt pressured to grab one before someone else claimed it, even though there was nobody else to compete against. Her eyes set themselves on a sapling, not far from her friends' trees. It was a young birch with a young soul inside. She tore at it with her bare hands. Her stone fists beat the white bark, sending it to the ground like early snow. Garth used the same technique on his tree. He called for the Queen to get started on Francis's. Slowly the birches gave in to this primitive method, letting out great cracks as they gave in to gravity.

But the one under the Queen's hand stood strong, like an impenetrable wall. If Helena and Garth could make progress, there was no reason she shouldn't have been able to. Garth went to her side and executed the same tactics he'd used on his tree, but didn't make a scratch. They began using other branches and rocks from the ground. The tree showed no sign of weakness. Its bark was as smooth and as white as it had been when they'd first arrived.

"I'm going to find something larger," said Garth, but as he went to forage, he fell over the giant bag he'd been burdened by for so many days. Pieces of his friend spilled across the ground. He winced at the gruesome sight, as if he were seeing lacerated flesh. Francis' arm lay before him. It had broken at the shoulder and bore a razor sharp edge. Garth furrowed his brow.

Then he picked it up and struck the tree. Sounds of cracking wood wailed into the night. With Francis' arm on Francis' tree, they were able to conquer the mighty birch.

As the last tree fell, the sun began to rise. Before they took their scheduled naps, they grinned at one another. They'd done it.

Garth didn't dream that day. His body was working on something else. There was no room for silly dreams.

I ran out of Bryant's apartment in a haze of euphoria, disappointment, and dread.

I awoke in Asher's apartment screaming at the most harassing light I'd ever seen.

My eyes were unable to adjust, thanks to a steady burn in my retina. My breath tightened from the heat. My skin itched from quickly developing hives. The curtains weren't thick enough so I spent the majority of the day in the bathroom with a "sour stomach" because it was the only room without a window. The sun poisoning and a craving for the rarest burger on Earth lead me to believe that I was, indeed, infected.

As expected, a detective called me in for a blood sample. "You see, we've found some DNA in your apartment that matches DNA from a crime scene a couple months back. We can't be too careful."

"And you think it might be mine? Am I a suspect?" I asked, playing dumber than ever.

"I can't say. But it'd be a good idea for you to come in and cooperate. If it's a match then we'll have a conversation. If not, we'll try and get you back in your apartment as quickly as possible."

I had to wait until sundown to go in, for fear of bursting into flames or melting into a puddle on the sidewalk. Even though spring had warmed the air, I dressed in too many layers to appear normal. I looked like a fanatical follower of an undetermined Orthodox faith. Or a Jedi. Yes, let's say that I looked like a Jedi.

The lab's fluorescent lighting further confused my eyes and I threatened to pass out. My sunglasses would have to remain on. Upon removal of my burka, the lab technician gasped. I was as pale as plaster and the whites of my eyes were a medicine pink. The poor guy was really thrown through a loop when my blood slid through the needle like half-dry nail polish. "Would you like me to send this over to our medical unit? Frankly, I'm a little concerned," he whispered.

"Really? Looks fine to me." I said.

He grimaced and walked away.

Garth awoke with a gasp, unable to tell if he was choking or screaming. He felt his lungs; the crisp evening air filled them so quickly they almost bust. Their natural rhythms were forgotten and needed to be relearned.

In. Out. In. Out.

He emerged from his gray, dark shell and was born again with skin untouched by sunlight. It was as soft and white as the birch he'd brought down. Discovering his human body was painful...and beautiful. Water ran from his eyes and nose, tickling his cheeks and neck. Every movement cracked a new joint and stretched a tender muscle. In his sobbing, Garth felt his tears wiped away by what he thought was a cool breeze.

It was Francis' cold, foggy fingers. They were no longer stone. They were not flesh, either. He was made of some element from the spirit world. He embraced Garth, who shivered under his friend's chilly embrace.

❖

Garth's newborn skin was more sensitive than ever and required Francis's bag to keep him warm. Garth clumsily wrapped his naked body in the dusty burlap. Then he quickly wished it wasn't burlap.

Rubble littered the ground. Francis picked up an unidentifiable piece of his former self. "I can't believe we were *this* for so long. We're free."

Garth looked *at* Francis and *through* him at the same time. Spirits are funny like that. "I hate to bring this up, but we should get you on your way," he said.

"Would it be terrible if I didn't go forward? I can stay with you and Helena."

"Soon you'll be with everyone from our past. You won't even notice that we're not with you."

"I doubt that," Francis said. His head fell sadly, like a settling mist. "What will you do, Garth? You're still alive and young. You'll see many more years, I'm sure. Where will you go?"

"I don't know, Francis." Garth hadn't put much thought into it yet, but when he looked at his hands he saw the youth that Francis had mentioned. His façade was that of a young man with the world ahead of him. Inside he felt like an old crone. A whole lifetime had passed but his body was unscathed. The family and friends he'd left in the village were not so lucky. They'd probably lived long lives and died natural deaths. He hoped they were able to look down on him. Surely they'd recognize him without the grotesque costume he'd been wearing for years. If not, Francis could point him out when he became reunited.

A seed of fear began to sprout inside of Garth as he thought of starting over as a human. There wasn't much left for him on Earth. He'd be a stranger in a new, sun-filled land. What would he do? Where would he go? "I guess we'll see."

The Queen was consoling Helena near her young tree, or what she thought was her tree. She was still stone. The spell hadn't worked.

"After we see him off, I'll return here with you. We'll find your tree. I promise," Garth said. That comforted her some but not enough to bring back the brightness she had once possessed. She tried to pull herself together for Francis's sake.

"Don't leave so quickly," said a voice. A crooked black cat strolled out from behind a birch. "You don't know where you're going next. Fools."

The Queen recognized the cat's crackling voice and general crookedness. "You're the hag," she said.

The cat arched its back in repulsion. "Is that what you call me?" it screeched.

"We don't know your name."

It spat out a sound more gruesome than Garth's former face. "That is my name. I told you that you wouldn't be able to say it." The hag-cat slithered towards Francis, the only spirit of the lot. "What do you consider to be your home, soul?"

Francis thought about the places he'd been. Home had been atop the King's palace for so long, he'd almost forgotten to consider the tiny village in which their story began. That was home, even though the roads that would bring him there were probably long dusted over by time's passing.

"Go to your home," purred the cat. "That is where you will find the door to the other side. Spirits must always go home to say goodbye before they move on."

"Will we be able to accompany him? Is that where we must part ways?" asked Garth.

"Can you walk through a door?"

Garth nodded

"Then you can go with him." With that, she hopped up a tree and out of their sight.

They didn't waste any time, for Helena and the Queen were still victims of the sun's curse. Garth knew where home was. He'd meditated on its surroundings all those years high above the world. It lay far beyond the plains of battle, past the hills of his forefathers' graves and along the river where life began (according to the old beliefs).

They kept a steady pace, but Helena and Francis often fell behind. Their time together was short and their love unexplored. The Queen walked beside Garth. "You are a true friend," she said. "You don't have to stay with us."

"We're in this together. Who else do we have besides each other?" he asked.

She laughed to herself. "I've always thought that the events in our lives happen for a reason. What we experience teaches us things, both good and bad. Sometimes terrible things happen to spark change." She looked up at the velvety sky. They were in the middle of night's stay. The blackness and openness of the world at that moment was deafening. "I also think that people don't meet by chance."

"We were all destined to be together?"

"Yes. If the Prince hadn't been killed, you wouldn't have met me. If you hadn't met me, Francis wouldn't have fallen. If Francis hadn't fallen, you'd still be stone and the King would still be alive. These happenings have not been ideal but they're contributing to a greater good."

He supposed she was right but thinking too much about it made his head hurt. "What will you do when this is over?" he asked.

She shrugged her shoulders. "I guess we will see."

11. The Past Haunts

The forests around the sacred river had been burned. The skeleton of their town met the horizon like a nightmare city. All was black. All was dry. All was dead.

Garth's eyes welled at the sight of his unrecognizable village. Any hopes of stumbling upon an elderly Evie were snuffed out by the still lingering stench of decades-old fires. He wondered if she had lived to see the flames, left before them or perished in their fury. Nature tried to reclaim the remnants but the earth had nothing left to help it thrive. Only boorish, ugly plant species were able to grow on the cursed land.

But a new smoke billowed from the old town center. The prospect of finding answers sent Garth there before the others could even notice the cloud. Soot, dust and dead things swirled in the air as he ran towards the square.

It was nothing more than a simple campfire, part of a crude kitchen. Garth kicked a pot filled with murky water and extinguished the pitiful flame.

An old woman ran out from a pile of rubble screaming and yielding a singed stick. "Back, ye! Back!" she cried. "That took me'all day to kindle, sir!" She swung her stick at Garth but his hand broke it before it could find his face. Her eyes filled with terror when she looked upon his face.

"Who did this?" he demanded.

The old woman balled up and rocked to a tune in her head. "Should've stayed home, should've stayed home," she sang.

"What are you singing?" Garth yelled. "Speak up, you old loon!"

"Garth, leave her alone. It's no use," the Queen barked as she ran to meet them.

"Tell me!" he screamed, grabbing the woman. "Tell me!"

She continued her singing:

"Ring-a-ding-ding, here come-a-King.
Ra-ta-dum-dum-lis'nen for the drum.
Men for the crown make a happy town.
Boys outta bed, girls end up dead."

Garth wobbled away and gasped for fresher air. "I was just a little one," the woman continued. She looked at him with knowing eyes and murmured, "Evie." Her tone was long and taunting, a creaking door in the middle of the night.

He lunged for her throat and demanded that she tell her secrets. The Queen wrestled him away before he'd caused any damage, but the woman was left shaken. She panted and grunted on the ground like a spooked animal. Helena attempted to ease her fears, forgetting that she and the Queen were probably just as scary to the woman as Garth's anger.

"Please, tell us what happened here," said Francis, joining Helena in her efforts. He patted to old woman's back in apology for his wild friend.

She stood and brushed the ash from her hair and face. "You boys. We know you. You were our brothers. Our fathers. All us little ones remembers you even though we never saw you come back," she gasped. Her glazed eyes darted back and forth, incapable of finding focus. "Evie was a good girl. When she was livin'. All good girls. Good friends. I'm all that's left. I'm a good hider, you see." She walked to Garth and touched his soft face and began to sob. "I'm so old. Why are you so young?"

Disturbed, he brushed her off. "Francis, we need to leave. Go find your home," he coughed through tears. The old lady sang to herself as they walked away from the square. It was a song Garth remembered but immediately tried to forget.

They found the remains of landmarks to guide them to what used to be their houses. Garth's was located behind the water well, which had been reduced to nothing more than a dry ditch. He had many memories of lugging water from it to his garden, where his father taught him how to grow their supper. Garth hoped Evie had paid attention to the routine. He was delighted to find that she had. Shadows of her work remained. Even under years of neglect and layers of soot, a few tiny buds still showed their heads. Garth rubbed the herbs between his fingers and inhaled their pale perfumes. Afternoons spent harvesting with his father came to mind. He could almost taste the rich soil on a hastily picked carrot.

As Garth lost himself in the past, Francis rummaged under rotting timber for something that might resemble his home. It had once been three houses to the left of Garth's, but there were no property lines or fences left to tell where one pile of junk ended and another began. Finally, under many charred beams and bricks and shingles, Francis saw something familiar.

The front door of his family's home was still intact. It even had remnants of blue pigment stained to its surface. When Francis went to move it, damp air blew out from underneath. Long ago, the door had led to a cozy room with a fire. In their journey to the other side it had become a passageway to the end of the world. The smell of salty surf cut through their town's stench of death.

The doorway took them beyond any chart, to a land deader than the town behind them. The ground was pale and rocky with crags scattering the landscape like old fingers pointing towards the heavens. Garth looked back at his home for the last time before the passageway closed. Although saddened, he found solace in the answers his visit had unearthed. His old home and his old life were finally put to rest the moment the door sealed and disappeared behind him. The light in the new world was dim and the air misty from the briny water ahead. Surely the bridge was nearby.

It was the first truly cold night of their journey and Garth finally had the skin to feel it. He tried his best to cover the violent shivers but his haphazard garment proved inadequate. The Queen clutched him under a heavy arm with hopes of warming him. The simple sensation of being held made her cool touch bearable. Helena gripped the basket of fruits, which shined brightly through the night and served as a beacon in the thick fog. They carefully maneuvered over the rocky shore but their concentration was interrupted by an alarming grumble.

"That's it! That's the Bridge Keeper. I feel it," said Francis. The sounds ahead confirmed that the Bridge Keeper was not of the human variety.

The fog became thicker. The rumble crept closer. They nervously followed the groans, holding one another tightly so as not to get separated. Their closeness eventually muddled their legs, sending Helena to the ground. The radiant orbs rolled in all directions, spilling light into the darkness and illuminating fallen trees, boulders, a cliff side, and the wooden post of the bridge. Helena ran ahead to scoop up the fruits before they could escape off the side. Just before one was lost to the drop, a giant, slimy tongue appeared and snatched it up.

"You have brought payment for my bridge," said the Bridge Keeper, chewing on the shining fruit. Helena raised her basket of the remaining fruit. She met a giant, cloaked figure that seemed to be of both land and sea. It had crawled out of the water and up the slope to meet them. "Throw another to me," it demanded.

Helena did. The little fruit lit up the sky before the Keeper's long tongue grabbed it, mid-air. It chewed sloppily and then opened its gaping mouth. The pulp coated the orifice, vividly displaying inhuman teeth and an oozing tongue. The light produced cascaded over them so that the Keeper could assess them before crossing.

"You are not all dead," it growled. "What makes you think I will grant you passage to the other side?"

Francis spoke up, "I am the only one making the full journey. These are my companions. They wish to take me as far as possible to bid me farewell." He looked at the Queen. "And attend to some business."

"This is sacred land, soul. It is contrary to the Way of Things for live ones to know of this place, let alone visit it."

"But we have already traveled very far and met with the witch in the woods. We've brought more than enough fruits to satisfy you, have we not?"

It thought for a moment and licked its lips. "Indeed, soul, you have. For that I will grant you all passage. Just know it is not for me to decide whether you make it across the bridge or not. *It* makes the decisions. Look upon the water below." The Keeper opened its mouth towards the river, revealing a filthy substance that looked more like the contents of a million chamber pots than water. "The water is tainted with the sins that souls must expel in order to go across. When you reach the middle of the bridge, you must confess all of your offenses, all of your secrets and regrets. The delights of the other side are reserved strictly for souls who have freed themselves of the grime acquired during their human lives. Only those with a clear conscience and a good heart may pass. Now, who will be first?" The Keeper moved aside and extended an appendage resembling an arm, inviting them to proceed.

Francis stepped forward. He left them with a reassuring smile before setting foot onto the bridge. The others barely moved an eyelash as he disappeared into the fog. They could hear the bridge creak as he made his was across, then how silently it stood as he stopped in the middle. It didn't take Francis long to clear his conscious. He was a good man. They listened as he steadily made his way to the other side. There was no buckling, no splash.

"I made it!" he yelled from a not-too-distant shore. "Just do what the Keeper said and all will be fine!"

Helena was next. She predictably made it across without a problem, not having experienced enough to be guilty of anything. The Queen and Garth looked at one another. "You go first," she said.

"No. I want to make sure you get over safely," he said.

"And what if I don't?"

"Don't be silly. Helena made it across. You will, too." Garth stared awkwardly at her, knowing why she was afraid. "What happened at the palace was bad, yes. But we did what we had to do. Just tell the water."

"Garth, that's not—"

"And if that bridge throws you over…well, let's just say that it hasn't seen the likes of me," he said, only half-joking. He'd already been a worthy opponent of the Way of Things and was no longer afraid of it.

"You can't always be a hero. Remember what I told you? Sometimes bad things need to happen."

"What are you talking about? You're enchanted, just like Helena. You have nothing more to be guilty of than what we did together."

"You don't know me, Garth."

"Tell the water about the twins and the King. The Horse let you go, you've already passed the test. Just confess to it. You know what you did was for good." There was a slight growl in his voice from irritation. Her stubbornness was finally wearing on him.

Her mouth began to say a million things before settling on, "I'm sorry." Her last glance before becoming engulfed in the fog was filled with pain. As soon as her eyes pulled away from his, she ran towards the bridge's center. Each step of her heavy body met the wooden planks with unnecessary force. Garth grew nervous as he heard her barrel ahead without stopping.

"Don't forget to stop," he called. The footsteps continued. "You must slow down."

Francis and Helena heard her too. From the other side, Garth heard their pleas. "You *have* to stop! Don't come any further!"

Garth's heart flew into his throat. She wasn't planning on stopping. She wanted to fall. He yelled out for her but a great crackle devoured his screams. An oily splash was the last they heard of the Queen.

"That one didn't even try! She must have had too many demons to even bother!" guffawed the Keeper.

"She's enchanted! She has no demons! There's no soul in her to go anywhere!" screamed Garth. "Where is she?"

"The Underworld. The Dark Place. It has many names, human."

Garth ran onto the bridge. As soon as he reached the center, he hurled himself over the side, into the thick, dark water below.

All I could do was wait: wait for DNA results, wait to go back to my apartment, wait for my symptoms to go away, wait for Robbie to speak to me again. We were broken up, even though we were never really together to begin with. It was a shame, too. If I was leading a normal life and he wasn't so crazy, I think we'd have worked out. Bad timing, I suppose.

A friend told me he had seen them out together. I figured that would happen. It's always easier to make a decision when there's no choice to be made. Nick won a game against nobody but himself. Hardly a triumph. I imagined them pretending to be happy for a month or two, until they realized that their relationship consisted of nothing but a few laughs and decent sex. Face-to-face, they'd try and stay strong. Behind each other's backs, they'd patrol the Internet for future flings and hang out with friends whose friends were fuckable. Soon, resentment and the poison of their lies would bubble to the surface and explode in their faces. They'd be miserable after the breakup. Even the rewards of singledom, like reentering the dating game and one night stands, would feel routine and unexciting, for they'd exhausted those activities while together. Those thoughts made me feel better. They made me feel human.

The days began to grow longer and Central Park's lawns and meadows called to me. Unfortunately the sun was still too much for my almost translucent skin. Just minutes of exposure would have me running for cover. My appetite dwindled to cravings for nothing more than a single block of the food pyramid. I ordered steaks rare. If the chef overcooked, I just sucked out the juices or carved out the little bits of pink. My cravings weren't specific to humans or even blood, just primitive yearnings for a fresh kill. Anything else wouldn't digest. I was a raw foodist of sorts. Thankfully, my high-protein diet was easy to disguise in New York. With all the muscle-hungry gays and extreme diet trends, I just looked like an Atkins follower with pale skin.

"You're a ball of energy tonight," Garth said to me.

"I've adopted your schedule. Since I can't do the sun thing, I sleep. I'm even considering a bartending gig," I said.

"I'm surprised that you're still suffering."

"*You're* surprised? Me too." I chomped on a piece of beef jerky and pretended to like it. I began to swallow but that didn't work out. Too cooked. "Do you think we could talk to Rita? Maybe she knows how long this will last."

"I think it's different for everyone. Depends on your immune system...dosage."

"If you're trying to get the dirty details about Bryant, forget about it." A smile crept across my face as I said his name.

"But it looks to me like it was a pleasant experience. Why don't you ask him?" I could have but the situation was awkward. I didn't have his number...I couldn't show up uninvited for fear of death... He kicked me out...

"Messy details." We sat on a roof overlooking the East River, searching for something else to say. "I think our trail is dead. I gave a DNA sample. Haven't heard anything."

"That's good. One problem solved."

Some asshole walked down the street rapping too loudly for the middle of the night. "Hey buddy, keep it down! This isn't Madison Square Garden! It's a residential street!" I yelled down. Did I mention that I'd had a confidence boost?

"Shut up, you faggot!" he hollered back, arms flailing in his oversized clothes, in an attempt to look larger than life.

"What'd you say? I'll come down there and rip your goddamned face off, you dizzy twat!" I hissed back. My eyes burned hot and my teeth bore like a wolf. The rapper repented and then ran in the other direction. I was proud and embarrassed and sick to my stomach.

"I see your vocabulary has improved along with your temper," Garth said snidely. "Maybe you'll be alright after all."

"Garth, who is trying to kill me?"

His head darted back towards the water. The lights of Astoria twinkled on the river. "We don't know yet," he whispered. He shifted uncomfortably, his gaze bobbed from me, to the river, back to me. "I'm sorry, Jeremy. I should have left you alone. After New Year's, I should have just brought you to safety and let you live your life."

"Why would you say that? You've saved my life *more than once*. I'd be dead without you."

"There shouldn't have been a more than once. Everything that's happened since then has been the result of our friendship. I can't help but believe that I've exposed you to a menace without even knowing it."

Another spark of anger began to ignite within me. Maybe not anger. Frustration? Either way, I felt a fury coming on. A new chemistry flowed through my veins that made me feel like I could take down a buffalo if necessary. I began to lunge for him but stopped myself. My wretched hand hung in the air, then retreated back to my lap. What would I have possibly done to a gargoyle? "I need to know what's going on," I said through gritted teeth.

"Nothing is certain. Remember how I told you about that conversation with the Queen? Events in our lives, our experiences, all happen for a reason. *That* is the Way of Things. The world is working something out, and you, unfortunately, are getting the brunt if it. Until we know for sure what or who is involved, we can't do anything. There's no use speculating. It'll only make you paranoid."

"I'm already the most paranoid person I know! Tell me what you know!"

"It is a feeling, that is all. Like touching trees and knowing which one has a soul. The same intuition has been drawing me to you. It is unexplainable."

"So I just have to wait? I have to stay indoors and eat sashimi and wait for someone to tell me what's going on, providing this 'menace' doesn't kill me before then?" I stomped around and pulled my hair like a three-year-old having a temper tantrum. "How did you finish off the King? Did he go to the Underworld like you planned? Is he the one torturing me?"

"That is *not* it. He is of no concern."

"He killed his son. He killed Francis and your mother and your sister."

"Jeremy, please."

"Well, did the Queen's plan work? Where is she? Why are you still a gargoyle, Garth? What happened? If we are being haunted by something from your past, tell me. Tell me!"

"Sometimes life doesn't work out the way you have planned!" he exploded. "I wanted to be a farmer with a family and be hundreds of years *dead* by now. Look at me. Look at you. I doubt you wanted to be the thing you are tonight. We are nothing like our ideals. Sometimes our failures are too painful to face. And sometimes our failures are not entirely our fault. Until someone can help us, we wait. Neither of us needs to be more desperate than we already are."

❖

The initial splash through the surface of the water was shocking. Perhaps it was because Garth hadn't been submerged in ages. Maybe it was because the water wasn't really water. Whatever substance it was, he sank quickly. Eventually he couldn't hold his breath any longer and had to accept the grimy fluid into his lungs. He became heavier and sank faster. The speed began to rob him of consciousness...

Why did you follow her?

I'm a good person.

Good people feed the hungry. They don't do things like this.

We'd come too far to abandon her.

Sacrifices must be made.

No. That doesn't make sense.

She made you feel alive. That's why you follow.

But I am alive. I'm human.

When you weren't. She made you feel—

Stop. I know what she made me feel. There was something missing. She helped.

Now you've lost that something.

No. I'm going after her.

She will be glad.

Will she?

You've thrown it all away. You're both doomed. She will be mad for that.

Will she?

And she will be glad.

Am I dying?

Does it matter?

I don't want to die.

I think you do.

12. In the Company of Souls

Meg and I were relocated to another apartment a few blocks north because the old one was still uninhabitable. Slowly we tried to get our lives back on track. I had all of my old furniture back in a room of my very own but I couldn't bring myself to sleep there. Even with Garth probably lurking nearby, my brain refused to let go of the heebie jeebies that made themselves present when the lights went out.

Instead, I situated myself on the living room couch near a window without a fire escape. The TV constantly blared to keep me company. TV Land's line up of everyone's favorite shows was a non-threatening companion. Even programs that creeped me out as a kid, like *The Adams Family* and *Tales from the Crypt*, were tame compared to the chaos inside my head.

Several hours later, I awoke in complete darkness. The TV wasn't running up my electricity bill, the streetlights were extinguished and the hall light failed to annoyingly seep in through the cracks around the front door. I'd been dragged to an unfamiliar dream realm. This place was not a version of my life, like dreams past. There was no bedroom with a murderous laundry pile, no burning Union Square. It was just an ominous, cavernous blackness. It made me feel small and exposed, like being trapped in outer space without a suit or ship nearby to cling to. The lack of everything would pull me apart. I'd explode. I hyperventilated at the thought. My breath echoed through the expanse and returned to me as a revving engine. It came at me at one hundred miles an hour, forcing me to duck into a ball to get out of its path.

I searched for a distinguishing anything; furniture, a rock, a hole, a pillar or a wall but felt nothing except the flat, wet ground.

Frustration mounted, setting me off crawling in one direction, hoping to slam into something to give me my bearings. The nothingness was endless. I choked on sobs, which wailed through the cave with one million times more intensity than upon leaving my mouth. I tried to scream for help but only a whisper came out for fear of hearing how the new world would morph my speech. Silence and I sat together for an undetermined amount of time until I worked up the courage to finally mutter, "Hello?"

Before the ugliness of echoes reached me I heard another voice answer, "Hello!" It was a voice I'd know anywhere. It was Garth's.

"Garth, where are you?"

"I can't tell. The echo is…the echo is…the echo is…"

Our voices flew around the cave in place of bats.

"…where are you…where are you…"

"…the echo…echo…"

Aggravation threw my fists to the floor. They landed in a puddle that splashed my face with lukewarm water.

"Garth, there's water on the ground." I waited several beats until my echoes disappeared to continue. "Splash the water into the air. I'll walk around until I feel it on me."

I removed my shirt to expose as much skin as possible to the droplets. My walk through the cavern was delicate. I didn't want to splash water onto myself by accident.

It didn't take long to feel him. I flinched the moment that I felt the splash first land on my cheekbone. "I feel you! Keep splashing!" I screamed. My arms extended for him, fingertips ticking the air as I thought about touching his rough stone arms. Instead, my hand caught something else. It was warm and soft.

"Garth?"

"Yes."

I latched on to what I thought was an elbow and worked my way to fingertips. I engulfed his hand—palm-to-palm, fingers entwined. He gasped.

"It's me. It's okay," I said. "Are you…human again?"

"Yes, silly. It was the tree," he replied before pulling me into his mortal arms. His nose pressed into my neck and then proceeded to my temple. His lips brushed my cheek until they met mine. My hands grasped his face and searched for features. I found eyes, a nose, and a mouth. All were in their right places and all were human.

"But you," he began. "You're, you're—"

I hushed him like he'd hushed me the first time we'd met. I kissed him.

All was still. Our lips were made for each other. I wanted the dream to last forever because I knew that kind of interaction was impossible in real life.

His hands brushed through my hair and down my back. They returned to my neck and then around, down the front of me. Then up again. Then down. Then up. He grabbed at my chest, squeezing my torso in search of something. He stepped backwards.

"What are you?" he asked. He sounded repulsed.

"Garth, it's me. You know me."

I felt him move further away. He tripped over something that knocked and rattled. I sprung for the spot where I thought he'd fell and found a pile of what felt like rubble.

From above came a horrible retching, hacking, snorting and gagging. A glowing mess cascaded from above and illuminated the cavern. It splattered in a soupy pile that gleamed onto us. Finally, our underground captivity was revealed. The cave was so dark and so endless, light dissipated into nothingness before it could find a wall or a ceiling.

"What is that?" I asked Garth. My eyes twitched as they tried to adjust to the new light.

"The Bridge Keeper must have brought up the fruits for us to see," he said.

Bridge Keeper? That's where Garth had left off when he told me his story. Was I in Garth's past, completing his history? No. That's ridiculous. I was simply dreaming. Or was it a dream...of the past?

My attention was quickly removed from that awareness when my eyes found his figure. Garth was wrapped in a burlap sack and lurched over, inspecting the rubble on which he'd tripped. He knelt in a sea of red that soaked his robe and freckled his white, white skin. Everything was saturated with blood.

As he rummaged through the broken stones he began to cough through maniacal laughter. The laughter soon turned into tears. He dusted off a piece of broken marble and held it up for me to see. A fraction of a face stared back at me. "This is you," he said. "The Queen?"

I extended a trembling hand towards the broken face. I never did take hold of it, though. For when my arm came into view, I saw right through it, down to the bleeding floor.

❖

My eyelids flew open like cartoon blinds. I wrapped my arms around my body, desperate to confirm a composition of flesh and blood. The arms and legs at my fingertips were mine, but deep inside I wasn't me. I wanted to reach under my skin and muscles and bones and pull out whatever lurked below. "What are you?" I asked myself.

My heart beat rapidly against my kneecaps. "I'm alive, not a spirit. I'm alive. I'm alive."

I was at home, not underground. The shower curtain I'd rigged for a window dressing awkwardly hung nearby. My cheap brown sheets, damp from night sweats, were tucked into the couch I'd always hated. The TV was blaring. I was home, not underground.

But I needed out. I needed *out*!

My legs wobbled down an East Harlem street as I tried to decide on a sanity-saving mantra. Dreams were not nonsensical waste bins. I'd learned to trust what I saw in sleep. That's why I was scared. Why couldn't I dream of money or ponies or never ending birthday parties?

Garth's habit of dropping by just in the nick of time had spoiled me. Just five minutes spent looking for him was excruciating. I looked crazier than the crazies I passed on my journey to find him. The usual suspects—crack whores, schizophrenics, and giant rats—flew through my periphery. A year earlier, I would have flinched but I was able to zoom by without noticing their pathetic mumbling, scurrying, and pleas.

"Hey, what's the rush?" asked some riff raff in a doorway. "Help me out, won't ya?"

I failed to acknowledge his existence. As I passed, his filthy hand grabbed my shoulder. "Hey, don't pretend a fellow's not here," he rattled with breath soaked in booze and Newports.

That was a mistake on his part. One should never touch a stranger, especially one in the state that I happened to be in that evening. My Night Creature infection had heightened my emotions and physical abilities, making me the equivalent of a nuclear bomb manned by a rabid chimpanzee. The details of what I did to that man are fuzzy. All I remember are the sounds of cracking bones as I swung him to the ground. When I looked down at my victim, his arm was bent in an inhuman direction within my hand. The body attached to it was sprawled on the ground, moaning. A smile tickled my cheeks as I observed him. Adrenaline blocked any sensation besides power. Taking him down was as simple as opening a door. My almost-attacker (or just a crazy man with too much gusto) cussed into the pavement as a pool of blood poured from his head. I found the wound and coated my tongue with its secretion.

He screamed a crackled smoker's scream that jolted me back to reality. My stomach lurched at the dirty iron taste. His blood spoiled fast.

A cat cried and hopped out of a nearby garbage can. It strutted over to the man and finished slurping what I could not. When it had had its fill, it looked at me and meowed. It was an ugly, skinny thing. The bum rolled over and roared incoherent obscenities as he swung for me. A swift kick sent him down again.

The scrawny cat ran down the street and disappeared under a chain link fence that blocked an empty lot from men like the man I'd just assaulted. Garth was in there. I could feel it.

I scaled the fence. The lot was overgrown and seemed to double as a dump yard for apartments above. An old tricycle, plastic toys, and empty bottles of beer hid in tall grass and young trees. It looked like a pedophile had exploded.

Garth sat on a discarded air conditioner. "You found me," he grumbled.

"I think this is a first."

"I thought that you were angry with me."

I tried to formulate a real sentence but settled for just not answering.

"You are still angry."

"What happened in the Underworld?" I finally asked. "Who was the Queen?"

"She was my friend. She was a very dear friend."

"She was a man," I blurted out. The conversation wasn't going as gracefully as I would have planned, if I had time to plan it.

"How did you know that?" he asked. He was barely able to utter the question.

"I had a dream. I was with you in a dark place. I was dead." His face compressed to contain his feelings. "A cat brought me here. It was Rita, wasn't it? She brought you news tonight, didn't she?"

"Yes. I did not believe her."

"What did she tell you?"

"You already know."

"No, I don't. What did she say?"

"It does not make sense."

"Nothing does. What did she say?" I demanded by kicking a green bottle. It shattered against the building.

"You are the Prince."

"Great. Perfect. Just what I need."

"There. You know," he spat as he paced wildly around the lot. "I was trying to figure out why all of this is happening. I tried to figure out why you are the constant victim, why I feel…but it cannot be. You are all dead, all dead and passed."

"Shut up!" called a tired, angry voice from upstairs.

"Garth, I don't understand. You need to help me," I begged. My tough veneer was melting.

He pushed me into the shadow of the building, against a wall. "You are supposed to be dead," he growled. "I sacrificed everything so that you could pass. Why are you here?" He shook me.

"I don't know—"

"I am," he looked down at himself and tried to tear at his impenetrable skin. "I am *this*…still. For you. I look like *this*; I still *live*, for you. And here you are." His eyes pierced mine, breaking the tear-dam that I'd been building. He backed away. "Please leave me."

❖

"Garth, It's still me. It's still me. I've been with you."

For the first time, Garth noticed deepness in the voice. With the physical version of the Queen gone, he could finally recognize it.

"I thought you were an enchantment. What have you done with the Queen?"

"The Queen was just a statue in the garden. She's broken now. I was the soul that inhabited that shell."

"But you are a man!" screamed Garth. Bile tested the back of his throat at the mention of that word, "man."

Was it because *he* was one?

Because he had never grown up to be one?

Had just kissed one?

He didn't know. The Keeper's light shone through the spirit before him. It fragmented strangely on his blood-covered face and body.

"I couldn't tell you the truth. It would have inhibited me from doing what needs to be done," said the spirit. His eyes hopped around the cavern like an injured bird. "Now it's taken care of. Leave me be and go back to your friends above ground."

"How? I came here because of *you*. Where will I go? Twelve paces this way or that way? This is the Underworld! We're stuck here together. For *eternity*!"

"Not necessarily," said another voice from a place beyond where the light could reach. "There are ways out of here. But I can't say those ways are the most pleasant, I'm afraid. There's recently been a feeding, that's why it's so empty. And bloody."

Garth remembered that voice. The last time he'd heard it, it had been screaming. It had been dying. "I know you," said Garth. "You're one of the twins. You murdered the Prince."

The voice laughed. "And *this* is my punishment. This place. That thing. It's coming for us, you know. But it hasn't got to me, yet. I found a hiding spot." He broke into a sob. "My brother was not as fortunate. I haven't heard from him in days. I think it got him. Brother!" he called. "The rest of us are hiding. Don't move! Save yourself!"

"There are others here?" asked Garth.

"Yes. Many, many. You think you're dead now...wait until *it* comes. Then you'll know why we hide."

"Whose blood is this? Souls have no flesh to bleed from," Garth said.

"It's the blood of the Demon. You see, it has no face. Its head is covered by skin, skin that has to be peeled back to reveal its eyes to see, its nose to smell, and its mouth to eat. But ripping away flesh is painful. The Demon will only peel it way after it's played with its meal first. The pain has to be worth it. Many souls end up ripping its mouth open themselves to end the suffering."

"Stop telling them everything. Let them fend for themselves!" called another voice.

"I think it's much more fun if they know what's happening to them, don't you?" cackled the twin. "And don't worry. It can smell sin, which the Prince is soaked in. Oh, I always knew I'd see you down here. It's nice when family is reunited, even after the toughest of times."

Garth stared at the fragile soul next to him. He'd never seen the Prince's face before. The King's shame had kept it hidden in the palace. That face tried to show bravery.

"Yes, it's me," said the Prince who was once the Queen. "I didn't start my journey to the other side when I should have. I inhabited the statue in my garden, like Joseph did with that old tree. I used her image to seek vengeance. Stone does more damage than air."

"I suppose you feel quite accomplished, cousin. Killing the men who killed you. I hear fulfillment of vengeance is an intense emotion," teased the twin. "Oh, wait, your vengeance is not complete. Let me ask you a question. What is worse: committing a murder or watching one happen? Worse yet, *ordering* a murder." The twin laughed madly. "He was our king, after all. We had to obey! We were the sons he wished for, not a sodomite in fancy clothing!"

The Prince charged in the possible direction of his cousin. "*I* killed my father, just as *I* killed you! You all thought I was weak but *I* brought you down. You couldn't stop me, even after death, and you never will. He will soon meet the same end as your brother. Both of you will, I'll be sure of it!"

The twin laughed, again. The other souls, who had been so quiet, began to stir. "Impossible. You are just as weak as the rest of us here," the twin scoffed.

"The Demons of the Underworld can be bribed. I have been guaranteed this," corrected the Prince.

"What are you talking about?" asked Garth. "We have nothing to give."

"Me, Garth. I am the gift. A sacrifice. The witch in the woods told me how."

Garth reeled at the thought. After what they'd gone through, after all of the ridicule the Prince had received in life, it was all to be thrown away? He deserved to rest in peace, not rot in the belly of a Demon. There was no way Garth could let that happen.

"I'll do it," he said.

"Absolutely not," argued the Prince.

"I'll take your place."

"No you won't, Garth."

"A lovers spat?" called the twin. "You degenerates sure aren't the decisive kind."

"I will make the sacrifice!" screamed Garth in the twin's direction. "I'll give my soul. But before that, I will find you and feed you to the Demon!"

"Garth, you must get out of here. This isn't the place for you. You're still human," cried the Prince.

"No, your Majesty, this isn't the place for *you*. You deserve to pass on with Francis."

Screams howled through the caverns. "It's coming!" one spirit said. "Shut up and stay hidden!" shouted another. Darkness encompassed them as the bile's light began to extinguish. Garth felt the cool rush of souls running past him, searching for safety in the shadows.

A muffled screech surged from deep within the cave. The Demon warned the souls of its arrival by shrieking behind its flesh. Their scattering made it easier to pluck them out of the darkness.

Garth couldn't tell how far away it was until a soul was thrown into him. Despite the spirit's airiness, it sent him flat onto the bloody floor.

"Don't let it get me!" pleaded the unknown soul. "I can repent. I must be forgiven!"

The Demon's giant footsteps shook the cavern. Garth cringed at the click of overgrown toenails. Out of the blackness, a giant hand brushed him aside. He watched the soul shout and squirm as the slimy fingers contorted it. Contrary to what Garth thought of ghosts, they could feel pain. He thought it unfair that a person could die so many times.

"Let me be! Let me be! Eat me already, it's too much!" begged the soul.

The Creature laughed behind its skinmask. The stifled snicker became a clear scream as its skin ripped, revealing a mouth with sharp, craggy teeth. The light grew fainter and it wasn't clear whether the soul or the Demon was responsible for the tear. The clicking nails came closer, allowing light to finally pour over its disgusting form. Blood dripped into large pools from the crevice across its face, the accompanying smell rancid. Garth and the Prince ran from the scene and into the unknown.

"You cannot hide forever! You *all* shall meet your end this way. I am not the only one. No, I am not. We will find you, torture you, and devour you!" roared the Demon. Moments later, it had done just that to the soul in its grasp. The cavern was silent as it ate.

Garth had been repressing sickness ever since he discovered the Queen's true identity. While witnessing the Demon's feeding, he threw up. He was thankful he hadn't eaten any glowing fruit.

The Demon called up to the Bridge Keeper, "Thank you for the light, brother!" It swatted its long arms into the surrounding darkness in search of its next victim.

"Take me!" cried the Prince.

"A volunteer?" bellowed the Demon as it pulled the lithe Prince from hiding.

Garth ran to the Demon, commanding it to leave the innocent soul alone. The Demon cowered at the sight of a human in his world.

"You. Boy. How are you in my domain?" it asked.

"Garth, please leave," begged the Prince.

"Silence, soul!" said the Demon. It threw the Prince to the ground and honed in on Garth. "You want to see Hell? Do you? Scary, yes? You want to tangle with an Immortal? Do you?"

"Yes."

"This isn't a game, human. I'll rip you limb from limb, I will. Start at your toes. Pluck you apart. Slowly, slowly."

The Prince yelled for Garth. They met against the fading light, where they could see each other one last time before the end. The

Prince's eyes were bright, his hair dark, and face still beautiful. "Don't do this," he said. His arm landed on Garth's shoulder.

Garth felt courage bubble within him. After years of regiment and obedience, he had bloomed into the man he'd always wanted to be. He finally stood, free-willed, for something good and true. The Prince was not a monster like the King. He was someone worthy of Garth's guard, worthy of Garth's soul.

But their tender moment was interrupted when the Demon stepped forward and revealing its full ghastly form. A giant, twisted body with long limbs and enormous hands crept closer. Its blanched, cave-grown skin was stained with its own red fluids. Scars ran across areas where features should be, although its mouth and one eye peeked through the overgrowth. It slowly inspected the two men through flaps of skin and steady trickle of blood.

"It's me you want. I am a pure soul," announced the Prince.

The Demon inhaled the Prince's essence and flickered its tongue to taste him. "What trickery is this?" it hissed. "You are clean and undeserving of this place. You will taste terrible."

"I am sacrificing myself in exchange for the Sacred Magic."

The Demon growled with anger. "Trick. Trick. Trick. Indeed. Who told you of that?"

"The crone in the woods."

"She expels too many secrets, she does!" The Demon paced around them, unhappy with its ruined meal. "What then? State the magic," it commanded.

"The sacrifice of a pure soul to purge the world of the evil ones. My father is avoiding the Way of Things. I offer myself to ensure his place here."

The Demon approached the Prince to make the proper negotiations. "That is indeed a great sacrifice to be made. It is the oldest and noblest of magic. At the dawn, there was light and there was dark. Good and evil. The good sacrificed many of themselves to bring the dark ones down, to trap them here. These battles happened before time and all memories. I am a descendant of the first brought to this dark place."

The Prince raised his head to the world above, to the Way of Things. "I am rekindling that magic!" he declared.

The earth rumbled in agreement. The Demon cowered and spoke to the air around it. "Fine! Fine. I will agree." It turned to the Prince. "I'll choke you down. A small price for the feast ahead of me. Your father's treachery will be well enjoyed." The Creature reared up in preparation to devour him.

"Stop!" cried Garth as he ran in front of the Prince. "Take me instead! I am also a pure soul!"

The Demon froze and growled with annoyance.

"I am purer than him," Garth continued. "My soul has not even been tainted by death. Take mine and free this man who was robbed of his mortal life. He deserves the paradise that surely awaits him." The Prince shook him to reconsider. Garth turned to him. "The soul inside of me is foreign. I've grown used to living without it." He stepped forward and spoke to the heavens. "A trade!"

Once again, the ground shook.

"Take my body, too. Surely that will make the magic even stronger," Garth suggested.

"Just your soul, human. You're body is of no interest to me," said the Demon. "Your sacrifice grants you a fate worse than death, you know. Go back to the world above. Go back without a soul."

Without a mortal soul, the flesh and blood husk he'd so briefly enjoyed began to revert to the Immortal form it had grown so accustomed to: one lacking sensation, warmth, or the ability to die. Once again, Garth was set in stone.

13. Clarity

On the other side of the bridge, the night sky of the limbo-land never gave way to day. The world they existed in was not the one they'd know. It was a place in between life and death, on the doorsteps of both Heaven and Hell. A brown and purple darkness swallowed them, allowing Helena to spend as many lucid hours with her beloved as possible.

"Can you really love me through this stone?" she asked Francis.

"You found affection for me through stone *and* deformities. I think I can manage getting over just one," he replied with a smile on his face as wide as the river behind them. He would have kissed her but the chilly softness of his ghost kisses would be lost on a statue like her. The smile would do.

Garth's short time inside the earth felt like ten times its length aboveground. What could have been minutes became hours or days or weeks. Who knew? Time wasn't something to worry about anymore. All Francis and Helena knew was that they were slowly becoming the unofficial greeters of souls after crossing the bridge. They offered congratulations and condolences, depending on the ghosts who crossed. Patient mothers, pious monks, gallant knights, jesters, and farmhands all walked the same path. Even a few heretics who'd been persecuted by their churches wandered across that ancient bridge. If those souls were cleared for entry, Helena wondered if the holy men who hanged them on the gallows would one day walk the same path.

The unmarked passing of time made waiting easier. It was a long uninterrupted dream. Their devotion to waiting for their friends never wavered. They knew they would return. They had to. Hopes bubbled with every creak of the bridge, although the faces of strangers were the only things that met them. Eventually their patience paid off and two figures emerged from the misty walkway. A tall man glided toward them with an arm extended across the back of a creature caught between man and monster. The joy they felt for their friend's return to the world was quickly eclipsed by his return to form. But they tried not to let it show.

"Where is the Queen?" asked Helena. She ran to Garth but he stumbled away with a tragic numbness that stopped her from embracing him. Helena looked at the foreign soul that accompanied him and whispered, "Who are you?"

Francis scurried to her side. "I know you. From nights above the palace, I know you."

The Prince nodded, sending Francis into a bow. "Your Majesty," he grumbled.

"You don't have to do that. You should be paying homage to Garth," said the Prince.

Helena went to Garth and forced him to look at her. "What did you do to yourself down there?"

"It's for the best. The Prince will explain. I'm tired. Sunrise can't come fast enough," he said, barely able to look into her eyes.

"There's no sun here. We could have gone on but we waited for you. Francis could be in paradise by now but he waited for *you*," said Helena with a tone that was anything but celebratory. "Garth, the man. What happened to him?"

A horn blew somewhere in the distance, kicking up a rancid breeze that rolled across the water behind them. Even in stone, Garth could smell it. The pitched sky smoldered with electricity. Like a new wound, crimson lightening bled from its clouds, followed by a band of winged chariots.

"Those won't do," said Garth, darkly. "They failed the last time."

As Garth slipped into hopelessness, the Seekers arrived. In addition to the army in flight, a dust storm announced a battalion by land. A throng of lanky, ancient beings marched past them.

"That ought to do," said Francis.

The Sacred Magic was real. The sacrifice had reawakened the protectors of the Way of Things. Pride washed away misery as Garth realized that his measly soul could ignite such power. He looked up at his Prince and saw sparkling tears well in his eyes.

The legions dispersed in search of the world's wandering souls. Even so, Garth felt a pang of doubt. He'd seen Immortals just like that torn into pieces by a sinister ghost. But his fears dissolved after the dust settled, for the Seekers were but a precursor to the titanic warriors behind them.

A second unit, one made of giants and other behemoths, made their way above the treetops and over the river. Their strides were awkward and stiff, and rightly so. The archaic race had been sleeping under mountains and riverbeds since the Sacred Magic had last been used. Even the primeval trees they walked through weren't old enough to remember the last awakening.

The battle panned out just beyond the bridge, in the badlands before the end of the world. War cries in lost languages and flashes of otherworldly light filled the sky during the siege of the world's wicked souls. The river swelled to the slats of the bridge with the sudden surge of new residents.

The Prince looked out over the filthy water and knew his mission had been accomplished. He tried to find himself a grin but his face was too heavy. Why did he feel no relief? His family had turned on him and, in turn, he had turned on his family. "I did this," he said to Garth. "It was ultimately your soul, but I was behind it. Just like my father was behind my death. I killed him and I brought him down. Yet I feel sick. Do you think that he ever had such pause?"

Garth was a foreigner to that kind of turmoil. He knew his family didn't have the capacity for so much hate. There was no use giving advice or comfort, for he had none. He simply wrapped his large arms around the soul and hoped the gesture said something.

It was time to finish their journey. The tests were passed and the end was no longer a distant thought. Francis and Helena eventually learned of what occurred between Garth and the Prince deep within the Earth. They didn't mind, though. Nothing seemed to faze them anymore.

❖

"Have you been tested recently?" Asher asked.

"Have I what?" I said with a tone of misunderstanding even though I knew exactly what he meant.

"You know, for the gay plague."

"Christ, go on and say it. We're not talking about an evil wizard. Yes, I was tested in the spring. For HIV. I was tested for HIV. Why?"

"You're not acting like yourself. You're being a prude. I thought you were hiding something contagious or leaking or—"

"No! I'm just being careful. Is anything wrong with that?" I wasn't lying. I was being careful. Not necessarily of spreading microbes or viruses, but of spreading a taste for blood and a hatred for what most find pleasurable. We were in the thick of summer, when the presence of hormones and mojitos are tripled compared to cooler times of the year. Abstaining from the pleasures of the flesh while Bryant's poison ran its course was the great test of my life. "I'll just stay in tonight. We'll do something tomorrow," I'd say. Then when tomorrow came I'd reschedule for tomorrow. And tomorrow. And tomorrow.

No wonder he thought I was dying.

Hells Kitchen, Chelsea, Greenwich Village, the East Village, and Union Square...Actually, the entire city was to be avoided because there were no longer distinct gayborhoods. The whole place was crawling with homos in short shorts and tank tops. But certain subway lines, ones that went to undesirable areas, had significantly less temptation. I spent a lot of time on those trains. One day a beautiful boy wandered onto my car, clearly making the obligatory visit to an unfortunate friend's new place. He held a fancy paper bag with a fancy red wine in one hand; his sub par boyfriend's hand in the other. The boyfriend's anti-attractiveness belittled the beautiful one with great hair, smooth skin and just enough scruff to make me swoon. I began thinking terribly bitchy thoughts like how they must have started dating in college when they were both in their prime. The boyfriend's genes had a lousy shelf life and expired in 2007, leaving his gorgeous partner to spend many hours at the gym and hundreds of dollars on clothes and products to overcompensate for the tragedy he'd been bound to. The attractive one looked at me as if to say, "If it weren't for this one, I'd get off at your stop." His eyes were apologetic for not being able to advance beyond stolen glances and corner smiles. The thing next to him glared in my direction then slid closer to the Adonis. The train stopped and I exited, trying to escape simultaneous thoughts of murder and ecstasy.

The doors closed and left me on an above ground platform—a clear sign of a neighborhood's disparity. The sun was setting but the air was still sweaty. Condemned warehouses and discount stores littered the street below me. For a second, I wished for Garth to be near, but I knew our last encounter made that impossible. It had been weeks since I'd last seen him. I had the feeling he was, for real, done with me. The reason was beyond my control, something I didn't even realize about myself until I'd met him. The most important part of me breathed only in his presence. He was meant to be in my life. If only he'd realize that.

An actual meat market resided on the corner of that outer-borough street. My stomach grumbled so I figured that a quarter pound of ground something or other would suffice. But as I crossed the street, a fragrance so decadent and flavorful that I needed to spit to relieve the drooling, danced past my nostrils. Fried chicken finally won my appetite back from the dark side. The breaded, seasoned and most importantly, *cooked* artery-clogger managed to stay in my gut. My days as an infected half-breed were coming to a close so I hopped on the next train back to Manhattan and met my best boys on the Dancebelt.

The Dancebelt is a stretch of Ninth Avenue that houses an entire evening's worth of homo bars. There isn't necessarily dancing at every establishment but the area is adjacent to the Theatre District, creating a virtual fruit salad of chorus boys and the like. The gays make mandatory stops at each place, even if it's just to use the bathroom. It's all part of thoroughly scoping out prospects and maximizing potential for phone numbers, email addresses, or even real live human contact.

About an hour into our romp, I was appropriately hammered. I'd been on the bench for so long, I felt that I had nothing to lose. In the past, I'd be the guy making awkward glances at the object of my affection. My newfound freedom (along with four gin and tonics) upped my courage levels, allowing me to speak to anything with a pulse. Asher observed in horror as I shamelessly received names for later Facebook stalking.

Some little bleach blonde number even asked me into the bathroom. I had enough sense to decline: One, because it was tasteless and two, because I wasn't one hundred percent sure that I couldn't pass along a contagious bloodlust syndrome.

"Well-played back there," said Bryant from behind a pillar supporting the second floor of the bar. "If you could refuse such an illicit transaction, you must be better. Welcome back to your life."

He was as striking as the last time I'd seen him. The wall of decorative tea lights cast a romantic glow and added to his mystique.

"This is the last place I'd have expected to see you," I said, half scared and half beside myself with aphrodesia.

"I don't go out much here. Anymore. But I was interested in seeing how you're faring. I spoke to Rita. She's concerned."

Of course he had to dampen my mood. "Why?"

"She told me that your Guardian has abandoned you. Things may seem like they're under control but I assure you, they aren't." He leaned into me and locked me in a very serious gaze. "Something's out there."

Thanks. Exactly what I wanted to hear. Being a half-breed vampire had finally given me the ability to function without a bodyguard. I hoped I'd be able to carry some of that bravery with me, but no. The moment I'm on the precipice of life, Bryant had to come and drag me back into the insane asylum. My anxiety skyrocketed to a level that should have given me a stroke. I had to play it cool, though. I couldn't freak out in front of the sexiest man on Earth. And by that I mean I had to be combative. "So why hasn't Rita done anything about it, huh?" I asked with my eyebrows raised practically to my hairline.

"These things take time. Soon she will be able to lend you counsel. Until then, she just wants to know you're safe."

"*She* wants to know or *you* do?" I asked, sensing he found pleasure in seeing me.

He silently confirmed with a smirk.

"I'm fine," I said. "I've managed to get through a few weeks without Garth. I'm not helpless."

"I believe you. But some souls are bound to each other."

"But Garth doesn't have a—"

Asher crept up from behind and almost made me lose my drink in his face. "We're going to head to the next place, okay?" he said, scoping out what he thought was a successful cruise on my part. "Bring him. He's niiiiice."

"Maybe. Please leave," I said, pushing his face anywhere but there.

"I'm gonna pee. Be right back." He ran into the bathroom, winking at me before the door swung closed.

"If I'm in danger, why can't you protect me? I know you're capable," I continued, once Asher was gone.

"Because that is not the Way of Things. He is a Guardian. I am not. In the old times, I am what he'd be protecting you from," he said, painfully. "Goodnight." He turned to walk through the crowd.

"That's it? All I get is a warning?" I yelled after him.

"It's more than you got when you were murdered a few hundred years ago," he said. I blinked and he was gone.

"He's sexy," Asher slurred, poking his head back around the pillar.

"Yeah, he is. We slept together a while ago."

"I can't believe you never told me about him. Wow. Who'd have thunk you'd be in the ranks with someone like that. He must have low self-esteem."

"Thanks a lot."

The hours leading up to my encounter with Bryant were blissful reminders of my life before Garth, when I was in the dark about the ancient Way, spells, lost souls and vampires. But all the cute boys and dance beats in the world couldn't tear me away from the new world

I had become entangled in. I wanted to flee to a little town and settle into a life of Wal-Mart and reality TV. Fading into obscurity would allow me to escape. Surely there were no gargoyles in the Midwest.

In the vestibule where the bouncer checks for fake ID's, I passed my nemesis. Nick. For just an instant, we met and my soul sizzled. His brown eyes were so dark they almost appeared black. He looked straight into mine, or maybe he didn't. There was no reflection, no glimmer of life to distinguish the exact placement of his gaze.

On the street, after my head stopped spinning and I'd freed myself from the confines of that testosterone den, Asher squawked too loudly about what had just happened.

"Shut up, he can probably hear you," I snapped.

"Jeremy," said a familiar voice. I turned around and saw Robbie reaching for the door, about to go in. The words "How are you," awkwardly stumbled from his mouth. His eyes darted looking for his date's proximity.

"On my way out," I said before my legs impulsively took off back towards Ninth Avenue.

Usually after several drinks at a bar full of attractive men who haven't spoken to me, I feel needy. Add in a run in with a former obsession and my version of Voldemort, I was feeling needy and... absolutely insane. I brushed aside concerns of infections and mental health and I forced myself to go home with an understudy of a show I'd never see. Surely, that could make me feel better. I managed to recover from blood lusts and so could he. Luckily, nothing supernatural was transferred. We woke up to a sun-filled room and enjoyed a morning stroll for iced coffees before I did the walk of shame back to Spanish Harlem.

When I got home and plugged in my dead phone, I had received a "Good to see you" text from Robbie. I felt no need to respond.

The sunless land didn't force the stone ones into hibernation but that didn't mean they couldn't get tired. After a brief rest, the Prince shook Garth. "Get up. Francis and I walked ahead. We're very close."

Garth opened his eyes and saw the Prince's willowy silhouette, blackened by a vibrant light behind him. His jaw dropped as he searched for words, "The sun…how…?"

"Can you believe? It's not the sun," laughed Helena. "It's something else. Something magic!" They walked through the trees, following the light. The chalky sand gave way to rich, damp soil. Soon, golden blossoms poked up their funny heads from the fertile earth. The flowers swayed in the wind like a wave of treasure as they walked into a seemingly endless valley. The moonlight couldn't help but reflect brilliantly off their amber petals, granting the sky daylight even in the darkest hours of evening.

Helena was made of the best marble, and in that light, it made no apologies for its finery. Colors swam across her curvy form like paint in a rainstorm. Francis looked at her with eyes as proud and as loving as on a wedding day. They danced through crystal pollen that broke the light into a spectrum of colors reserved for only the dead. It was, indeed, the gateway to paradise.

Who could resist rejoicing in such beauty? The sprint to meet the plain's end began with vigor. Prancing in the flowers was a simple joy, the perfect reward for their recent trials. Memories of their last moments together would be beautiful and happy. After running and running to a place still unseen, Francis wondered where they were actually going.

The Prince observed the never-ending yellow glow. "There should be a marker, something to tell us where to head," he said.

"Surely, it's just over the horizon. I'll walk until I'm rubble as long as it gets you to where you need to be," Garth said to the Prince. He found pleasure in pledging allegiance to someone again.

They stood motionless in the golden sea of rustling flower heads. When the air became still, their clapping heads silenced, the sound of a steady trickle nearby caught their attention. "Hear that?" said the Prince. "It's water."

Hidden beneath the canopy of petals ran a softly babbling brook. The stream passed under them, snaking backward to the dark river that held all of their secrets and lies. The water was so clear, so pure, it hardly looked like water at all. The riverbed could be easily mistaken for a shallow trench until the tiniest splash from a downward reaching foot or hand made it visible.

"We have to find its source," the Prince decided, and they all followed.

They waded against the rushing current for miles. "Where is it coming from?" asked Helena. "There is no sea or mountaintops nearby for it to flow from."

"Someone's been paying attention to her lessons," said Francis with a grin.

"Of course I have. You've made me quite knowledgeable about the world, you know. It's a shame I didn't get a real body back there. I'd make a perfectly good human." She allowed herself a second of sadness before continuing, "But I have much to learn still."

"Don't worry, Helena. I'll continue with your lessons," Garth said. "You'll learn more from me without Francis's joking and flirting."

She settled into a good laugh. A single tear streamed down her cheek as she grinned. Francis inspected it with much bewilderment, thinking that a human Helena would soon break out of that stone shell. Then a second and third tear rolled toward the ground.

But the tears were not falling from her eyes. They fell from the sky. As they walked along the water-path, the rain fell with a force that more resembled a waterfall than a downpour. It beat the flowers flat against the soil and enveloped the landscape with a thick mist that forced each pilgrim several steps into solitude.

In that bright blindness, souls and statues were left alone with their thoughts. The souls found contentment in the silence of the final leg of their journey.

The stone ones were left with the unhappy reality of feeling their loved ones slip from their grasp. Like the fear of falling, a crippling nervousness caught in their throats. They would be alone, left to wander the world with undefined futures and never-ending lives. Their minds were exposed to the secrets of the world, which proved to be more poison than antidote. What to do with so much knowledge and nobody to share it with?

When the haze lifted, a steady and sensible rain washed away their fears. Clarity opened their eyes and hearts. Uneasiness trickled downstream into the murky waters under the bridge.

The stairway rose out of the ground. It was made of ancient stone and stood taller than any mountain and reached higher than the sky.

They walked forward.

A great roar came from above.

They stopped.

14. Into the Lonesome World

A ugust flew by in what felt like seconds, as August usually does. I resented the recent goings on for keeping me indoors for the majority of summer. I was paler than the *Twilight* posters in every tween's bedroom. More so, I hated the forty-five jobs I was forced to take to make up for several weeks in darkness. I spent nearly every waking hour behind the front desk of a yoga studio or bussing tables at a cocktail lounge or tearing tickets at an off-Broadway theatre. I could see my social life making its few last, desperate attempts to revive itself. It twitched like a dying bug the world was about to fully smash. In the movie montage in my head, I walked home from every shift with a cover of "All By Myself" playing in the background.

I finally earned half a day off. After a moderately successful tanning session at the piers, I returned to my apartment and checked messages on my phone. I'd left it at home to grant me some peace. I still hadn't heard anything from the lab about my blood and that made me anxious. A sane person would have assumed my supernatural efforts had worked and I was in the clear. My far from normal brain was wracked with a fear that the C.I.A. had gotten hold of my samples and decoded what I'd done. I was on the alert for Gillian Andersen, Will Smith, or Hugh Jackman to show up on my doorstep with a warrant for my termination. My thumb stumbled over tiny buttons to access a possible summons from them to appear in a secret government courthouse that dealt exclusively in the world of magic. Or a voicemail—whichever came first.

"Hey Jerm. It's Robbie. I know that you probably don't want me calling you but...I just wanted to talk. After I bumped into you last month, with Nick...sorry. I bet that was awkward. Um...he got really weird. It continued until, well, now. Needless to say, we aren't together anymore. Not that you care. This isn't a plea to return to you. I'm not that crazy. I just wanted to let you know that he's in a strange place. In case he tries to contact you. It's actually kind of creepy. Sorry. I hope you're well. Um...yeah, bye."

I replayed the voicemail for Dan and Asher over drinks.

"How tragic," Dan said with a roll of the eyes.

"Do you think he wants to get back together?" Asher said, even though the answer was so obvious it didn't need to be mentioned.

"He sounds like a serial monogamist."

"I thought only straight people with low self-esteem from single-parent households did that."

"Gays, too."

"I don't know about him," I said. "He's probably just lonely."

"Rebound."

"Rebound."

"Yes, yes," I scrambled. "But what if he's really trying to warn me about something?" I quickly took the world's largest gulp from my martini to cover up my nervous smile.

"What? You think Nick's a serial killer? I mean, you *were* a threat to their relationship, but come *on*. You're no Brad Pitt," Dan said, putting me in my place. Then he mocked me: "Look at me, I'm Jeremy, everyone is trying to kill me."

"Hey, if someone tried to kill you in the middle of the night, you'd be just as—"

"Paranoid," Asher suggested.

"Yes, paranoid," I cowered.

"Rightfully so. I guess," Dan half-agreed. "You should probably be medicated."

After several beverages we stumbled to the sidewalk. The poor boy that I was, I decided not to continue to bars numbered two, three, and four. I'd rather spend my money on a cab to avoid the potential attackers that I seemed to be so prone to attracting.

"For the money you're going to spend on this cab, you could buy two drinks," Dan scoffed.

"Yes, but Spanish Harlem isn't exactly the most inviting place after dark. And it's starting to rain."

"The whole city's a risk. Nowhere is safe."

I knew that all too well but decided to cab it, anyway. TV screens had been installed in the back of every taxi, which made me sick to my stomach. If I didn't turn it off immediately, I'd end up glancing down and watching a weather forecast or the review of a movie that I hadn't planned on seeing. Then I'd get sick. Luckily, that cab didn't possess a working screen and my driver didn't play music, leaving me to a ride home in almost-solitude. I closed my eyes and listened to the soothing sound of raindrops on metal.

We eventually came to a red light and I felt the usual jerk as the car stopped too short. Nothing uncommon. I began to drift off, dreaming of nothing in particular…probably tomorrow's lunch or the barista at the Forty-Third Street Starbucks. Just as my dream man handed me my latte, I was jolted out of my haze by a rapping at the window. Through water droplets, I saw a face staring at me. A hand wiped the glass to reveal the maniacal grin of Nick.

"Hello, Mr. King. Hello, Your Highness," he taunted through foggy breath.

The light turned green. "Go!" I yelled.

The cab took off, leaving Nick on the curb. After several blocks he was just a shadow on a far off corner of my window. I sunk into my seat, closed my eyes, tried to catch my breath, and waited to be home.

Then the driver called back, "Your friend! Your friend!"

I swung my head around and saw Nick lit in the blazing red of our taillights, running in quick pursuit of us.

"Just drive!" I demanded. The car turned down a street, then an avenue, then a street, until that crazy queer was out of sight. "Take the FDR, just in case," I demanded.

We zoomed up the highway, along the East River. The long stretch of speeding cars helped put my mind elsewhere. It was like fleeing the country, even though I was just traveling a few miles northeast.

The cab dropped me off at the end of my street. I sprinted to the door, still spooked. I knew it was impossible for Nick to be nearby but I could feel imaginary breath making my neck hairs raise. When I was little, I used to scare myself on the way up the stairs to my bedroom. Even though nobody was behind me, I imagined little hands grabbing at my ankles. I'd run so quickly that I'd usually end up falling and waking up the entire house. I almost pulled the same stunt on the front steps of my building. The door couldn't close fast enough behind me.

September had tricked us into leaving the air conditioner off even though the air was still thick with residual summer. I felt like a swamp monster in that sticky apartment. I tore off my wet shift and checked my armpits for B.O., which was kind of ridiculous because my bed didn't care if I smelled. "Anyone home?" I hollered. My roommate was still out. It was too quiet. My phone chimed with the arrival of a text message, nearly sending me into cardiac arrest.

YOU'RE NOT SO PRETTY WHEN YOU'RE SCARED.

Another chime.

DOES ROBBIE KNOW THAT?

One more.

I BET YOU'D BE DOWNRIGHT UGLY WITH YOUR FACE SPLIT OPEN.

❖

With wings whiter than the clouds it came from, an Angel descended, heralded not by its heavenly choir, but by its inhuman roar. When the Angel finally came into view, they could see why: the noble head of a lion sat atop the graceful body of man.

"Welcome, friends," the Angel spoke from the first of many, many steps up the staircase. His voice purred from a deep register. "You've taken longer than many before you. I hope you find the rain refreshing."

"Yes. Yes we do," Francis eagerly replied.

"And I am glad. It is your final cleansing before you ascend the stairway to Heaven."

Heaven.

The word sat solidly with Garth.

It was a place where his friends would go.

A place where his family resided.

A place that he would never see…

He tried to savor those last, precious moments with Francis and the Prince. He desperately burned their ghostly images into his mind. He'd carry those pictures with him forever. The light of paradise cascaded down the epic staircase and made his stone heart heavier than it had been for decades. He reached out a hand to find comfort from the souls, but they had already begun gravitating towards the Angel. Garth stepped forward only to be met by another roar.

"Guardian, you know well that this is no place for an Immortal. Our tasks are for Earth. Mine is at the bottom of the stair, greeting souls and ensuring only souls shall pass."

"But they have no souls," argued the Prince as if it would grant them special permission.

The Angel looked down on him sadly and said, "The human form, though great, is not everlasting. Your souls grow weary of their time here and must retire above." His attention returned to the stone ones. "We need not ascend the stairs for we are strong and made for *this* world. We do not expire. That knowledge, the ability to live on, is our Heaven. They watch over us from above just as we watched over them here."

"I had a soul," Garth blurted, unable to find the required eloquence for speaking to an Angel.

"And it was not meant for you. Sometimes the Way of Things change as time passes. Humans show strength, Immortals show weakness, and souls tire of paradise. The rules of the universe are strict but not definite. One speck of dust can create a world and one exceptional man can make an Immortal."

"But I know too much," Garth cried. "How can I go through life knowing all of its secrets?"

"Hardly," laughed the Angel. "Knowledge doesn't ruin wonder; it inspires it. Live and help others do the same."

Garth took a step away from the stairs, a step towards a new life. The Angel's advice filled the place where his soul should have been. A new purpose flowed through him. He took Helena's hand and smiled. Together, they would learn how to let go. They would help others to live.

The Angel looked again at the two souls. "It is time."

15. Answers

The Prince was retired to his bedchamber long before the sun went down. Time crawled slowly after his doors were locked. Boredom set in too quickly.

He sat at the end of his bed and thought on the day's lessons.

Then he looked out the window into his garden and admired its grandeur.

Eventually he lulled himself into a trance, listening to a strand of pearls beat against itself when tossed from hand to hand.

Click, click, click.

Click, click, click.

He thought he had been hypnotized for an hour. It was more likely just a few minutes. The moon had barely risen and was still mistakable for a cloud. Soon the torches would be lit, all except the one in his room.

Reveling from the halls below echoed through the ancient palace's corridors and into his bedchamber, where he finally decided to close his eyes for the night. "Dreams," he thought, "dreams will pass these hours much more efficiently than life can." His hands ran across his warm skin. No need for a blanket that evening. His fingers grazed the place where a scar would form after the scabbing fell off and the tenderness subsided. That skin had felt a blade, on a night much like that one. But it had also felt dressings from a kind handmaiden. In his dark room, the memory flushed his face with embarrassment. "How could I have been so weak?"

It was a silly question, though. Of course he felt weak. Father, mother, uncles, aunts, cousins, and court all turned their heads, backs, and sympathies away from him. The boy Prince was peculiar, the adolescent was questionable, but the man was intolerable. Their new religion was strict, the stringency useful for keeping the people at bay. A King with a son like that would cause discourse. A King with a son like that could not be a god. So the King did not have a son *like that*. He was pushed to the back, hidden in shadows, never spoken of. Eventually the simple men and women of the kingdom forgot about the once future heir.

Despite all of this, the Prince went on sitting at the end of his bed, looking out his window, and tossing pearls from side to side. "One day, it will change…" His optimism was necessary. Many boys lacked that courage and disappeared to even darker places than he. For them, he would live. He was, after all, their Prince.

The drinking and singing carried late into the night.

The Prince dreamed.

Vile schemes were developed.

The Prince dreamed.

Two men broke down the door.

The Prince awoke.

"Why?" he asked. The men said nothing, simply snickered. Then kicked, then hit, then broke, and then crushed. "But I'm your kin," he said with a mouth full of teeth. When they finally spoke, their words were harsh. They could have killed him with their words alone.

The world was quiet as he began to die. Not even the smallest bird dared chirp with the rising sun. They bowed to their Prince while he dragged himself to the Queen near the water. In her arms he would lay until angels came to greet him. Oh, how strong she was. He'd modeled himself after her. "I tried, my lady. I tried."

Were she real, she'd know he had. Were she real, she'd have replied, "Yes, you did. You were very strong. You were very proud. But so were they."

"Then I will be stronger," he said.

Then he wretched.

He screamed…

I awoke weeping and twisted in my bed. The dream was vivid. Too vivid.

"Garth!" I yelled, knowing fully well that he couldn't hear me. He was somewhere else, maybe not even in the city. He could have been in a different state, a different country, found another staircase and climbed it.

"Garth!" I threw on some clothing.

"Garth!" I ran out the door.

"Garth!" I hurried down the street.

The homeless people thought I needed money. The deranged wondered what my disturbance was.

"Garth!" Maybe I could beckon him to my side. Possibly we shared some kind of ESP?

I came to a place where the streets were empty, save for me. I wanted Nick to come after me. I dared him. I was at once incredibly weak and insanely strong. "Come on, you piece of shit! I'll tear your face off, you pathetic freak!" My articulation and vocabulary disappeared beneath my rage.

"I wouldn't go inviting your enemies to your side. Not just yet," said a man from behind me. I turned around with closed fists and swinging arms. It was probably the gayest sight on Earth, but damnit, I committed to those punches. Bryant caught my hands in his. Their coolness was shocking. I'd forgotten the sensation that our conflicting temperatures had on my heart.

"How are you here? How is there *always* someone here?" I cried.

"Because you need watching. Garth is not here for you. I'm stepping in," he said, coolly.

"He asked you to?"

He shifted contrapposto and swiped an imaginary wisp of hair. "After he found out that I'd been doing it anyway, he asked me to continue."

"Excuse me?"

"I have been observing you. Since that night."

I wanted to be angry but the idea was too arousing. Finally, a stalker I was into. "Why?" I asked. "You said that you couldn't. I already have a Guardian."

"I know. And I'm not him," he said as he advanced toward me. The expression he wore began to frighten me. Bryant was going to a dark place, a place I'd never accessed while I had his poison in me.

"Bryant, stop. You're scaring me."

"I'm older than I look Jeremy. I've seen many souls leave this world. I've been the reason they've left."

His presence was paralyzing. Even though he hadn't touched me yet, I felt like he was holding me down. My feet were stuck.

Then something funny happened. His eyes began to glimmer with tears. His jaw bobbed for words. "If you are really who they say you are, I am given hope that not everyone is truly lost," he said. The tears escaped his eyes and began to drip down his face. "Many innocent lives were taken. Do you remember anything from before you came here? What was it was like there, in Heaven? Who was with you? Is it easy to come back?"

He was clutching me, desperate for answers.

"Bryant, I don't...I don't know anything."

"Nothing? Would photographs help? Names? There are some people whose fates I *need* to know about. Maybe you can remember... Please, you have to remember."

My heart splintered as I watched him break down.

"So many people died."

"I'm sorry," I said, beginning to cry myself. When others get emotional I tend to absorb their energy, even if I have no clue what they're crying about. "I can't help you. I don't know anything. I can't control this thing inside of me."

He sniffed away the remaining tears and straightened. "Of course. Nothing about the Way makes sense. I don't know how anyone can begin to understand it. It isn't fair."

"You're right. It's not fair. All I have are dreams about people I don't know. I smell or hear things and have memories that aren't mine. I can't place half the things that my mind comes up with."

"Sounds downright magical."

I ignored his cynicism. "Garth was the only person I could talk to about it because...well, he knows. He knows what I know. What I think I know. Somewhere deep down I'm contented being with him."

"You love that grotesque?" he asked. There was no repulsion in his words. He was genuinely wondering. Or accusing.

"Part of me might," I said. "I wish Rita would help me figure this out, already."

"Well you're in luck."

I peered at him curiously.

"That's the other reason I'm here. She's ready."

Rita's apartment was cleaner than the last time I'd visited. The mess of papers, bottles, keepsakes, and plain-old junk had been removed or simply stuffed into the periphery. Even a scented candle burned, masking the old air with a sugary stench. "I went through a phase in the seventies when I made them," she said. "I'm sure it's chock full 'o lead or other toxic shit. Be careful breathing," she coughed.

"What's the occasion, Rita? I've never seen this place so orderly," Bryant said. He did the obligatory index finger swipe across the table, looking for excess dust. The fragile man I'd just seen was replaced by the strong vampire I'd known.

"Don't be smart with me. I don't think you understand just *who* is coming tonight, do you?"

We shrugged.

"She is one of the oldest. When the world was new, she was there. She was my teacher's teacher's teacher. And if you know anything about witch life spans, that means she's really goddamn old." She went to a mirror and applied more lipstick. It was the definition of pink. She probably intended for a less severe look by changing from her usual red but it was an equal trade.

"So, she's dead?" I asked, always the mortal fool.

"We witches aren't Immortals but it takes us abnormally long to pass on. This broad has powers and knowledge beyond anybody else, so she's taking her sweet time."

My stomach turned thinking about what she'd look like. The witch in front of me wasn't exactly the picture of beauty. I could barely imagine what façade such an ancient one could manage to put up.

Rita came to me and grabbed my arm. "She was there, chickadee." She spoke with rancid breath that'd been sweetened by way of sugar-free gum. "She was the witch who lent counsel to Garth, and to you, so many moons ago. If anyone knows the Way of Things, it's her."

Garth entered quickly, carrying a bag over his shoulder. I flashed on what he must have looked like slinging Francis through the wilderness.

"Perfect timing," sang Rita with hands over her head, bracelets rattling.

"He's good at that," I said, feigning disinterest. Really, I was never gladder to see him.

Garth gently put down his bag and walked to me. He took my chin in his hand, bringing my face to his. Our foreheads kissed. "I am sorry," he whispered.

We didn't need another argument over the things we couldn't help. So I just smiled.

Rita harrumphed. Garth went to the bag and pulled out an ornate leather box. Gold lettering spelled out something in an unfamiliar alphabet.

"My stars," said Rita.

"Where did you get that?" asked Bryant.

"The Institute. In Prague," she rang.

"I thought the fires—"

"Only part of it. There are vaults below."

Bryant looked at the box in awe.

"Bryant did a bang-up job destroying the place in the eighties," she boasted. "He's quite notorious for it."

Garth brought the box over to the table. We gathered around it like participants in a séance. "I'm warning you, it isn't a pretty sight," Garth said with hands still protecting its contents.

"Will we need some snow orchid?" asked Rita.

"Yes, definitely. I'd almost forgot. She is near the end of her time here. I'm lucky to have found her when I did. Needless to say, she is quite groggy."

"Wait, wait, wait…she's in there?" I asked.

"Yes, dearie," said Rita. She snapped her fingers and a small jar flew from the kitchen into her hand.

"Well, not entirely," said Garth.

"Was she in the head collection?" wondered Bryant. "That's repulsive."

"Yes. And under sharp supervision. Apparently strange occurrences have taken place in recent years."

"Stop it," I demanded. "Stop assuming that I have even an inkling as to what you're talking about. Is there a witch's head in that box?" It sounded even more ridiculous actually coming out of my mouth.

"I told you, it takes us a long time to pass on. And some parts die before others," Rita said to me. With a magic word, she unhinged the latch on the box. It creaked open. The smell was enough to kill a man. The sight was worse. An ancient, wrinkled, and bald head sat neatly on a velvet bed. Its eyes were closed so tightly, the creases were lost amongst the raisin-y skin folds covering the hag's face. Rita opened the jar and sprinkled a white powder over the approximate location of eyes and lips, uttering another incantation.

The old hag's eyes peeled open and her lips un-stuck from one another. She crowed something in an extinct language. Everyone laughed.

"What? What?" I asked.

"She asked if she was dead yet," said Garth. Rita spoke to the head again in the same dialect.

"Fine," said the head. "It is not a pretty language, but I will oblige."

"Thank you," I said.

The head looked at me with clouded eyes. "It is true. You are an old soul. These eyes can see what you cannot. They can see what they cannot. Fetch me flora!" the head commanded.

"What kind?" asked Rita.

"Any kind. As long as it has grown form the earth."

Rita ran into the kitchen and rummaged through the refrigerator. The head continued to examine me.

She returned with a ball of lettuce, brown and soggy. "I forgot about this one. Meant to make a salad last week. It's organic, too."

"Feed it to me!" barked the hag.

The head chewed on the sluggish leaf and moved the contents of its mouth from side to side. Its old eyes closed for a solid minute. Then it gasped. "There is a great upheaval. You," it said, looking at me. "Your kind has done too much."

"I sensed this," whispered Garth to Bryant.

"Honey, I've been sensing it for a long time. Why else do you think I stay inside all day?" joked Rita.

"It is no laughing matter," continued the head. " Man's progress, his disrespect for the Earth and disregard of the Way of Things, has thrown it off course. The seals between worlds are breaking. I know what haunts you, young Prince."

"What? What is it?" I pleaded, answering to a title that I didn't feel was mine.

"Your kin. Garth's sacrifice brought down your father. The Demon devoured one cousin. But another remained. Through these centuries, he lurked in the darkest corners of the Underworld, avoiding his soul's death. Finally, a light from above. A crack in the seal. He escaped. Many did."

"Jesus, Mary, and Joseph," gasped Rita. "I thought that'd been remedied."

"So there are legit evil spirits walking around?" I said, my tone droll.

"Put your brain in the real world and you will notice the rise of evil here. The damned seek out faint bodies to inhabit and complete the unfinished atrocities from days gone by. Some begin new ones, grander in scale, utilizing what did not exist in their time." The head's eyes continued to search me, like I had the answers written plainly on my face. "Your cousin has been searching for you for longer than you've even existed."

"Then I'm not just a beacon for bad luck. The same soul has been trying to kill me for the past year, just in different forms?"

"Yes."

"All because there is another soul inside of me? One that's not really me?" I was stumbling over words, nearly crying.

"It is you. Souls can complete many life cycles, my dear. Yours has only lived once before," said the head, trying to comfort me. Rita put a hand on my shoulder. "Sometimes a soul will tire of the other side and decide to begin a new journey. Sometimes it leaves to do work here on Earth. Only the soul knows for sure. All we are certain of is, twenty-two years ago, the Prince decided to try again. Here you are."

"Judging from your visions, it seems like your soul is trying to make its former identity known, possibly in order to perform a particular task," suggested Rita.

"Yes, witch," said the head. "You are an astute one, you are."

"Thank you," Rita said, blushing. She turned back to me. "I suspect you wanted to find this one," referring to Garth.

"Well, I picked a pretty shitty time to visit." I said. "There's a pissed off ghost trailing me."

"I believe that is your plan," the head said.

That decapitation was beginning to get on my nerves. "Why would I plan to be pursued by something that wants me dead? Sounds a bit redundant, no?"

"Because you knew it would bring me to you," Garth piped up from next to me. "I've been avenging your death for centuries. You knew I'd come to the aid of someone like yourself."

"A tragic gay kid getting beat up on Twenty-Sixth Street?" I said, hoping it would come off as self-deprecation instead of the sad fact it was.

"A person singled out for being himself," he asserted.

My attempt at infecting sarcasm into the conversation had stopped it cold.

"But remember the chain. Remember a soul's place in it," spat the head. "From above, he looks down on the Immortals who looked over him in life. You've been watching Garth. You have been watching all of them battle the change in the Way. You are here for more than a visit."

"You're here to repair the balance," said Bryant. "Because we Immortals aren't enough. I know your legend, Garth. You could do nothing against the King until you had a mortal soul to offer."

"That is the Sacred Magic," confirmed Rita.

"I will be so bold to suggest," said Bryant. He cleared his throat, "That the Prince intended to—"

"Sacrifice myself?" I asked. "I came here just to kill myself?"

"Sacrifice is the oldest magic. It has done miraculous things," marveled Rita. "It saved you, it made Helena. You, more than most, are connected to it."

"Garth, you said the Prince was a brave soul. This would be a brave act," Bryant added.

Garth came to me, "No. You will not perform the task."

"I can't say that I'm really considering it," I said.

"But you were. Up there, looking down, you were. That's why you've come here. You might not be sure about it now, but when you are faced with the choice you will give yourself to the Way."

"I don't want to do it."

"But the Way of Things," murmured Rita.

"The old ways are dead! The humans have their own rules now. They do not need us to look after them and we do not need the souls to watch us," exclaimed Garth. He pulled me into him. "He was already killed once. I will not have it happen again. This boy deserves to live."

"I agree. There must be another way," said Bryant.

"I thought the point of me coming here was to avoid dying. How did this conversation turn into the complete opposite?" I asked, on the verge of giving up and taking my chances with the evil cousin-ghost-person.

"Then find another pure soul," said the head. "Jeremy, you may sacrifice another. The magic will work. But when your time comes to cross the bridge, I guarantee you will not make it to the other side."

"But he'll have had a chance to live," Bryant said.

"A damned life. Murder doesn't go away. The face of his victim will stay on the back of his eyes, forever. Nobody wants to live that life. You should know that, Night Creature," said the head.

The room fell silent as the magic folk brewed in their thoughts. The cheap candle flickered in the breeze from the filthy air conditioner in the alley window. They were a sad lot, reduced to tenements, rooftops, and boxes. How could such powerful beings be pushed into such obscurity? Was it us, the mortals, who mistreated our gifts and ignored our protectors? If we were so bad, maybe it was best to let it all fall apart. Let the world be overrun with demons and become polluted with our wasted and deformed young. If I gave myself to death in order to exterminate one rogue soul, would the world really benefit?

"The Deep Magic must be used again. It will bring order to the Way of Things like it did in the beginning," said the head.

"This one sacrifice will do all that? The seals will be fixed?" asked Garth.

The head rolled over from exhaustion. The lack of essential organs made all the explaining understandably taxing. "I cannot be sure."

"What do you mean, you aren't sure? I'm not jumping in front of a gun based on the hunch of that...that dead head-thing," I said. The others looked at me like I'd just stepped on the baby Jesus.

"He is right," the head agreed. "The boy is right! The Old Magic, Original Magic, Deep Magic...it has those names for a reason. Millennia have passed since its inception. The world changes. So does magic. We cannot be positive about its outcome." Again we sat around the head in our own thoughts.

Nobody had an answer.

Everyone wanted to disappear.

"But there is something to say about faith," offered the head. "You may not always know for sure but you can hope for the best. Believe in the best. You cannot see the soul inside you, Jeremy, but you know it is in there. Don't you?"

"You're right. I can't see it. But I know it's there because it constantly gives me proof. Every time I close my eyes, round a corner, wake up in the morning, there's proof." I walked away from their huddle and looked out the window, even though it faced a dark alleyway containing absolutely nothing interesting to observe. "Life isn't Sunday school, there's no room for faith. Facts, that's what I believe in. Show me something real. A live gargoyle, a talking head in a box; those are real. Killing myself for a magic that hasn't been seen in my lifetime isn't. Until you show me the instruction booklet or bring down whoever makes this *Way of Things* from their castle at the top of that staircase, I can't. That's asking too much of me. My life has already changed so much…"

I couldn't. There wasn't anything left to say. I needed either a drink or a smoke or a life transplant. I stomped over to a cabinet that, in a normal person's home, would have contained the makings of a bar. Since I was in a witch's den, this thing was stocked with mason jars filled with newts and bottles of oddly colored fluids with unreadable labels.

"I mean…what do you…?" I mumbled. Again, I couldn't…

Then I spotted a package of long cigarettes on Rita's end table. My hands trembled as I tried to pull one from the tightly packed container. Once I finally placed one between my lips, I couldn't bother searching for a light. Who know what I'd have found. I just motioned at the cancer stick with my hand, hoping one of them would have the courtesy to help me out in my moment of need.

Rita was the first to approach. She held up her fist, presumably containing a lighter. But then she flicked her crooked index finger in the air and produced a flame at the end of her nail, no match or fluid necessary. Pure abracadabra. "Here, baby," she offered.

I stared at the fire dancing at the end of her finger. Of her *finger*! Then I looked at a gargoyle. And a vampire. And a severed head still chewing on old lettuce. None of them even flinched at the sight. That kind of behavior was *normal* to them. "What has my life come to?" I asked in the quietest of whispers.

That's when the tears came.

And the heaving.

And the hyperventilating.

The head went back in the box. I went onto the couch. My dreams retreated to the quiet place within me where the Prince slept. He had finally arrived…we just had to learn to live together.

16. WRESTLING

Morning in Rita's apartment was odd. The moth-eaten curtains were pulled, barely shrouding us from the bright world outside. My face found warmth in a puddle of sunlight as my legs stirred up dust on her couch. With each inhalation I smelled my grandparent's house…open windows, childhood accidents, and out-of-date perfume. Most people would find it disgusting but I was comforted by the familiarity. I tried to flip over and steal a few more minutes of sleep but I stubbed my toe on what I assumed was an end table. When I sat up, I saw it was Garth hunched on the floor.

I'd never seen him in his true statue form. He'd always gone to one of his secret spots to retire before daybreak. He was so still, I found it hard to believe he possessed the range of motion he did come sundown. My hand ran over his brow and pointed ears. His vulnerability in that state was scary. I imagined someone raising a hammer or throwing him over the side of a building like his friend, Francis. The thought made sick. "Thank you," I whispered. "I'm sorry for being a terror recently."

Dust floated about the room in dense plankton clouds. It whirled around as I walked through to the kitchen.

Rita sat at her small table drinking coffee the color of sin. "There's some left in the pot," she hummed. Her hand mechanically went from ashtray to mouth. She'd be able to milk a long five minutes out of that morning cigarette.

"What are you reading?" I asked after glancing at papers that had nothing to do with news.

"I inherited these after my teacher passed on. That witch has no head in a vault. That witch is in the dirt like everyone else," she said before flipping the pages. The writing made no sense to my eyes.

"They look very old."

She chuckled. "Oh, yes. These pages have lived through a lot. Wars. Famines. Great upheavals. Things you've never seen. Too young." She reached over and patted the other end of the table, a motion presumably for me to sit with her. I did. She leaned in toward me. "You secretly smirk at the fact...that your way of life has never been threatened. Bombs never went off in your city. The great wars of men over the last hundred years, I lived through them. I lost family to them before I found my calling."

"I'm...I'm sorry." I didn't know how to respond. It wasn't my fault I'd been lucky enough to be born in a relatively peaceful time. Well, from what I'd experienced, at least.

"Life got better once I recognized my powers, my worth. The goings on of humans became no concern to me. I thought I'd always have my spells and my obligations to the Way of Things because they were unchanging." She inhaled her cigarette and held the smoke inside of her for a moment. She smiled and blew it out her nose. "I secretly smirked at the fact that my way of life couldn't be threatened."

"So the Way made your life better?"

"Sure." She shrugged. "But I'm realizing nothing is unchanging. At first, I hardly noticed the magic slipping through my fingers. Now, I see it. As if the world is crashing down around me, I see it."

So no matter what path I pursued, I'd be screwed. Good to know. "What are you seeing? How is it different?"

"This," she said as her knuckle knocked on the table. The same hand ran across its linoleum top, yellowed from smoke and decades of use. Her nails attempted to dig into the impenetrable plastic. "Witches used to have magnificent homes in the natural world. Mine is artificial—five levels too high and filled with memories of dead ages. Not just of witches and Immortals, but of humans." She pointed her smoking fingers to one of the crowded walls. "There. See that picture?"

There were a million photos haphazardly hung over one another. There was no way I could know what one she was referring to. I pretended. "Yes. I see."

"It was taken in the Twenties. We were carefree. I did my fair share of dancing and boozing. See that girl with the white cap and the saucer eyes? That was me, a young witch then. I was very beautiful."

Her detail helped me find it. She was a gorgeous woman, with an expression that was the textbook definition of happiness. I wondered if someone were to take a photo of me, if I would be able to look that elated by my newfound relationship with the Way of Things. Probably not. As she said, it was different then. I tried to compare the bright eyes in the picture to the ones in front of me, but they wee hidden. She never looked at the portrait. Her cigarette lingered in its direction as she tried to save herself from a teary state. Her hand withdrew and met her shriveled lips for one last puff before the filter burned.

"Rita, do you think Garth's disappointed in me?" I asked.

"How so, dear?" she asked, sweetly.

"I mean...I don't know what he expects now that I'm...back. Am I much like I was in that past life?"

"I wasn't here then. But the old one in the box, I saw a glimmer in those dying eyes. I see the same one in Garth's. You're in there, all right. Nothing to worry about. As for him, I can't say what he expects. The two of you never met on the same plane. But love is love and it endures. It endures time, form, death, and rebirth. It isn't always the same and it isn't always attainable in a traditional sense, but it's there. I'm sure he is thrilled."

He'd promised Helena they would return to the birches. She was sure magic could be found there. It was a border place, where the worlds of men and spirits collide, but Garth didn't have much hope. Still, he had all of eternity to get where he needed to go. A stop at the trees surely wouldn't hurt. Forever was filled with possibilities and there was plenty of time to figure out the details.

The trip to the stair had been arduous but backtracking was even more so. The land was in the thick of winter hibernation. Ice in their porous skin made them heavy. The whitewash in the air made them clumsy. Garth supposed they were lucky to be made of stone, for humans would have perished in such conditions. When the sun rose, they huddled together and hoped to be mistaken for a boulder or a snowdrift by unfortunate travelers who were destined for sickness or starvation.

They spent nights mostly in silent reflection. Helena's usual optimistic attitude was wearing thin as reality set in. The idea of living an Immortal life was hard on her. At the fountain, she'd heard men speak of love as the greatest of human emotions. She thought she experienced it with Francis but he was gone. His absence burrowed a deep hole in her center. She wanted to fill it with him, to experience the whole gamut of sensations the hag had promised months ago when she poured that vial of tears over her head. The thought of going back to that fountain as people lived around her conjured impulses of flying off a cliff and smashing into a million pieces. At least, then, she'd be at ease. There'd be no soul to go anywhere. She'd cease to exist and rid the world, Heaven, and Hell of her sadness.

Garth had always thought of himself as cursed, not special. But being Immortal was extremely remarkable. He hadn't realized it until the end, but it was. "Immortal," he kept murmuring under his breath, unaware of his doing so. Helena would ask if he was all right and he'd just shake his head and keep walking. So together they traveled and longed for humanity but settled for their assigned lots.

He still felt it, though. That brief rendezvous with mortality invigorated senses he thought he'd lost. Unfortunately those feelings were quick to leave him, scattered along the path behind them, lost in the heaps of white. Should he have let them go so easily? Forget all humanity and give himself completely to the Way of Things? Was the Way good or bad? Did it provide structure or keep them confined?

He looked at Helena and saw the terror in her eyes. "Don't let them go," she seemed to say. At least for her sake, he wouldn't. He strove to remember...

He loved his mother, always happy even in the saddest of times. He tried to recall how her eyes would gloss with a smile when she looked at him.

He loved his sister, Evie. She looked up to him even though he'd done nothing in his lifetime worth looking up to. He hoped she still thought of him. He would think of her often.

He loved his father. Their time together was brief but it was happy. He tried to hear his cackling laugh.

He loved Francis, his oldest and truest friend.

He loved Helena, who reminded him to remind himself of happy times.

And he supposed he loved the Prince. But it was a new kind of love. A kind he'd never felt before. It was emergent. Foreign. Scary. Painful. Ridiculous. Breathtaking. Easy. Natural. Perfect. Aching. Desirable. Missed....

It was a memory striving to be retained.

There was an awkward hour and a half between my two part-time jobs. Back when I pretended to have money, I would have gone shopping...or at least pretended to go shopping with my pretend money and I'd have just ended up buying a pair of underwear to gain a sense of accomplishment after wasting an hour and a half of my life doing nothing but pretending. But it was a crisp fall day and I decided to be outside. The weather was perfect for meandering. It was so prefect that five minutes indoors to buy a simple cup of *regular* coffee made me feel ashamed. I'd finally acknowledged that I couldn't afford lattes, hence the multiple careers.

New York was making its best efforts at being green, resulting in a welcome bombardment of fruit carts and farmers markets. I found a quaint, five-stand market not far from Rita's lair and ventured in, feigning interest in newly harvested vegetables I never order when I'm out. I had no intention of buying anything but I did like to imagine myself purchasing organic spinach and making a splendid salad for dinner. That's what real adults did. I always saw them strolling through the booths, commenting on how *gorgeous* the week's offerings were. They had real jobs with real incomes and real apartments with real lovers. When would my life become real? Would I ever grow up? I kept thinking about what Garth had said. What the hell was the point to me? Was I supposed to start a lecture series on the Way of Things? Train with Night Creatures and become a vigilante? I had to find my purpose.

The usual suspects, half-crazy/half-brilliant individuals, stood behind folding tables advising on recipes and bestowing their farmland knowledge on the trying-to-be-so-progressive-they-have-to-regress-into-having-an-interest-in-farming city folk. I turned my name brand coffee cup around so the logo branded my palm with the love of consumerism. I couldn't be judged by the anti-consumers. I contemplated, for a moment, throwing it away and opting for the hot cider at one of the tables. Then I remembered cider could do nothing for keeping me lucid though my next shift. I'd also read somewhere that people who drink coffee are less likely to commit suicide. While I wasn't particularly suicidal (in the traditional sense), I was having thoughts of giving my mortal soul to a Hell creature (fairly untraditional). Technically suicide. To make sure I made the right choice, I drank coffee like mother's milk.

"Jeremy!" called a voice. I was growing tired of people beckoning me, as they usually had something way too interesting to divulge. The culprit was Robbie. He stood behind a stand piled high with wholesome goodness. The heather grey hoodie I'd always loved on him peeked out from behind a forest green apron. His face was flushed from either the cold or excitement. I assumed both.

I'd learned that after he broke up with Nick, he decided to take some time to himself. There are only a few options available to accomplish time to oneself. Some go to a religious or spiritual center surrounded by deserts, jungles, mountaintops, or civil unrest. Some get back in touch with the land. Since Robbie was an atheist who read Richard Dawkins like the words of Jesus Christ, a farm just outside of the city was the most sensible option.

"I've been involving too many people in my life instead of involving my life in other people's. For good. To help. It's been nice getting away from everyone and everything. Learn how the world works. All you need to live is food and water. Everything else, the Earth provides," he said with a small smile. He could have sounded like a vegan, environmentalist drone but he didn't.

"You seem happy," I said.

"I am. I really am." He picked up a crate of green things and arranged them neatly on the table. "What about you? It's been a while. Since summer, right?"

"Yeah. I'm well. I'm just…thinking about stuff. I'm not on a farm. I manage to think pretty well here in the city. All this bullshit is inspiring, I suppose."

He laughed. "That's good. At least you still have that sense of humor." And he still had that crooked smile and big brown eyes. For the first time I saw him without a veil of muddled thoughts and secret lovers. I doubted he could see the same thing when looking back at me. I'd always been muddled and felt especially muddled that autumn as I waited to seal my fate in one world or the other. Could he see that? Could anyone see the ghosts and ghouls and vampires and witches and magic in my eyes or did I just look like a regulation schizophrenic?

"What did you say?" he asked. Apparently I was talking to myself.

"Um…nothing. I was just thinking. Out loud. It's my new thing." I felt compelled to tell him everything. It would have been nice to have someone outside of the Midnight Society knowing my troubles. Instead I asked, "Do you believe in magic?" Ugh. Who asks that? Life was suddenly a scene from a made for TV Christmas movie. I waited for a lousy C.G.I. star to shoot across the sky.

He looked at me like one would look at something being pulled out of thin air. "Ah, I believe in science," he said. Typical answer. "Why?"

My mouth became taffy. "I'm just wondering if anyone really does. Anymore. We know a lot about things…the world. It's hard to find people who believe in magic. Not the bible magic. Not the magic of science. Magic magic. Do people really believe in it?"

"Well, I'm sure there are some."

"Like when we talk about religion. We all secretly know what we're talking about didn't happen. Noah's Ark didn't happen. But we pretend it did."

His head tilted at an extreme angle. "What are you getting at?"

I didn't know, really. I mean, I did. I wanted to find someone who believed in genuine magic. Someone who wouldn't look at me like I was crazy when I told them I'd spent the last nine months listening to a gargoyle spin tales of wonder. And, oh yeah, that I'm a reincarnated prince from the year 500. *That's* what I think I was trying to get at.

"You don't look well," he said, coming around from the other side of the table. "You realize you've been muttering to yourself, right?"

"No. Yes…probably so." A great rumble tore through the sky. The haze of incoming storm clouds darkened it to green and then back again. Something wasn't right. "I need to go," I said as I turned and began to bolt towards Rita's. Robbie called something after me but I continued my zoom in her direction.

I had reached the end of the block when the rain began. In seconds, drizzle turned to pummeling drops the size of avocados. The storm covered the sun. Evening looked like it was upon me but I couldn't be sure. The downpour became so intense, seeing my own hands in front of me became difficult. I stopped on a corner so as not to get hit by oncoming cars. Traffic had exercised the same caution. A hand came from behind and grabbed my shoulder. Robbie pulled me into him so closely, our faces were the only things visible.

"What's happened to you?" he said loudly over the roar of nature's fury. "Where are you going?"

"You wouldn't understand," I said. What could I do, take him with me to Rita's? To him, she'd just look like an old show queen. He followed me despite my manic pleas to get off my back. When we arrived at her building the doors were appropriately locked. I rang up. Nothing. I rang again.

"Whose place is this?" Robbie asked.

"Robbie, please go. I'll talk to you later."

"Yes?" hissed a voice from the intercom. It wasn't Rita.

"Where's Rita?" I blasted into the speaker.

"She's unavailable at the moment," said the voice. "Goodbye."

"Wait a second," said Robbie. "Was that Nick?"

The mention of that name sent imaginary knives into my side. My face turned momentarily white. I braced myself against the doorframe just in case I passed out. It was Nick, but not the Nick I'd known. The hag-head was right. The cousin my former self killed five hundred years ago had definitely crept his way inside of him. "No, no, no...it can't be...he's just angry, not a ghost...no, no..." I mumbled to myself.

"Is this some kind of joke? Are you seeing Nick now?"

"Just shut up," I roared. "I'm going around back." I ran to the condemned building next door. The landlord had carefully blocked all entries to avoid squatters. New York's finest may be those in public service but its second finest are its homeless. They can find a way into practically anything. Thanks to them, the front door had become perfectly accessible. Robbie ranted behind me. He was convinced Nick and I were in cahoots to get back at him.

"This is crazy. You can't go in there by yourself," he said as I slipped inside. He followed. My autopilot took me to the back alley that connected all of the buildings on that block. The rain still poured but the high walls around us diffused its violence. Hundreds of waterfalls cascaded down the bricks and ran towards drains. I pointed to the fire escape five stories up. Robbie tried to say something but I forcefully put a finger over his lips.

"We aren't dealing with Nick, anymore. You should go," I whispered.

"You city faggots are sneaky," called Nick from the highest window.

Before I had time to look up, he was gone.

"What's he doing, Jeremy? What's going on?" Robbie asked.

Nick soon reappeared with a lifeless old waif in his arms. "She's who you were looking for?" he asked before letting Rita go. Limbs and costume jewelry flapped against giant raindrops before hitting the ground. A stream of blood and makeup joined the river towards the drain.

Robbie stood frozen in shock but I still commanded him to stay put before committing myself to the shaky iron structure above me. The fire escapes of old buildings are more for show than anything. They're comforting to look at but if an evacuation were actually necessary, the sudden plummet from five stories above would kill people faster than any fire. I made my way up, slipping and swinging like a contestant on a televised obstacle course. Nick watched from above with a grin so evil, it couldn't possibly belong to anyone but an escapee from Hell.

For his amusement, he shook the ladder just enough for me to lose my footing, but not fall. He didn't want to kill me that way. He wanted flesh on flesh, like he'd done centuries ago. I'd be tortured more than the first time he put me in the grave.

He was waiting in Rita's dim apartment. Her collection of multi-colored hurricane lamps illuminated our faces like stained glass. I could see the toll my cousin had taken on Nick's body. His eyes were bulged and bloodshot, skin clung to muscles so tightly it was almost transparent. His friends must have attributed the change to a drug problem, as possession isn't the first thing to come to people's minds.

"It really is you," he said.

"Yes," I answered…the Prince answered…we both answered.

"You know not the terrors I have endured these last centuries."

"Deservedly so."

"You killed us. You sent us there."

"You would have gone there anyway."

"No, cousin. You are mistaken. For our knowledge of the Way of Things would have far surpassed your father's. Our father's. He loved us more."

"I am not that boy anymore. I have a new body, a new life. My father is nothing like that. The old days are over. You have no business here."

"You are just as foolish as always. Those days are back. I will make it so," he growled before lunging at me.

❖

The birches were near but sunrise was nearer. Garth and Helena settled down for the day amongst scruffy pines. She remembered him saying "goodnight" to her.

Goodnight didn't have the same meaning to them as it did to humans. While the mortal version translated to "safe night," the Immortals' was congratulatory, as in their night had actually been good. Many miles were traversed and their new lives had begun to settle. Helena had a feeling the orchard would bring nothing they didn't already have. She was positive Garth secretly thought the same, that he was just humoring her. He was a good friend for trying. It would be a beautiful place to visit, though. Especially on a snowy evening. This acceptance had made for a good night.

That day, her mind raced as her body slept under the sun's cold stare. She dreamt of love and loss and the two times she'd experienced those feelings. She had no idea how lucky she was to know them. Men live their whole lives yearning to feel such things. Many fail and go through life alone and numb, cold and contented. But she had known them. In stone she had done more than many men.

She saw herself an old woman. Her hair, whatever color it was, had dried and streaked itself grey. When she looked in the mirror she wondered where her youth had gone. When Francis looked at her he wondered why she wondered. His eyes were swollen with love for her. Sometimes he'd think of her and get sick to his stomach with feelings. He kissed her ageing hair and face and she kissed his.

Together they'd made a home, a family, and memories of their own, not borrowed. Their house was filthy from children's feet and children's games. They didn't mind, though. The pair reclined and looked out at their ramshackle kingdom of spilled meals, broken toys, soiled towels, dried bouquets, love letters, and dust. It was all theirs, all created by their human hands and finally existing in their human minds.

Helena awoke from the dream and began to cry.

Our battle was quick. I wasted no time in pinning Nick to the ground. My hands clamped around his neck and tried to squeeze the life out of him. I don't know how I became so strong. My eyes seared his, helping me concentrate my strength on ending his life. He growled and tossed. For a second his eyes cleared and I saw Nick, the real Nick. Then my cousin. Then Nick. Then my cousin. Nick spoke, "Stop, please…"

I threw myself off him as he tried to fill his lungs again. I couldn't do it, not to Nick. I didn't like him but he didn't deserve to die.

"Pathetic," he said, not Nick anymore. "That is why you could not reign. You were weak. Like a woman." He stood up and rolled his shoulders, cracking every joint. "The soul in front of you killed you. The man in front of you fucked your boyfriend behind your back."

"He was *never* my boyfriend!" I bellowed. "Because your crazy ass was always in the picture ruining everything. And you're *still* in the picture but now with a freaking ghost inside your body. I'm tired of you."

"What are you waiting for? God, you are weak."

"I am not weak! I killed you once. I killed your brother. I killed my father. I've watched you scream and cry and beg for mercy but in the end, it was I who tasted blood. You were nothing but a pawn in a failed game, you piece of shit!"

He ran at me, sending me through furniture and god-knows-what. Blood surged, insides moved, and hot iron began to fill my mouth…

Someone threw Nick off of me. Another tossed him into Rita's photograph-covered brick wall. Punches and bodies flew. He was no match for the two Immortals on my side. Nick regained his footing and managed to jump out of the window. He landed like a cat on his feet. He smirked at Robbie, who was still waiting with the gnarled body of a witch. "Hey, babe," he said, before running through the vacant building and into the city.

"Jeremy, are you alright?" Garth asked, leaning over me, brushing my hair from a gash on my forehead.

"Here, drink this," Bryant said. He held out an uncrushed vile from Rita's collection. "It will stop the bleeding."

"Let's hope. I don't want you getting hungry," I grumbled. The potion burned a good burn that let me know it was working. I was up in less than a minute. "Rita..." We climbed down the escape and met Robbie.

"Jerm, what's going on?" he asked with eyes and mouth wide from shock.

"You should go," I said. "I'll find you later."

He looked at Garth. Garth looked at him. They shared something strange and uncomfortable. "Yes. I'll do that." He backed into the building and disappeared.

Bryant was kneeling next to Rita, crying. He did his best to untwist her body and lay her out like the lady she was.

"Why did he do that?" I asked Garth.

"He did not want her to help you," said someone. The masked Angel of Death was at the end of the alley. It walked towards us. "Guardian, we meet again."

"Greetings," said Garth.

"May I?" the Angel asked Bryant. He stood and let it near her body. The Angel knelt down, turned her head towards itself and gave her a deep kiss. Its hand grazed her body without shame or disgust. When it pulled away, Rita's soul came with it, lips still locked.

She finished the kiss. "Woowee," she said. "It's been a while since I've done that, let me tell you." She looked to her audience for a laugh.

I grinned.

"I guess you're here to tell me what to do next."

"I am," said the Angel.

"You're going to tell me to go see a witch, but honey, I'm the witch. So you'd better start directing souls to that broad downtown or else their gonna show up here and think this whole afterlife thing is a bunch of hooey."

"Then you know the path?"

"Those blinders are on tight, aren't they? Yes, I know. Thank you." She stood up and looked at her body. "Jesus Christ, I hadn't even put my face on yet. I'm sorry you had to see that. Bryant, darling?"

"Yes?" he said, wiping tears from his eyes.

"You're sweet to cry for an old thing like me. But you'd be even sweeter if you did something with this body."

"Would you like the traditional rites?"

"Where would you do such a thing, in the park? That'd be interesting. Just do something nice and respectful. That thing is old. Deserves to go out in style."

"Of course," he said with a smile. "Rita?"

"Yes, dear?"

"You were the only one left. The only one who knew me before I…" His tears returned with more intensity. "Everyone's dead."

Rita's soul put her arms around him. He shivered at her touch. "There, there, babyboy. It's over now. Fresh starts, right? New friends. New adventures."

The Angel had turned away and was about to take flight. Garth stopped it. "Wait!"

"Yes, Guardian?"

"How do you know it's me?"

The Angel turned. "I can sense your presence. How could I forget? This mask has not been removed since our last meeting," it said with a protective hand near the knot.

"I apologize for the offense," Garth said. "But I also want to thank you. Helena was a good friend."

The Angel stopped him before he could say any more. "No worry. I am glad for it. Your actions will never be forgotten, Garth the Guardian, Challenger of the Way of Things."

"The Way of Things is falling apart, isn't it?"

"No. The Way is changing. It is up to the few who know it to change it for the better," the Angel replied.

With one flap of its wings, it was airborne and fading into clearing night sky.

The winter sun had set early. Garth arose to a full moon; the brightest he could remember. The new fallen snow intensified its light, nearly blinding him in the first flutters of waking. When his vision cleared, he was alone. Hours prior his arms had held Helena, but now they were full of rubble. His mind was attacked with memories of Francis' tragic end.

It was happening all over again.

The King hadn't been brought down.

All of their sacrifices had been in vain.

Footprints in the snow lead towards the orchard. As he ran through the trees, he thought once again of the King. He didn't know how but he'd find a way to destroy him. That man had robbed him of everyone he'd ever loved. If there were anything virtuous about the Way of Things, vengeance would be had. He could still see the blood on his hands; hear the crushing of his skull beneath his fists. How satisfying it was. Would he be granted such satisfaction with a ghost?

The orchard was a mystical place, and the King could work great magic there. Garth had to arrive before the treacherous work could be completed. He sped faster than his legs had ever carried him, even faster than his war days when swords and fire were often at his back. As the glistening birches began to announce themselves with their stunning whiteness, the footprints stopped. Clouds darkened the sky and cast the evil King in shadow.

Garth stood before the ghost of the man who enslaved him, killed his friend, murdered the Prince, and forever changed his life. He growled, demanding that the vile spirit face his final demise head on. The shadow moved and found Garth's eyes.

Garth the Guardian was not was not met with the cold, malicious glare of the King; but the soft, beautiful gaze of a young woman.

The moon reappeared, gracing Garth with her full presence. Her skin and hair were as white as the birch bark, her figure as tall and lithe. She stood motionless, seemingly trapped in her own body. Pallid hair flew about her face and crystal tears froze in her marbled eyes and on her untouched cheeks. At last, Helena was human.

"Help me!" she screamed. "This body…I don't know how…" She didn't finish. She seemed to choke on saliva and sobs and air. Her body thrashed as the snow fell on her skin. Her arms braced her chest at the movement of her lungs. Her tongue dangled from her mouth, its wetness and weight apparently not what she expected. Wind grazed her long hair against her face and into her eyes. "No! It's too much! I should have stayed on my fountain…"

What could Garth possibly do? She was helpless, naked, and freezing. He could provide no warmth, no shelter. He was just as cold as the air that was killing her. Maybe death would the best option. Finally, she was a mortal possessing a mortal soul. She could join Francis and be happy.

His Immortal duties rang in his head. Allowing her to perish would be the antithesis of them. He was her protector. She needed to live.

Before he could reach her, she had fallen to the ground. The life was draining from her quicker than it had entered. Garth gathered her up and searched for shelter.

"Immortal," boomed a voice from the sky. "She is expiring." Garth looked up and saw the Angel of Death descending. Its huge wings scooped the air with thunderous claps.

"No! Leave us! Turn back," he yelled at the Angel.

Just like he'd been told, the Angel was blindfolded. It's head bobbed around in search of her. It laughed. "This is the Way of Things, brother. You know that."

"But this is different. She hasn't had a chance."

"Many don't; the still-born child, the victims of war. All things run their courses differently. She wasn't meant to live."

"That isn't fair! If she was not meant to live then I was not meant to be Immortal. We both can do impossible things."

"I am not a Judge, just a Messenger. I must rouse her soul from her body and lend it counsel. I wear these blinders so all are equal and my task is completed without corruption."

"She is new to this world. Help her. You have the power. As Immortals, our duty is to them."

"And *this* is my duty to them."

"You are more powerful than I. Take her somewhere safe. There is still time!"

The Angel grew irritated from the sympathetic picture Garth was drawing. "Be gone, brother. You must not interfere with the Way of Things. Let her die so I may do my work. You were not meant for this one." With a beat of its wings, it touched the ground and Helena's breath became short.

"I am tired of being told what I am and am not meant to do!" Garth screamed. A fury for the rules of the Way had been building within him for quite some time. There, in the snowy orchard, it finally showed itself. In a haze of flying snow, he jumped for the Angel. Before it even had time to realize it was being attacked, Garth had already begun to unwrap the binding over its eyes.

The Angel eventually regained ground but it was too late. Its protection against the human condition was stripped. Its eyes beheld Helena.

It saw a brand new being, hardly touched by the world, twisted and shivering in the snow. "I have never seen a death," the Angel said.

Garth had nothing further to do, even though he was prepared to do anything. The Angel picked her up and flew above the trees.

"Where are you taking her?" Garth yelled into the sky.

"To the witch in the woods. She will be safe there."

17. Variations on a Theme

Bryant left with Rita's body in a hurry. There was limited time to perform her rites. I asked Garth what they included but all he could say was, "Bryant is friendlier with the witches than I. Surely whatever he has planned will be appropriate."

Rita's apartment was an absolute wreck. I mean, it was always kind of a disaster but after that episode with Nick it looked like a refugee camp. We sifted through the surviving artifacts for anything that might be helpful but neither of us knew what to look for. Other witches would be there in the morning to claim her valuables. Then they'd wipe her existence from off the face of the Earth. Like everything else in the lives of followers of the Way, Rita would become nothing more than a memory.

"What should we do about Robbie?" I asked. I hoped he'd run home and was hiding under the bed. Or maybe drank himself into a stupor.

"I'm sure there is a charm or herb around here to help him forget," Garth said on his way into the kitchen. "I believe the Night Creatures use black rosemary to make their victims forget. Or is it white thyme?" He opened a cabinet holding hundreds of unlabeled ingredients. "We should just ask Bryant when he returns."

"No. I don't want to hide anything anymore. If we're supposed to help the Way, people need to know it exists. We'll start with him."

He stopped and clutched the filthy doorframe. His eyes concentrated on the floor.

"Are you okay?"

He perked up. "I am fine. I just find it surprising that you trust him after what happened between you. I did not know you were—"

"I ran into him earlier," I said, squirming with the uncomfortable duty of explaining forgiveness. It's a concept understood by few. "People have lapses of stupidity that hurt others. But I enjoy his company. I miss it. I think he's moved past whatever ate at him. I can, too."

"There are some things that are not forgivable."

"Yeah. But grudges should be reserved for bigger things than a twenty-year-old boy being…a twenty-year-old boy. There are worse problems in the world." I shivered from the breeze coming in from the broken window.

"Fall is here," he said as he impulsively came towards me. His hands reached out and then retracted. "I am sorry. I still forget I cannot provide much warmth."

"No," I laughed softly. "Probably not. Here…" I took off my wet shit and put on one of Rita's kimonos. It smelled like old Chanel and cigarettes. That smell would stitch itself in my sense memory forever. "How do I look?"

"I cannot decide if you are a geisha or a drag queen," he said. It was the first time I'd heard him tell a contemporary joke.

I pulled him close and placed his hands on my shoulders. At first, he tensed. I breathed deeply and he settled into wrapping himself around me. He definitely wasn't warm but he was comfortable. I felt better there. He noticed me begin to doze off in his arms.

"I am going to take you to stay with Bryant. You will be safe there," he said.

"I'm not safe anywhere, am I?"

"His lair is very secure."

"Stop calling it a lair." I thought again. "It is kind of lair-ish, isn't it?"

"You are easy to find, especially for Nick. He is not bound to the night, like I am. A Night Creature's lair will protect you."

❖

As one could guess, Bryant slept all day. Duh. But his relationship with sleep and daylight wasn't forced like Garth's. His aversion to sun made sleeping during daylight hours practical. While that giant star overhead burned cancer into our skin and boiled the oceans, he dreamt of whatever vampires dream about...probably blood and virgins and castles.

"Can I come over to your place? We need to talk." Robbie asked during a phone conversation. I'd been avoiding him because explaining the whole Angel of Death business was going to be awkward. Not to mention embarrassing, exhausting, and generally something I wished I didn't have to do. It was like coming out of the closet all over again: "Mom, I'm...I'm...a reincarnated Prince with a demonic soul-cousin trying to kill me every other day. And yeah, I might also be in love with a gargoyle. Or a Vampire."

Shit.

I looked around at Bryant's steel-trap apartment. The blue-white light from eco-friendly bulbs was giving me a headache. "No, you can't come over. I'm not staying at my place anymore," I snapped.

"Where are you staying?"

I peeked in the refrigerator for something to eat. As predicted, nothing but dead things. "I'm at a friend's. For safe keeping."

"We can get coffee."

"Yes, we can. Thing is...I'm kind of afraid to leave. Without supervision...an escort...possibly an armed tank."

"Wait, who's place are you staying at?"

"Um..."

"Is it one of those...?"

"Yes. The tall, pale one."

"That's what we need to talk about. I feel like a—"

"Crazy person? Yes, welcome to my world." I opened the freezer and found a pint of butter pecan ice cream with a note:

For you. We'll go grocery shopping tonight.

"At least it's a good flavor," I said.
"What?"

"Sorry. Nothing. Listen, the sun is going down soon and Bryant will be up. Then I can better gauge my evening."

"Are you staying with a vampire or something?"

"Something like that," I said. I could hear him grunt something related to frustration. "Don't worry. He doesn't suck my blood. This is an awkward conversation. I gotta go. I'll call you later, promise." I hung up and dug into my frozen confection.

"You're allowed to leave, you know," said Bryant. His sudden appearance nearly made me choke on a candy-coated nut.

"It's not dark yet," I coughed.

"Then don't open the shades. Besides, it was hard to sleep with all that beating around the bush," he said. He tied up his silk robe and sat at the kitchen bar across from me.

"Is it wrong for me to want a day or two of normalcy? Explaining all this isn't normal."

"Neither is living here. I don't think you'd be happy leading a normal life, anyhow."

He had a point. I had studied acting in college. I wanted my life to be just as theatrical, exulted from normalcy. As a child, I'd always gravitated towards the peculiar. From when I used to pretend to be a merkid by crossing my feet in the pool to when I pranced around the forest talking to imaginary elves, I was always looking for something out of the ordinary. Had I known being different would be so dangerous, I would have concentrated on fitting in a little better.

"How did you tell your family and friends about yourself," I asked. "Or did you fake your death like in the movies?"

Bryant laughed softly as he carefully plotted his answer. "It was about twenty-five years ago. A plague was tearing through the city. There weren't many people around to tell," he said as he nervously fumbled with the top to my ice cream container. "With the few people I had around, I became distant. Yes, the obvious confinements of my condition made socializing difficult, but I was also scared. And embarrassed. I didn't know what they'd think or if they'd believe me. I regret that." He looked at me to see what effect his story had had. "Tell your friends. They aren't your friends if they don't believe you."

"You're right. But I'm going to hold off on my family. For them, it's already weird enough that I kiss men," I said.

"Are they supportive?"

"Oh, yes. They're fine. It's just different. Unexpected. It's something *they* need to deal with. I've got my own shit." I snatched the ice cream cap back from him. "Like getting something *real* to eat. As much as I love ice cream, I can guarantee it won't be in my system in about 40 minutes, if you know what I mean."

"That's crass," he scoffed.

"Shut up. You drink blood."

He rolled his eyes. "I think we should be safe to open the blinds now."

I walked over to the two giant blinds and prepared to pull their industrial-strength cords. Before I did, I turned to him, "You have friends now, right?"

He grinned widely. "Yes. There are more Immortals here than you think. You just have to know how to spot them. It's been nice to meet Garth. Neither of us were meant to lead this kind of life, but it's the hand we've been dealt." He met me at the window. "Here, let me help. They're heavy."

The blinds rose and downtown sprawled below us. The sky was still painted with the slightest hint of pink, which slipped away in a matter of seconds. No matter how long I'd lived in the city or from what vantage point I'd seen it, the skyline could always entrance. Still does. Bryant's smile dropped and his eyes became more serious. "What's the date?" he asked.

"Um...I don't know," I said. I really didn't. Time had become slosh. "Mid October, I think."

"Must be. Do you know why we celebrate Halloween?"

"I watched a History Channel documentary on it once. It's like an old, pagan holiday or something."

"Yes. Souls can always show themselves to you if they choose, but they have no choice on Halloween. The veils that keep mortals from seeing spirits are thin then. It has something to do with gravity and moons and, well, I don't fully understand it." His hands tilted my face toward the street. "Do you see anything unusual out there?"

All I saw were crack whores, garbage pickers, and NYU freshmen trying to get into the bar across the street, "No. Nothing unusual." I turned back to him. "Am I missing something?"

"It's easy for beings like me to see the spirits. I see many more than usual." I watched him try and count the souls he saw. He got overwhelmed and took a gulp of vile-tasting fear. "Let's hope the veils lift sooner than later so *you* can see the ones who might be a threat."

I took the same sour swig from his fear-cup and announced, "I want a burrito."

❖

"So, you're an old soul," said Robbie. We were walking through the park, enjoying colorful trees and warm apple ciders.

"Yes," I said.

"This is a lot."

"You don't have to believe me."

"I wouldn't if I didn't see someone get thrown out of a window. And a vampire. And a rock man."

"That'll do it."

"This is challenging a lot of my beliefs. There's no such thing as—"

I stopped him. "That we know of. We aren't able to explain *everything* yet. The more you question it, the crazier you'll get. So take a deep breath. Yes, Virginia, there is a Santa Claus. Actually, there's not…but possibly flying reindeer." There were also invisible ghosts haunting my wake but I quickly shook the thought from my mind so I could function like a typical person and not go running to a church for sanctuary.

The pensive expression that had been plastered across his face for the past forty-five minutes cracked. A smile shone through. "So, are you like in love with him? Garth?"

"I…uh—"

"Then there's the other one—"

"Bryant," I said. "And, I don't know. There's something very familiar with Garth. There are the obvious limitations to any feelings I may have. And Bryant is—"

"You don't have to explain yourself," he cut in.

"I guess they're called feelings for a reason," I said. "Feel. Not speak."

He looked around at all the people enjoying the same beautiful fall day we were. He observed a young couple with a toddler, a first date chatting on a bench, an old woman fingering her wedding ring while looking out over the water. "You know, there are many types of love," he said. "And I think it's possible to have more than one great love. You can love many people at the same time, in different ways and capacities."

"Are you thinking of becoming a polygamist?" I asked.

"No. I'm talking about humanity, about life. To limit us to these boxes and rules is insulting. We're capable of feeling so much. There's so much love to be felt, so much love out there." He stopped us from walking and turned to me. "I'm not trying to excuse the way I acted this winter. There's a difference between experiencing love and being a dick. I was a dick."

I smirked toward the ground and placed my hand on the small of his back. We kept strolling.

Pain spread across his face with his next thought. "So do you have to kill Nick or something?" he asked.

"I don't want to," I assured him. "But we don't know. We aren't sure what to do."

"Nick's still in there," he said. "He isn't possessed all the time. The Nick I know is still helping plan a big Halloween party at that old church on Sixth. He's kind of a professional homosexual nowadays."

"What?"

"It's for that nightlife magazine he interned at. They have a big party every year. He invited everyone on his friend list. Maybe he'll be normal Nick there and you can talk to him."

"On Halloween? Something tells me he won't be."

"Oh. But maybe he will. And your friends can come, too. Everyone will be in costume. They'll blend right in."

I always knew Robbie was smart but that was downright genius. "You want to go?" I asked.

"I was thinking about it. Not that I'm seeing him again. I'm not. We're friends now. And it's supposed to be really fun," he said, brightly. "Will that be awkward?"

"Not at all. Start planning your costume."

Garth and Bryant whispered as we climbed the stairs to the roof. Bryant had convinced the doorman we were attending a Halloween party in the building. Being that it was All Hallows Eve-Eve, the likelihood of spotting a costumed twenty-something in the village was great. Garth had no problem passing as a grade "A" party attendee. It was his first time in a residential building as a guest. The elevator was apparently too much to introduce him to, so we used the stairs (all twenty flights) to get us to the top.

"Is there a reason you've dragged us here?" I asked in between pants of exhaustion. Their whispers drowned out my question. "Hello!" Finally, I elicited a change in attention.

"I don't know if it'll make a difference to you," said Bryant.

"We wanted to find a good vantage point," Garth added.

"To see Washington Square Park."

"It's down the street. Why don't we walk through? NYU's cleaned up most of the drug addicts," I offered.

"I don't think that's a good idea. Remember what I told you about Halloween?" asked Bryant.

Of course I had. I'd been living with the fear of ghosts roaming whatever hall, staircase, street, or bathroom I happened to be in. I even developed a habit of walk-running practically everywhere, thinking I could avoid them. To the layman, I must have looked like I was on the verge of pissing or crapping myself. All the time.

"Washington Square has a long, death-ridden history," he continued.

"Well, NYU has a *huge* suicide rate. Have you looked at the tuition costs?" I said with my usual lack of sensitivity.

"It was once a potters field. People were hanged on its trees and buried under its stone. Before that it was an Indian burial ground."

"That's disturbing."

"It's always a bit haunted, but this time of year especially so."

"And with the current situation, probably even more," Garth said.

We reached the door to the roof. "So this is just for the two of you? I won't see anything out of the ordinary?"

Bryant shook his head and opened the door. Below us Fifth Avenue met the park, which looked just like it should at night. The arch was majestically illuminated with the newly renovated fountain turned off for the evening behind it. Humans still milled about, as usual. Drifters sang on their guitars, old men played chess and kids got high. That park never sleeps. I was impressed by nothing more than a new aerial view of my city. The Immortals stood next to me in awe.

"I cannot believe it," said Garth.

"There are so many," Bryant agreed.

"Much more than usual. There is Dark Magic at work here."

"What's it like?" I asked.

"The souls are congregating. It is some kind of rally," Garth said. His eyes were fixed to the open space just beyond the arch.

I tried to see what they saw. I strained my eyes and wished Immortal sight to them but all I got was a headache. Soon, though, something became visible. A young man stood on a bench, preaching to nobody in particular. The pedestrians passed by with their usual blinders, trying not to provoke the crazy person. "Can either of you see that man over there? On the bench. He's yelling something," I asked them.

Bryant stood on the ledge of the building and peered off. "The young guy," he said.

Garth joined him, "It is Nick. He is speaking to the souls."

"He must be readying them for tomorrow," I said. "He knows we're coming."

"Where are we going tomorrow?" asked Garth.

"To a Halloween party. I know for sure he'll be there. I thought it'd be the perfect time to act. But let's just do it now," I said, running for the door.

Bryant was in front of it before I could reach the handle. "That isn't wise. We have no plan," he said. "That is what I wanted to discuss this evening."

"His forces are great," Garth said.

"I have been conferencing with other followers of the Way. They will come to our aid if needed. Garth's reputation will lure any Immortal into our fight. We can gain strength."

Garth was embarrassed but it was true. "Even so, we have no sacrifice for the Demon."

My heart sank. I'd been avoiding thinking about that part since we'd spoken to the head.

"That isn't true," Bryant said. "We have Nick."

"No," I blurted. "He doesn't deserve that."

"He is trying to kill you."

"He isn't. He's possessed."

"It's called a sacrifice. By definition, it shouldn't feel perfect. We need to sacrifice an innocent."

"And that's what he is. He's innocent. His actions are not his."

"I understand that," Bryant said. He guided me back to Garth. "I've been thinking about this. It wouldn't be fair to take someone unsuspecting, completely uninvolved. Giving Nick to the Demon will be the most direct way to end this. Your cousin's soul will be in him. There will be no chance for him to escape."

"But without a soul, his body will die and we'll be responsible. No, *I'll* be responsible because the two of you are Immortal and never have to face judgment," I said.

Bryant's face contorted with uneasy thoughts. "What if we can salvage him?" he suggested. Garth sneered, seeming to know where the conversation was going. "After the Demon takes Nick's soul, I'll take his body. With my blood in him, he can live on."

"You want to turn him?" I asked.

"I don't want to but it will save him. He'll have the opportunity to live. Your conscience can be cleared."

We silently processed the possibility. Cars grumbled below us. Nick's tirade echoed faintly through the arch. It all seemed terribly complicated. I had to speak up. "Why don't we just give my soul to the Demon? That's obviously what would work best. Then Bryant can turn me."

"No!" they both yelled.

"The Way would be healed, Nick would still be alive, and so would I."

"Hardly," said Garth. "I refuse to let that happen."

"Agreed. I'm not granting this existence to you." Bryant said. He was on the verge of getting weepy again.

"But you'd give it to him?" I argued.

"Yes, because he's awful!" he said. "You don't deserve this!" One tear fell down his face. "You will lead a normal life full of sunlight and love and experiences and you will die when you are old. When your life is up. You will be with your friends and family in Heaven, not trapped here and reviled for all eternity. Got it?"

Garth grunted in agreement. "Then it is decided. Tomorrow, Nick will be the sacrifice."

❖

For the amount weighing on my mind, I slept easily that night. Mere hours separated us from fate. Evil souls would go back to Hell, an innocent soul would be sacrificed, a man would become a monster, and I could continue living. I hoped I was worth all of the fuss.

But it wasn't just for me. It was for the Prince. He was worth it. My victory would be a victory for all of those unnoticed and underserved atrocities committed since taboo came into existence. Every sneer, every roll of the eyes, every harsh word, every raised hand against my people fueled me for what would go down in the old church on Halloween night.

Yes, my people. We are not a race or a religion or regional clan. We come from all walks of life; in all shapes, sizes, colors, heights, weights, sexes, and forms—we exist. But our common thread surpasses those things. It runs deeper than hair, than skin, than speech, than beliefs, than thought, and into the very thing that makes us live: our hearts. All humans have them but only some are chastised for using them, for feeling the most primal and important impulses our species can feel. My friends, my lovers, my community, *my people* were worth it.

"You slept well," said a voice at the end of my bed. The sun poured in on what I thought were two Angels watching over me. When I reached for my glasses, I saw them clearer. Not Angels, but two souls. A man and a woman stood at my feet. "Do you know us?" asked the woman, "From your dreams?"

"Helena? Francis?" I croaked, still groggy and slightly incoherent. She was as beautiful as Garth had described her. Francis looked just as warm.

"We have come to speak with you about your plan," Francis said.

"It will not work," said Helena.

My lips began to quiver. "But the hag, she said—"

"The one you call Nick. He is not strong enough to awaken the Old Magic," she whispered.

"His soul is weakened by your cousin's presence. He is tainted." Francis said.

"Why have you come to me? Souls are supposed to help the Immortals. Why haven't you gone to Garth?" I cried.

"We have," she said. "We come to you also."

"To prepare you for when the time comes," he finished.

"So I have to…"

"Quiet, Prince. Our time here is brief. You must ensure the sacrifice heals the Way of Things," she said.

With a slight bow, they dissolved into the air.

It was up to me. My newfound pride had to be re-channeled from living for others, to dying for them. I didn't even know how to begin justifying my sacrifice. Did people even do that anymore? I thought martyrdom went out of fashion with the Bubonic Plague. Despite the fact I was so young, was it possible my mortal experience was over? Was I full of life to the point of ending it? When an old person dies, people remark on how complete their life was.

What if it wasn't?

What if they had much more to do?

If we're all so different and unique, our capacities for life should be equally so. Maybe a person can reach their limit at a young age.

I was no longer the rainbows-out-my-ass, typical twenty-something little shit I'd been in January. I'd been shown things no human had ever seen. How could I possibly continue living in a world that's wonder had been exposed? Even though most of my experiences with magic had been stressful, terrifying, and generally unpleasant, I was lucky, at least, to know the truth. As one of the only witnesses to the Way of Things, it was my responsibility to use my knowledge and heal it.

The next day I finished my costume, confirmed my friends' attendance at another party, casually checked in with my parents, and sat quietly in my room. I watched the setting sun cast weird shadows on my world. I knew it would be the last I saw of it. I took a mental photograph and then left to meet Garth on a rooftop, just as I had done almost every night for eight months.

I wouldn't have had it any other way.

18. Deep Magic

I figured if it was going to be my last Halloween, my costume needed to be nothing short of amazing. I arrived at Bryant's apartment painted gold and donning dramatic eyes, cheeks, and lips. "What are you?" he asked.

"I'm King Tut," I said, adjusting my headdress. "I figured this is an ode to my two alter egos. I see you've embraced the vampire thing tonight."

"There's no better time," he said as he dribbled faux blood from his lips. He was dressed in Victorian blacks and burgundies. There was something terribly sexy about that fetishized version of him. Would one last romp be *that* terrible on the night of my death? "Garth's on the roof. He's in a weird mood."

As usual, Garth was perched on the edge of the building, looking over the city. "Are you stressed out about what to wear?" I said. "We can grab you a sailor hat on the way if you'd like."

He obligatory-laughed at me. "You look good," he said. "You are rightfully royal this evening."

I originally hadn't planned on mentioning my Christmas Carol-like visit that morning, but I was curious. "When was the last time you saw Helena?"

He turned around with defenses up. "Why do you ask?"

"Just wondering," I clucked, chickening out.

"I haven't seen her since she became human. The Angel took her to safety with the hag in the woods. By the time I got there, she had already left. I hear she lived her life quite fully."

Case closed. He wanted to move on.

"Oh. Why didn't you go after her?" I pressed.

"Humans need to be with humans. So they can do their work here on Earth. So they can live their lives on their own. Free will. After we aid you, we will do the same. We have meddled enough in your world." The eyes under his raised brows looked deeply at me. "I did not go after her because I cared for her.

Bryant coughed to catch our attention. "The church has many secret passageways. In the seventies they were used for sex and drug use, but tonight they'll be used to find our way belowground," he instructed.

"Where to, exactly?" I asked.

"Well, we're certainly not traveling all the way into the Underworld to summon the Demon, but we'll need to get close. We can lure Nick into one of the abandoned subway tunnels for the offering."

"The moon is getting high. We should utilize every hour of evening that is given to us," decided Garth.

Bryant agreed. "The others will be meeting there soon."

❖

Walking through the streets instead of above them with my Immortal friends was exhilarating. I flaunted them like new shoes or a killer haircut. Garth beamed through his occasional self-consciousness. "I cannot believe I have never thought of doing this before," he said.

"Awesome costume, man!" hollered a drunk guy. "Can we get a picture with you?" Garth looked at the camera like it was alien weaponry. I'd forgotten to mention that New Yorkers treat Halloween like a day at a Disney park. Pictures must be taken with every possible character, sometimes even video. Signatures are not required unless asking for a number or closing out a bar tab.

Among the unwelcome photogs was my unwelcome admirer, Robbie. I immediately began scolding him: "What are you doing here? I told you not to—"

Familiar faces popped their costumed heads through the crowd. Asher, Dan, and Meg, timidly smiled at my supernatural cohorts and me. "I thought you were all going to the party uptown?" I asked like I wasn't standing next to anyone/thing peculiar.

"I told them to come. We all wanted to be here for you," Robbie said. He grabbed my pinky finger and squeezed. "Don't try and talk us out of it."

I cursed under my breath before greeting them with stiff hugs. I tried to appear grateful but I couldn't have been more terrified for them. Introductions were appropriately weird. Meg looked at Bryant and impulsively said, "You're scary." His strange eyes looked sharply back at her. The color from her head drained, which was his cue to cut the act. A warm smile spread across his face sending her into uncomfortable laughter that may have actually been the precursor to a panic attack.

"I'm sorry," announced Dan. "Is anyone going to acknowledge how bizarre this is or are we going to pretend that these are his friends from summer camp? I mean, honestly."

"It is very strange," Garth said. He was the last person I expected to speak up. I thought he'd trail behind and grumble to himself for most of the night. Well at least until we needed to make a sacrifice. "This kind of union of worlds is very rare so…" he trailed off trying to think of something poetic. Instead he opted for the truth, "…so enjoy it while you can because it will probably never happen again. Let us get going."

After a brief stint in line, we entered the sanctuary of the old church. That cavernous space was one of the last giant dance clubs in New York. Its several levels of bars, lounges and dance floors were playgrounds for debauchery. A spectrum of lights blurred features, and sweet smelling smoke poured from hissing machines to mask the pungent smell of horny men. The costumes ran from barely there to permit-worthy construction sites. "Where are your friends?" I asked Bryant and Garth.

"They're everywhere," Bryant replied. His eyes danced from corner to corner.

We stood like Amish tourists in Tokyo.

Asher, without much knowledge on the situation at hand, critiqued us (as usual). "To seem less conspicuous, perhaps we should dance. Or drink."

"Yes, do that," I said. "We're going to survey the area real quick."

My human friends made their way to one of the overflowing bars as we maneuvered through the masses. "See that stairwell," yelled Bryant, pointing to a far corner. "It leads to the basement. The passageways to the tunnels are down there. When Nick gets here, that's where we need to lure him." The music was absolutely roaring and we strained to hear every word one another said.

A new song by that week's gay icon seared through the speakers. The boys went wild, like feeding time at a zoo. The entire club seized as the first eight bars of music pummeled us into unwilled dancing. Finding Nick and getting him in that basement wasn't going to be easy.

The crowd swelled with the arrival of more guests. From the looks on Bryant and Garth's faces, these weren't your average attendees. With a sudden cool rush over my exposed shoulders, I could finally see them. Spirits floated around every mortal in search of us.

The gays however, were unfazed. The sensual beat, the glitter, the booze, the sweat, and the thickly pheromoned air put them into a trance that wouldn't end until the lights went up at 4 a.m. Bodies writhed against bodies, smearing makeup and scratching skin. God, I wished I were lost in that daze instead of stressing out about which limb the Demon would devour first.

As I tried to join my brethren, Garth's cold hand grabbed me. He pushed me behind him, bore his teeth, and hissed words that sounded as threatening as they did foreign. He commanded the Immortals to ready themselves for the impending conflict with Nick's band of ghosts.

Dedicated to the party as they were, the gays couldn't help but notice the arising conflict between what they thought were just some rowdy partygoers. Was there really a fight going down in one of *their* establishments? Fists weren't meant to fly unless they were pumping to a decent beat. One man hollered for a bouncer then returned to his dancing. Security soon proved useless against guests with real fangs and ghosts made of real plasma. Nervousness rippled through the mortals, who seemed to sense something was a little off about that Halloween party. Claws came out and voices screamed at the highest possible decibel.

The attendees began their flee to the streets but the music and lights continued to blare. "What the hell is in these drinks?" hollered a brawny man dressed in gladiator gear.

A queen in Jackie O. drag grabbed his hand and rushed him toward the door. "I'm tweaking out. Let's go."

As the party drained itself of humans, the Immortals could safely face off against the ghosts and ghouls Nick had recruited. Meg, Asher, and Dan weren't much help in battle. They did their part by following the crowd to the street and convincing everybody that the crazy things they were seeing were the result of drugs in the fog machine.

Garth picked me up and threw me behind a bar. "Stay here," he commanded before jumping back into the scuffle. Surely whatever waited at the end of his fist would not be recovering. I peered my head over the sticky counter and spotted Nick, eagerly searching the crowd for me. It was obvious the real Nick had picked out the costume: sexy Harry Potter. Short shorts and a loose tie paired with round glasses and disheveled hair. It was probably the least threatening costume for someone looking for blood as eagerly as he was. Had my cousin any say in the dressings, Nick would be carrying a pitchfork. A real one. As his eyes scanned the room, he demanded a gruesome cohort help him in his efforts. The ghoul grumbled and set out on the hunt for me.

If I was going to act, I had to do it then. Garth had conveniently placed me near the stairwell door. All I had to do was make a mad dash and get into the cellar before Nick could see me. I grabbed a bottle, counted to three, and ran like the wind.

Just before hitting the doorway, Nick's minion had me in its clutches. I don't even know what breed of evil it was but it was ugly. The thing screeched in Nick's direction, probably alerting his master of a successful catch. My bottle came down over its head before the last horrid sound could escape its mouth. I'd never been so glad to be in possession of peach schnapps.

It was no wonder the club had been shut down numerous times for mysterious deaths and drug overdoses. Dangerous nooks and crannies were so easily assessable; they might as well have had neon arrows pointing toward them. I imagined corpses rotting for days before an unfortunate club promoter stumbled upon them while looking for extra postcards.

As soon as I closed the basement door behind me, I began tumbling down the rickety stairs into a box of plastic cups. The florescent lighting buzzed and flickered like it should near the climax of any story. The storage room was stocked with every kind of booze imaginable. Were circumstances different, a chorus of angels would have marked my arrival in such a room. Behind the warped shelving and twenty bottles of house gin, I could see a wooden door. In order to reach it, the shelf had to be removed. Since I didn't have my forklift with me, I simply turned the shelf over to grant me access. It was a real travesty for alcohol consumers everywhere.

Had diva number two not been bumping on the sound system upstairs, the shattering of hundreds of glass bottles would have been rather telling as to where I was. I kicked my way through debris and opened the door.

"Dammnit!" I screamed, and then kicked an unbroken handle of vodka. It was nothing more than an old cupboard. The shelving I'd just destroyed was its 2.0.

"That's not the right door," Bryant said from behind me.

"I know. Obviously," I said. "What are you doing down here?"

"I was going to ask you the same thing."

"Bryant, I'm…I'm the one meant to be sacrificed. Nick won't be enough."

I heard another crash in another part of the basement. We both ran for it. Broken boards lay in a heap next to a thin opening in the brick wall. *That* was the passage I'd been looking for. I needed to get down there before *whoever* broke down the door.

"Wait!" Bryant called after me. "We don't know who's down there."

"Even more reason to get there first."

We ran through the dark passages, holding cell phones as torches. The ground turned from cement, to stone, to dirt, to a watery mixture of everything. The tunnel rattled from the speeding trains around us. "We need to get lower," Bryant said. We searched out ladders and stairways to continue our descent. When we met a dead end, we tried another hallway. If there was a door, we opened it. If it was locked, we broke it down. Our navigation was occasionally aided by a distant clamor ahead of us. That may have made getting lost less terrifying but it made meeting our leader even more so. In the pit of my stomach, I knew it was Nick. He must have had his own scheme in mind. I reached behind me for Bryant's hand. Soon, I could tell we were deep under the city. The air was thin and hot. The subways that had once deafened us were reduced to merely a hum.

"Why do these tunnels exist?" I asked.

"Construction. Abandoned train lines. Who knows. This city is practically resting on a block of Swiss cheese," he whispered. "Shine your light over here. I felt something."

He guided my hand towards the wall and found wiring. "There must be electric running through here," I squealed. My hands searched for a switch.

A voice whispered behind us.

"That's the Sacred Language," Bryant declared in a hush.

"It is," said the voice. I shone my phone in its direction and found Nick. "The Demon has been summoned."

"Run!" commanded Bryant. I ran forward, barely allowing my miniscule light to illuminate what lay before me. I slid in the muck and lost my headdress to the tunnels below.

The air became cooler and the Earth itself grumbled. The clicking of nails and muffled grumbles from my dreams barreled toward us. I hysterically scratched at the wall for light. I found success. With a loud clunk, electric buzzed and illuminated one dim bulb after another. The chain reaction started with the fixture above my head and continued down the hallway, revealing the horrific surprise at the end of the corridor.

Garth crouched in front of the Demon as it slowly approached him. Bryant and I raced to meet him as Nick stood behind and cackled.

We'd barely taken three steps when the Demon lifted its talons and ripped open a mouth of razor teeth. Inky blood poured from the crevice it roared through, "Who calls me?"

"It is I," replied Garth.

I tried to stop him but Bryant took me in his arms as the Demon let out another roar.

"I am Garth, Guardian of Mortals and Challenger of the Way of Things," he announced like an ordained title.

"Yes," growled the Demon. "I remember you, conjurer of Deep Magic. Those powers are all but forgotten."

"I am here to restore balance."

"With what soul, Guardian? I ate it, I did. It rots deep in the hollows of the Earth. You have nothing left." It laughed. Nick heightened his own snickers to meet the thing's volume.

"And," Garth began over their noise, "to send this soul to Hell once and for all."

The Demon stopped and uttered a summons from antiquity. Nick fell to the ground and slid to its feet. The Demon picked him up with a bloody claw and held him to Garth for confirmation. He endorsed my cousin with a nod.

"This is a weak soul. It does no magic," bellowed the Demon. It threw Nick into the wall. He fell limply to the ground.

"Then take me," Garth said. "An Immortal offering himself, his whole being, will be strong enough. I am sure of it."

I collapsed in Bryant's grip and wept so deeply, no sounds came forth.

"You dare?" hissed the Demon.

"I do," Garth said.

"That has never been done, Guardian."

"I know."

The Demon purred with curiosity. It looked skyward and asked a question in a dead language. Bryant translated into my ear: "This Immortal seeks to bring down wandering souls and seal the cracks between worlds. For this he offers his existence. Do you accept his sacrifice?"

"No!" I screamed. Bryant held me tighter.

The Way replied with a deep tremor. The Demon grinned. "It is done," it said. "The Challenger will challenge the Way no more…" It reared up in preparation to devour Garth.

"Wait," Garth commanded. He turned to me. "This is for you. This is for all of us."

He didn't even get a chance to turn around and meet fate in the face. As the Demon was about to come down on him, Garth exploded into billions of particles of dust.

The Demon landed on the ground with a boom. "That one was mine!" it screamed to the Way. "That one was mine!" The floor shook once more, and then split. A light blasted through the crack and claimed the monster. A cold wind swept by us as the souls of the damned were sucked down behind it.

The last one to go down came from inside of Nick. His limp body heaved itself into the air. It contorted into gruesome shapes before falling into a jumbled heap of lifeless limbs. Nick, not my cousin, flickered eyeballs from under half-closed lids like someone experiencing the most horrible of dreams.

My world went dark. Every nightmare I'd ever had rushed past me and locked itself in Hell. I too felt myself slipping, like a toy boat towards an open drain. Bryant roped me in with his strong arms. His cold lips pressed through my hair onto my scalp, sending secret words into my brain. They came out like a melody without being set to music, lulling me into a sleep that was as clear and cool as his eyes. There were no visions or feelings or fears in that moment, just my soul and I taking a well-deserved retreat in preparation for the next leg of my life.

19. The Return of the King

The hospital room was expectedly bleak. The muted colors reminded me more of bile and pus than serenity and well-being. My gold face was turned a violent red from harsh soaps and my royal garb abandoned for a flakey hospital gown. A deep, clinical depression washed over me as I brewed in the foreignness of my sterilized skin, the crispy sheets and my memory-less brain. What upset me the most was not that I couldn't recall how I ended up there, but that I'd ended up there at all. Garth wouldn't have let that happen. Garth would have taken me somewhere anonymous, somewhere where I didn't have to face realities like gay bashings and breakups and death. Garth would let me live in his faerie tale. Garth...

I couldn't bring to mind all of the events in the tunnel. The sequence, the reasoning, and the visual of his destruction melded into nothing more than a feeling that forced my body into and intense, weepy catharsis. Both versions of my soul cried in that bed. Both love affairs were mourned. Both of his sacrifices were scraped deeply onto my insides, forming wounds that would never clot or scab or fade away.

A dry hand grasped my forearm. "You okay, Bub?" my father asked. He hadn't called me that since I was a child. Or maybe he had. Every time I'd seen or spoken to him or my mother, I'd been distant. I wondered how much I'd actually heard them say in the past year. Their presence at the end of my journey marked my return to reality.

My father's lips tightened as he tried to hold back tears that parental concern—no, parental *love* had prompted. To see his son laying so feebly in a cold hospital room was unsettling. What scenario had he constructed to explain my injuries? The tears he cried were the same tears he'd shed after I came out of the closet. They weren't tears of anger for having a faggot son or tears mourning the end of our family name. Most parents don't cry for those reasons. They may say they do but they don't. They cry out of fear. Their tears acknowledge that their children will face adversity in a world that only pretends to be accepting.

This was a foreign sight for the soul inside of me. His father didn't have the capacity for love that mine did. His father was the adversary my father was afraid of. As I watched dad cry for me, I felt the Prince squirm inside. He flinched with dread and burned with anger. But for the first time I felt in control of myself. "No," I told the Prince. "He's not like that. Those days are over."

"You're not coming back, are you?" Robbie asked me. We were walking through the state park near my parent's house. Mom, Dad, and the dogs kept a few yards in front of us. Seeing Robbie was a welcome break from the much needed coddling my family had been providing. The *incident*, as they called it, was still not entirely clear to them. When pressed for information, I usually had a semi-breakdown that granted me a few days of peace before more questions edged their way into casual conversation. The emotional ruptures were attributed to a combination of being unable to deal with loss and the stress of trying to figure out what version of the truth was acceptable to my wonderful suburban family. I tried to paint myself as the victim of a hate crime instead of a crazy person trying to sacrifice himself to a Hell beast. One route would bring me sympathy and the other would bring me to an institution. I chose the first option.

"I don't know if I can go back yet," I said. "I don't think I'm ready for that city again. Not yet, anyway." I took in the tall pines and the unseasonably warm winter sun.

"Maybe it's not ready for you yet, either. Your friends managed to lead a whole club full of gays to believe they were hallucinating. I think the club is under investigation."

"You didn't feel obligated to tell everyone the truth about their visions?"

"People already think I'm weird. Now it's their turn. Let's take baby steps in revealing the Way," he said. His elbow grazed my arm in a slight act of intimacy. "So you're not going crazy at home like you thought you would?"

"Surprisingly, no. I love it here. It's my home. I'm going to stay a while and figure out what I want to do."

"What do you think that is? Still want to act?"

"Absolutely not. I don't need any more attention called to myself, thank you." I started doing that thing where I let my eyes retreat to someplace else, hoping I'd disappear instead of divulging personal information. But Robbie was my friend, I could tell him. "I think I'm going to write. I have some interesting things to say, I think."

"Interesting, bizarre…"

I gave him a slight punch in the arm. "Hey, it's true."

"I know," he laughed. "I didn't say it wasn't. I think that's a great idea."

I smiled warmly at his dark brown eyes. They knew and loved me well. "Thank you for coming to visit," I said.

"Well I just wanted to make sure you're okay. I've missed you."

I'd missed him, too. My head nodded down to his shoulder.

"I also wanted to offer my help, if you need it," he said, turning slightly red.

"What, because Garth is gone you think I need a replacement?" The mention of that name, again, swelled my face and eyes with sadness. He let me brew in it for a second before I breathed the feelings back into the pit of my stomach. "I don't need protection, sir."

"I know. You're very capable. Now that I think of it, you've met your protection quota for your lifetime."

"Two lifetimes, actually."

"Yes, two. If a bullet comes your way, I'm going to duck. You're on your own from now on."

"Deal." I let out a genuine chuckle, ridding my eyes of their remaining sad glossiness.

My hand took his and we joined the rest of my family on a trek through sandy trails and along iron-stained creeks. Was I meant to be there, in that forest? Maybe I should have been in the grandest city on Earth? Did I belong in 2009 or fifteen hundred years prior? Was I destined to be with him, a former lover? A new best friend? With my family? Maybe a vampire? A monster? A man? I didn't know. How did a bunch of kids walk back through a wardrobe and resume life as…well, a bunch of kids? My childhood heroes couldn't have got along without medication or therapy or ending it all, right? Maybe they couldn't cope but I would. I had to. Life after magic had to stay just as magical.

The rules in which I'd once believed our world to exist within had been broken. The confines of old beliefs would do nothing for me anymore. No ancient witch or winged creature could tell me how to live and die, for that knowledge is too unique to harness. Each man's course is different. Each man's existence must be important. Time's been slipping through our fingers since the moment we first became conscious. There's no time left for wasting time.

The souls around me understand that. I look around at the people in my life and I don't feel so crazy. The pieces of Garth that blew to the wind on that Halloween night were dispersed into them.

They think in ways no modern souls can.

They're wise beyond the ages their bodies suggest.

They guard me after the sun goes down *and* while it blazes over our heads.

They count our love in years when they should be counting in centuries.

They may not realize these things but I do.

For the hands that I so often hold now are hands I know well, hands that are no longer set in stone.

The End

About the Author

Jeremy grew up in South Jersey, where his primary life goal was to become a mermaid. When that proved impossible, he decided the next best thing would be to move to New York City and study theater at Marymount Manhattan College. He lived an actor's life for several years before he realized he'd be more satisfied as a writer. And he was. Besides fiction, he dabbles in essays, screenwriting, and illustration.

He shares an apartment in Manhattan with his best friends and a strange little dog. *In Stone* is his first novel.

Soliloquy Titles From Bold Strokes Books

Timothy by Greg Herren. *Timothy* is a romantic suspense thriller from award-winning mystery writer Greg Herren set in the fabulous Hamptons. (978-1-60282-760-8)

In Stone: A Grotesque Faerie Tale by Jeremy Jordan King. A young New Yorker is rescued from a hate crime by a mysterious someone who turns out to be more of a *something*. (978-1-60282-761-5)

The You Know Who Girls: Freshman Year by Annameekee Hesik. As they begin freshman year, Abbey Brooks and her best friend, Kate, pinky swear they'll keep away from the lesbians in Gila High, but Abbey already suspects she's one of those you-know-who girls herself and slowly learns who her true friends really are. (978-1-60282-754-7)

The Secret of Othello by Sam Cameron. Florida teen detectives Steven and Denny risk their lives to search for a sunken NASA satellite—but under the waves, no one can hear you scream... (978-1-60282-742-4)

Andy Squared by Jennifer Lavoie. Andrew never thought anyone could come between him and his twin sister, Andrea...until Ryder rode into town. (978-1-60282-743-1)

OMGqueer edited by Radclyffe and Katherine E. Lynch. Through stories imagined and told by youth across America, this anthology provides a snapshot of queerness at the dawn of the new millennium. (978-1-60282-682-3)

Sara by Greg Herren. A mysterious and beautiful new student at Southern Heights High School stirs things up when students start dying. (978-1-60282-674-8)

Boys of Summer edited by Steve Berman. Stories of young love and adventure, when the sky's ceiling is a bright blue marvel, when another boy's laughter at the beach can distract from dull summer jobs. (978-1-60282-663-2)

Street Dreams by Tama Wise. Tyson Rua has more than his fair share of problems growing up in New Zealand—he's gay, he's falling in love, and he's run afoul of the local hip-hop crew leader just as he's trying to make it as a graffiti artist. (978-1-60282-650-2)

me@you.com by K.E. Payne. Is it possible to fall in love with someone you've never met? Imogen Summers thinks so because it's happened to her. (978-1-60282-592-5)

Swimming to Chicago by David-Matthew Barnes. As the lives of the adults around them unravel, high school students Alex and Robby form an unbreakable bond, vowing to do anything to stay together— even if it means leaving everything behind. (978-1-60282-572-7)

Speaking Out edited by Steve Berman. Inspiring stories written for and about LGBT and Q teens of overcoming adversity (against intolerance and homophobia) and experiencing life after "coming out." (978-1-60282-566-6)

365 Days by K.E. Payne. Life sucks when you're seventeen years old and confused about your sexuality, and the girl of your dreams doesn't even know you exist. Then in walks sexy new emo girl, Hannah Harrison. Clemmie Atkins has exactly 365 days to discover herself, and she's going to have a blast doing it! (978-1-60282-540-6)

Cursebusters! by Julie Smith. Budding psychic Reeno is the most accomplished teenage burglar in California, but one tiny screw-up and poof!—she's sentenced to Bad Girl School. And that isn't even her worst problem. Her sister Haley's dying of an illness no one can diagnose, and now she can't even help. (978-1-60282-559-8)

Who I Am by M.L. Rice. Devin Kelly's senior year is a disaster. She's in a new school in a new town, and the school bully is making her life miserable—but then she meets his sister Melanie and realizes her feelings for her are more than platonic. (978-1-60282-231-3)

Sleeping Angel by Greg Herren. Eric Matthews survives a terrible car accident only to find out everyone in town thinks he's a murderer—and he has to clear his name even though he has no memories of what happened. (978-1-60282-214-6)

Mesmerized by David-Matthew Barnes. Through her close friendship with Brodie and Lance, Serena Albright learns about the many forms of love and finds comfort for the grief and guilt she feels over the brutal death of her older brother, the victim of a hate crime. (978-1-60282-191-0)

The Perfect Family by Kathryn Shay. A mother and her gay son stand hand in hand as the storms of change engulf their perfect family and the life they knew. (978-1-60282-181-1)

Father Knows Best by Lynda Sandoval. High school juniors and best friends Lila Moreno, Meryl Morganstern, and Caressa Thibodoux plan to make the most of the summer before senior year. What they discover that amazing summer about girl power, growing up, and trusting friends and family more than prepares them to tackle that all-important senior year! (978-1-60282-147-7)